a novel by

courtney cole

dante's girl

Lakehouse Press, 2012

Cover photography and design by Dani Snell, Refracting Light Photography

Library of Congress Cataloging-in-Publication Data

Cole, Courtney.
   Dante's Girl/Courtney Cole --- Lakehouse Press trade pbk.ed.
   ISBN: 978-0615660691

Printed in the United States of America

dedication

To Gunner.
Because I want you to know that
anything is possible.
Always.
And I love you.
Always.

Other titles by Courtney Cole:

The Bloodstone Saga:
Every Last Kiss
Fated
With My Last Breath
My Tattered Bonds
House of Thebes

The Moonstone Saga:
Soul Kissed
Soul Bound
Princess of the Night (Coming soon)

The American Princess:
Princess
Glass Castles (Coming soon)

Guardian

Chapter One

It is impossible to look hot in the dingy fluorescent light of an airport bathroom. Or as my best friend Becca would say, hawt.

At this particular moment, I'm not hot *or* hawt. I make this revelation as I vigorously scrub at my arms and face and then use a wet paper towel under my pits.

And what is it about peeing in an airport toilet ten times in a day that makes you feel so completely scummy? I glance around at the crumpled tissues strewn about on the scuffed floor and the dirty toilets peeking from behind half-closed doors and cringe. That answer is clearly 'because of the germs'.

Ack.

Trying not to think about it, I clean up the best I can. After running a brush through my hair, I stick a piece of gum in my mouth, apply a thin layer of lip gloss and call it good. I glance into the mirror and cringe. It isn't good *enough*, but it will have to do. Very soon, I'll put this dreadful four hour layover in

Amsterdam behind me and before I even know it, I'll be in London.

With my father.

For the summer.

It would be torture.

Just shoot me now.

And it's not because I don't love him, because I do. My reluctance doesn't stem from lack of love. It comes from the deep-seeded fact that Alexander Ellis doesn't understand me. He never has and he never will. It's something that I've made my peace with and I'm not angry about it.

I'm his only child and he works his life away as some top-secret agent for the NSA. His job is so secret that I don't even know what he does. In my head, I imagine him jumping from helicopters and saving starving children in war torn areas. But in reality, I know he probably sits behind a desk and analyzes information from a satellite stream or a taped telephone conversation. I'm pretty sure that's what the NSA does, anyway. They aren't the cool kind of spies.

Also, he isn't exactly sure what to do with a daughter. I was supposed to have been a boy. Seventeen years ago, sonograms apparently weren't as absolute as they are today, because the technician told my parents that she was 99.9% sure that I was a boy. They painted my nursery blue and picked out my name and everything. I can only imagine the shocked horror on my father's face when I was born with lady parts.

Regardless, I know he loves me. Even though he had willingly given my mother full custody when they divorced years ago, I know he only did it because he works overseas so much and he isn't exactly sure how to raise a girl.

He does okay. But then again, I do have some reason to believe that he still pretends that I'm a boy, just to make it easier on himself. It's fairly easy to do since I still have the boy name that they originally picked out.

With my head down, I trudge back out into the congested halls of Schiphol airport. Weary travelers bustle around me and I shift my bags so that I can pull the stubborn strap of my tank top back over my shoulder where it belongs.

As I do, I crash into someone with enough force that my bags go flying out of my hands and scatter onto the ground under people's feet.

"Son of a –" I blurt before I even think.

"Buck?" a male voice offers helpfully.

Looking up, I stare into the most unique and beautiful shade of blue that a pair of eyes has ever possessed. Of that I am certain. Blue just shouldn't be that multi-faceted and twinkling. There should be a law or something.

Or at least a warning label:

Caution, these eyes may cause female knees to tremble.

Before I can help it, I scan the rest of him.

Sweet Mary.

This guy had lucked out in the gene department. Tall, slender, beautiful. Honey colored hair that had natural highlights that could even catch the crappy airport light, broad shoulders, slim hips, long legs. He is tan and golden with a bright, white smile.

I am surely staring at Apollo, the god of the sun. Probably with my mouth hanging open, which makes me realize that I must look like an idiot- the personification of what foreigners think Americans to be. I snap my mouth closed.

"I'm sorry," I say quickly, trying to still my racing heart. "Did I run into you?"

"Only a bit," Apollo says gentlemanly, with a shrug of his strong shoulders. I can tell he is strong even through his shirt sleeves, which are snug across his toned biceps. Sweet baby monkeys.

"How can someone run into someone else only by a bit?" I ask with a nervous smile as I kneel to retrieve my stuff.

Please don't let him smell me right now, I silently pray to any god who cares to listen. I am sure that at this point in my travels, I probably smell like soiled hamster bedding.

He bends next to me and picks up the contents of my spilled purse. He smells like sunshine. And rain. And everything beautiful that I can think of. I try not to cringe as his fingers grasp a tampon and slide it back inside my bag. He doesn't even flinch, he just casually continues to pick up my things like he's used to handling feminine hygiene products.

"Oh, it's fairly easy, really," he answers. He has an exotic sounding accent that I can't place. "At least, when you're not looking where you're going." My head snaps up and he laughs.

"I'm kidding," he assures me as he extends an arm to me. Even his hand is graceful. I gulp as his fingers curl around mine. "You can bump into me any time you'd like."

"Thanks," I mumble. "I think."

"I'm Dante," he tells me, his impossibly blue eyes still twinkling.

"I'm Reece," I answer with a sigh, already anticipating his reaction. "Yes, I know it's a boy's name."

"You're not a boy," Dante observes. "Most definitely not a boy."

Is that a note of appreciation in his voice? Surely not. I look like a bedraggled Shih Tzu.

"No, I'm not," I agree. "I just don't know that my dad ever got that memo."

I look past Dante and find that he is alone. He seems to be about my age so that's a little unusual in these circumstances. My parents had flown me as an 'unaccompanied minor' across the ocean for years, but other people's parents are usually a little squeamish about that.

"I'm sure that fact hasn't escaped him," Dante tells me in amusement. Why do his eyes have to sparkle so much? I usually go for brown-eyed guys. But this boy is most certainly making me re-think that stance.

"That's debatable," I sigh. Realizing that we are impeding the busy pedestrian traffic like a dam in a rushing river, I smile.

"Thank you very much for helping me pick up my things. Safe travels!"

I turn on my heel and pivot, walking quickly and what I hope is confidently in the other direction. Hitching my heavy purse up on my shoulder, I fight the urge to turn and look at him. Something about him is practically mesmerizing.

But I don't look. I keep walking, one foot in front of the other. When I reach the moving walkway, I hop on and focus ahead of me, eyes straight forward.

Don't look back.

Don't look back.

Don't look back.

Regardless of my silent chanting, when I step from the walkway, I discreetly check behind me. Apollo is nowhere to be seen. With a sigh, I continue on to the British Airways terminal. Only three short hours left until take-off. Plugging my earbuds into my ears, I settle into a seat and close my eyes.

* * *

"Excuse me, Reece?"

Before I even open my eyes, I know the sexy accent is coming from Apollo. I can feel his epic hotness emanating through my eyelids. I only hope that I haven't been drooling in my sleep.

"Yes?" I ask as nonchalantly as I can while my eyes pop open. I try to discreetly smooth my hair down. In my head, I envision myself as Chewbacca from Star Wars and wince.

Dante hands me my phone, which must've fallen from my lap as I napped.

"Are you on the flight to London?" he grins. "They're boarding priority travelers now. I just thought you should know."

Yikes. I had slept for three hours? In a noisy airport? I must have been super tired.

"Thank you," I reply quickly, gathering my things in a rush. "I didn't mean to fall asleep. I'm not a priority traveler, but I probably would have slept through general boarding. Thank you for waking me."

I glance at him as I stand up and can't help but do a double take. It isn't easy to get used to his particular brand of sexy. He is laid-back, handsome and casual, which is a formula for utter female devastation. The impossible thing is that he doesn't seem to realize it. He's effortlessly sophisticated and chic.

"Well, you're awake now and that's the important thing. Have a nice trip, Reece," Dante grins once more before he joins a group of men who are apparently waiting for him.

I was wrong, I guess. He isn't alone after all. The men close around him in a tight circle and they board the plane with the other passengers with first class tickets.

He's on my flight.

I gulp and find a place in line with the other travelers flying coach.

As the richer, better-dressed passengers file past us, I feel a little like a bumpkin in rumpled clothing. Even though I travel to London every summer to visit my dad, I live in rural America the rest of the year. And all of a sudden, I feel like I am wearing a blinking neon sign proclaiming that very fact. The clothing that had seemed sophisticated to travel in this morning now seems like it was hand-made in someone's backwoods shed.

And it *so* makes sense that Apollo is in first class. He smells like a beautiful sunrise in a wooded meadow. Oh, my gosh. What is wrong with me? Where did that come from? I am totally being as corny as an erectile dysfunction commercial.

I roll my eyes at my own absurdity and hand my ticket to the heavily made-up flight attendant who is waiting to take it. She glances at it and then at me before she stamps my passport and hands it back.

"Have a nice flight, Miss Ellis," she tells me before turning her attention to the passenger behind me.

Yeah, right.

I like flying almost as much as I like having dental work. Or having my fingernails pulled out one by one. Or having paper cuts sliced onto my legs and then lemon juice poured onto them. Just about that much.

Filing down the narrow aisle through first class, I can't help but search out Apollo. It doesn't take long to find him. He is situated by the window in a wide, leather first-class seat. He's already covered in a warm blanket and looks like he is settling in for the hour long flight.

As I move closer to him, his eyes pop open and meet mine, the electric blue of his almost causing me to gasp aloud.

He smiles slightly as I pass and his gaze doesn't waver from mine.

I find myself wishing that I could sit next to him. Not only because of the lavish first class seats, although those would be nice too.

But rather, there is something in the air between Dante and me. I can feel it, an instant connection. I can practically reach out and touch it. I've never experienced chemistry like this in my life. It's the kind that seems corny when you read about it in books, but in real life, it is anything but. It is simply electrifying. Ripping my eyes from his, I continue down the aisle and find my seat.

Taking a deep breath, I stash my carry-on in the overhead bin and slump into the window seat, trying not to hyperventilate as my fear of flying suddenly overwhelms me while the cramped airplane closes in around me.

Deep breath in.

Deep breath out.

Repeat.

I watch the flight crew below me loading the bags into the belly of the plane. What if they dislodge the landing gear while they are messing around down there? What if they don't check the systems well enough and we die in a fiery crash? What if the metal holding the plane together rips off in the air and peels away like tissue paper?

Deep breath in.

Deep breath out.

Repeat.

I might die.

Seriously.

I listen impatiently as the flight attendants give their safety spiel and motion toward the exits like they are NFL referees with dumb tiny scarves around their necks. I just need for them to get on with it. Just let us taxi out and take-off and then I will be perfectly fine once we are in the air. My hands get clammy and my ears start to roar. Why am I such a freak?

Deep breath in.

Deep breath out.

Repeat.

You freaking flight attendants.

Hurry.

Up.

I'm just getting ready to shove my earbuds back in to distract myself when Dante appears next to me like a savior or an angel or something of equal beauty and importance.

"Is this seat taken?" he smiles and I notice a dimple in his right cheek that I hadn't noticed before. How had I missed a dimple?

"Um, not that I know of," I answer weakly, trying not to die from heart palpations. "But the seat belt sign is on. You're not supposed to be out of your seat."

Fabulous. Now I sound like a hall monitor with a heart problem.

Dante shrugs without seeming worried.

"I think it will be okay," he answers. "We're not even on the runway yet."

"Good point."

"Can I sit here? I'm bored up front."

I nod, my palms instantly clammier. "I hope you brought your blanket. You won't get much back here except for a bag of peanuts."

And now I sound like a cheap hall monitor with a heart problem. I'm presenting myself better and better by the moment.

Dante smiles yet again and sits next to me. He brings his charming accent with him and the scent of his amazing cologne. I take a deep breath. He smells far better than the stale airplane air. *Far* better. I fight the urge to jump into his lap and inhale his neck, a maneuver that just might make me appear slightly insane.

"You look pretty pale," he observes as he buckles up. "Are you afraid to fly?"

"Is it that obvious?" I ask quietly. "As much as I've flown in my lifetime, I should be used to it. But

I'm afraid that's never going to happen. Once I'm in the air for awhile, I'll be fine, but until then... well, I'm terrified. I admit it."

"Don't worry," Dante tells me quietly, his voice calm and reassuring. "There's nothing to be afraid of. You're more likely to get into a--"

"Car crash rather than die in a plane crash," I interrupt. "Yes, I know. I've heard. Where are you from?" I ask curiously, half out of genuine curiosity and half out of the need to distract myself. "You have the most interesting accent."

He smiles, his teeth brilliantly white. I decide on the spot that I could watch him smile all day long.

"Caberra," he answers, reminding me that I had asked a question. "It's an island near Greece. And you?"

"Like you don't know that I'm American," I chuckle. "I know it's written all over me. I'm sure you're a fan, right?"

"Of Americans?" he raises a golden eyebrow. "Of course. I love them. I have no reason not to. They bring a lot of tourist dollars to Caberra."

"Well, we are a land of excess," I admit. "But that's usually what foreigners seem to hate about us."

Dante stares at me for a moment and then smiles.

"Well, I can't speak for all foreigners, but I don't hate Americans. And you're not in America right now, are you?"

I shake my head. "No, I am most certainly not."

"Well, then. You're the foreigner now." He grins and I can't help but smile back. He has a point.

The pilot gets on the intercom and his nasally voice drones on and on, but I am able to tune it out as I engage in conversation with a boy who is surely a direct descendent of the gods. There is no other plausible explanation for his good looks or charm.

I barely even hear the words that come out of Dante's mouth, because I am so mesmerized by the shape of his lips as he moves them. Pathetic, I know, but true.

One thing about me: I don't lie to myself. I might stretch the truth for my parents from time to time when necessary, but never to myself. And I'm pathetically fascinated by this boy.

Finally, the aircraft shudders a bit and noses forward and I startle, gripping the arms of my seat. My fingers turn white and I am certain that I am leaving permanent indentions in the cracked vinyl arm-rests.

"Don't worry," Dante says quietly, unpeeling one of my hands and grasping it within his own. "It will be fine."

The feel of his hand distracts me. Strong and warm, it cups my own carefully, like he is holding something very fragile. I close my eyes and enjoy the feeling. I only have a couple of minutes to soak it in, however.

As the plane moves down the runway in preparation for take-off, something happens. Something isn't right.

Our plane rocks a little, then quivers, like it is being moved by a strong gust of wind. I feel it a brief moment before Dante tightens his grip on my hand, a split second before light explodes from outside of my eyelids. I open them to discover fire tearing down the runway past my window. Before I can react or even scream, all hell breaks loose.

Chapter Two

Things start happening more quickly than I can even register, all of them occurring in a huge colorful blur.

First, it is as if things are in slow motion as I struggle to make sense of what had happened.

Flight attendants rush around the plane as fire continues to blaze around us. The pilot speaks into the intercom again, but I can't hear him now because of the din in the cabin.

Everyone is chattering nervously, wondering what had just happened as sirens immediately begin to wail in the distance. And then, when the sirens start, a hush falls over the plane. And even in the fog of my shock and confusion, I have to give the emergency workers credit for their quick response time.

I gather up my courage and look out the window. From the edge of the runway, half in and half out of the grassy dirt, the skeletal remains of another airplane burn. I can see the white shell of its tail melting away and revealing the metallic bones of the aircraft. Black, toxic smoke billow from it into the heavens but perhaps the most troubling was the absence of one thing.

The rescue slide doesn't emerge from the side of the plane. The carcass is still and silent, with only grotesque, loud popping noises coming from the flames.

"Oh, my god!"

A woman in the back of our plane breaks the eerie silence when she starts screaming.

She cries, pointing out of her window, her hand shaking. The people on the burning aircraft are clearly dead. We can't see them, but we know. There is a pall in the air, a shocked and unspoken sentiment that ripples through every passenger on our plane.

"What happened?" a little boy across the aisle asks his mother.

His mother is ghostly white, all color leached from her face as she stares outside of her window. Shaking her head grimly, she slides her plastic window-shade closed. Glancing my way, her eyes meet mine for a scant moment, before she lowers her head.

We just witnessed a tragedy. The problem is, I'm not sure exactly what kind. I'm not sure of anything at all.

"What happened?" I ask Dante frantically. "What happened to them? Were they taking off or landing?"

He peers at the wreckage. "I don't know," he admits. "I can't tell."

The men in suits appear out of nowhere by Dante's elbow.

"Come, Dante. We need to move." A tall man with a blonde buzz cut and tanned skin commands Dante urgently. "We can't stay here."

"What?" Dante answers blankly, staring up at the man. "How are we going to go anywhere?"

Buzz Cut grasps Dante's arm, his fingers thick like sausages.

"There's no time to discuss. We have to move." He leans down and murmurs something into Dante's ear. The only word I catch is "terrorists."

I gasp and Buzz Cut looks at me, his flat blue eyes solemn. Raising a beefy finger, he pushes it to his lips, cautioning me to be silent. I bite my lip and Dante turns to me.

"Get your bags, Reece."

"What?" I ask in confusion.

"Just grab your things," he says quickly as he stands up. "I'm not leaving you here alone."

Grasping the handle of my carry-on as I heft my purse onto my shoulder, I file down the aisle quietly and quickly after Dante. I don't even know this guy but for some reason, in this moment, I trust him. I'd definitely rather be with him than out here on this flaming tarmac. That much is certain.

The flight attendants close around us in a protective barrier as we wait by the door. Behind us, I can hear the dismay of the other passengers as they loudly voice their concerns over why we are able to leave and they aren't. It's actually a valid question and one that I don't know the answer to.

As the airplane taxies slowly across the tarmac toward the opposite side of the airport, I stare out the window in shock.

Pieces of the burning aircraft are scattered everywhere. Small twists of metal, bits of clothing, burned rubber. My gaze flies to the aircraft itself and I find that a jagged hole has been torn into the belly of the plane. I gasp again and tear my eyes away. But that doesn't help.

For one thing, I catch a glimpse of a blackened doll lying in the grass by the airplane's wheel, its face melted away. For another, the images have been seared into my mind, probably forever. I squeeze my eyes closed and wait for the plane to stop moving.

A few minutes later, we draw to a stop. I open my eyes once again and find that we are docked in a quiet, dark area of the airport.

Buzz Cut moves quickly to open the aircraft's door. Glancing outside, I find that a tall mobile staircase has been dragged out to the airplane, the same kind as you would see the president climbing for Airforce One.

I gulp.

How is Dante able to garner this kind of special treatment?

But there is no time to ask. The men in suits are hustling us down the steep stairs and it is all I can do to keep up, to keep my feet moving so that I don't fall. These guys clearly mean business. I can hear the loud protests of the passengers still on the plane, right up until the door is clicked closed behind us.

"It's alright," Dante tells me quietly as we walk toward the terminal. "Don't be afraid."

"Where are we? Where are we going?" I ask. "Why are you taking me with you?"

"I didn't want to leave you back there," he explains calmly. "No one knows what happened. They think it was terrorists. They're locking the airport down. You could be here for hours or even days. I don't want that. We're in a secure, unused terminal. I promise you that you are safe with me. We're going to cross back under Schiphol through a security tunnel and then we'll take you wherever you need to go."

"Well, where are *you* going?"

"I *was* going to join my father in London," Dante says, his eyes slightly concerned. "But now I will probably return home."

"But how?" I ask in confusion. "You just said they're closing down the airport."

"I'm not sure," he answers. "Russell? How will we be getting home?"

Buzz Cut turns around.

"Private helicopters are en route to meet us as we speak. We'll fly to Thessaloniki, then charter a boat to Caberra. We'll be home in no time. And we're not making any detours, Dante."

"Home?" I cry out, before I can stop myself. "As in, *your* home? Caberra? My father is going to kill me. Can't you just drop me off? I can take the Chunnel."

I've always liked riding the train underneath the English Channel, anyway. And it's name, Chunnel, is fun to say.

Buzz Cut is already shaking his head.

"Obviously, if the airports are closed down, they'll close the Chunnel down too. I'm guessing that all public transportation will be closed until they ascertain if this was a terrorist attack."

Dante stares at Buzz Cut. "We have to drop Reece off," he says calmly. "Her father will be worried."

"It is not that simple," Buzz Cut answers. "I'm sure the ferry won't be running. Your father wouldn't want me to detour, Dante. I'm sorry. Your safety is what I'm paid for. We will all travel home. Reece can call her father from there. End of story."

"Russell," Dante begins, his gaze turning icy. "You do not get to order me. I wish to drop Reece off safely with her father. Make it happen."

"Mr. Giliberti," Russell replies formally. "I do wish I could accommodate you. But we have specific evacuation procedures in place to ensure your safety. Per your father's direction, I am never authorized to deviate from the plan in these situations. I apologize. In this situation, your father's order trumps yours."

Dante stares at him silently for a moment with daggers in his eyes.

"Very well," he finally answers with icicles dripping from his words.

Yikes. There is no love lost between these two. That much is apparent. Should I be worried? This guy isn't in the witness protection program or something, is he? And these guys are his handlers? What the eff?

Dante turns back to me, the tone of his voice changing to congenial and charming.

"Reece, I apologize. It appears that we must return to Caberra per safety protocol. I assure you, however, that we will get you to your father at the soonest available opportunity. I give you my promise that you will be safe with us."

I nod and gulp, a loud sound in the silence. And then I remember my cell phone. This is the twenty-first century. I can call my father.

Right now.

And if I am, in fact, traveling with a psychopath or criminal, my father can come and get me. I mean, he works for the NSA. He has to have connections of some sort and satellites to track down my exact location.

Yanking my phone out of my pocket, I power it on and slide my finger across the screen to unlock it. I punch in my father's number with shaking hands.

No dial tone.

I try again.

This time, I connect with an automated message which wavers in and out, first in Dutch and then in English. *All circuits are currently busy. Please try your call again later.*

Great.

"Don't worry," Dante reassures me quietly, his hand on my shoulder. "It will be okay."

"How do you know?" I challenge him.

"I just do," he shrugs. "It always is."

I can't argue with that logic. In my seventeen years of life, there has never been anything that didn't eventually turn out alright. But to be fair, I've never left an airport with a complete stranger who might possibly be an ax murderer before, either.

Holy cow. I'm such an idiot.

I'm totally screwed.

My dad is going to have to identify my body parts.

I'm sure of it.

We step out of the darkened terminal and find two large black SUVs with tinted windows waiting for us. An airport security person stands to the side. He takes our passports and ushers us on our way after speaking hurriedly with Russell.

I briefly consider telling Dante that I've changed my mind, that I want to stay, but something holds me back. I'm not sure what. Some niggling little thing in the corner of my mind tells me to just hang tight. My mother has always told me to trust my gut. And right now, for some reason, my gut is telling me that Dante is okay, that I am safe with him.

I sincerely hope my gut isn't crazy.

The other four men in suits take the front SUV while Dante, Russell and I climb into the second one. I settle into the cushiony seat, the leather cool against my skin. I pull my shirt down to cover the exposed skin on the bottom of my back and then turn to Dante, who was sitting next to me.

"Who are you?"

"Dante Giliberti," he answers, pronouncing Giliberti as Gili-Bear-ti and looking confused by my question. But he has to know why I'm wondering.

"Why does Dante Gili-bear-ti command such special treatment?" I demand impatiently, staring him straight in the eye. "I'm sorry if I seem rude, but I'm an American speeding away from an airport with a man that I don't even know. You are clearly important or we would be stuck back there with everyone else- probably even still on that plane." I shudder at the thought. "And while I'm very grateful to you that that isn't the case, I would like to know who you are."

"My father is Dimitri Giliberti. He's the Prime Minister of Caberra."

Dante says this calmly, casually and matter-of-factly, as though he is speaking of the weather, as though it is something that anyone might say.

My mouth drops open and I'm pretty sure that my vision blurs for a second.

"Prime Minister?" I stutter.

I can see mild amusement on Buzz Cut's face, but I ignore it. At this moment, he doesn't matter.

Although, now at least it makes sense why Dante has a security team in the first place. Oh, sweet Mary. The guy has an entire security team. The realization makes me almost nauseous and I'm not sure why. I should be happy. Dante isn't an ax murderer.

"Are you upset?" Dante asks in concern. "Are you alright?"

"Your father is the Prime Minister of a country," I say out loud. Dante nods.

"Yes. Caberra. It's a small island country in the Mediterranean. It's not far from Greece."

"I know where it is. You already told me," I answer softly. "And your father is the Prime Minister."

Dante nods. "Yes."

I gulp. My father is a desk-jockey for the NSA. Dante's father is the leader of a country. It's just one more reason that I should feel inadequate when standing next to him.

"Don't be intimidated by that," Dante adds graciously. "You're not sitting next to the Prime Minister of Caberra. You're sitting next to me. And I'm a normal person."

"A normal person with billions of dollars," Russell mutters beneath his breath. Dante shoots him a glare.

"Billions of dollars," I repeat weakly. "You have billions of dollars. You're a billionaire."

Dante doesn't answer yes or no. Instead he says, "My family has been in the olive business for quite a long time. We export gourmet olives."

He's diplomatic, too. It must run in his family.

"Giliberti Olives," I murmur, absently picturing a name that sits on a jar in my very own kitchen cabinets back home. My grandmother loves their garlic stuffed olives. If we even have them in Kansas, then they must be a huge company. Clearly, they ship all over the world.

"Yes, Giliberti Olives," Dante answers pleasantly. "You've heard of us? We sell pretty much any kind of olive you can think of, as well as gourmet olive oils."

"You're a billionaire," I repeat again.

I feel stupid, but I just can't wrap my head around it. This handsome, sophisticated boy is a billionaire. And the son of a Prime Minister. It makes total and complete sense. The realization that I am safe barely registers with me. It is overshadowed by the fact that the beautiful boy that I am with is a billionaire.

"Does it matter?" Dante asks with a smile. "Money is money. It is only that. It doesn't define us, does it?"

I'm pretty sure it does. I'm farm girl from Kansas and he's the wealthy son of a Prime Minister. We are from completely different worlds. So different, that we are probably separated by two or three galaxies. He's way out of my league. In fact, he's in a total league of his own.

Chapter Three

"Why did you bring her in the first place?" Buzz Cut demands of Dante.

They are standing approximately five paces from the SUV as we wait for the helicopter to prepare for our flight. They must think that I can't hear them over the whir of the helicopter's engine. I want to tell them that I'm not deaf, but instead I cringe from the agitation in Russell's voice.

"Because I couldn't leave her there," Dante answers icily. "And I don't answer to you, Russell. I do as I please and you will do as I say."

The bodyguard glares at Dante for one long moment before he pivots on his heel and stalks over to speak with the crew chief of the helicopter.

Honestly, I'm impressed with how quickly the flight crew had reached us.

We'd only driven for a half an hour before the helicopter met us on the road, touching down in a field next to us. We'd pulled over and now, ten minutes later, we are about to board.

It's surreal.

Larger than life.

And if my mother knew this, that I am about to travel to an island nation with someone I've never met before, or in fact, about any of it, she'd have a heart attack. As it is, I still don't have a cell signal so I'm safe for the time being. I'm with the son of a Prime Minister, after all.

Dante strolls back to where I am leaning against the car, his shoulders all wide and strong and distracting. He smiles casually and you'd never know from his face that he had just gotten into a little verbal altercation with his massive bodyguard.

"Are you alright?" he asks politely. "Do you need anything?"

I shake my head. "I need to call my parents before they kill me. But other than that, I'm fine."

Dante nods. "The cellular circuits are jammed because everyone is on their cell phone in this area, trying to check on their loved ones. When we reach Caberra, I'm sure it will be clear. You can call them then."

"Okay," I answer, fiddling with the strap of my purse. Dante's casual good looks aren't something I have gotten used to yet. He still causes my tongue to tie in knots. Actually, I don't foresee that dissipating anytime soon.

"Are you upset that I brought you with me?" Dante asks, his forehead wrinkling in concern. "I didn't mean to cause you any trouble with your parents. It's just that we didn't know at the airport what the problem might be. I thought it was terrorists and something inside of me said that I couldn't leave you there."

"You *thought* it was terrorists," I repeat in confusion. "It wasn't?"

Dante shakes his blond head. "The helicopter pilot tells me that a volcano erupted in Greenland. The ash has carried in the air and it is wreaking havoc on airplanes. It gets sucked into their engines and clogs them up. Airports all over Europe are closed down."

"Will a helicopter be safe?" I ask nervously, mentally picturing a fiery crash. Perhaps I'm going to die after all. My pulse speeds up.

Dante smiles reassuringly.

"Yes. It's safe. Helicopters don't have jet engines to clog, so we'll be fine." He glances at me. "I promise."

At precisely that moment, the pilot motions to us that he's ready and we quickly move to board. Dante lifts my hand and helps me step into the craft, like a prince and a princess. His manners are perfect. His mother should be proud.

"It will be fine," Dante repeats to me, patting my shoulder.

I'm such a baby. I know that. But in the face of what we'd just seen a couple of hours ago, I'm 99.999% sure that my terror is justified.

The co-pilot hands us headphones, which we all put on and settle into our seats. This is the biggest helicopter that I've ever seen, large enough to seat everyone in Dante's security detail.

That thought makes me gulp again.

Dante has a security detail.

He is my complete and polar opposite on the life-importance-meter.

I fasten my seatbelt and close my eyes. All of a sudden, I feel his breath on my cheek and his mouth next to my ear.

"I promise, it will be fine."

Everyone in the helicopter can hear, because mouthpieces are attached to our headphones. My cheeks burst into flame. Now everyone is well aware that I'm a big baby. Perfect.

"The people on that plane. Are they all dead?"

It is completely silent around me as I ask the question. No one wants to answer and that is answer enough. Dante's face is grave as he leans toward me.

"Yes. They are."

The breath freezes in my throat as I remember the grotesque popping sound as the plane had burned. And the doll with no face.

I close my eyes but I still see the visions.

Dante reaches over and squeezes my hand.

Perfect.

For real, this time.

I feel my heart flutter a little at his nearness and at the way his cool hand feels within mine. And then I instantly feel silly.

Just because I'm a small-town farm girl does not mean that I should make a fool of myself over this boy. I have to have some self-respect. I am *not* going to fawn all over him. He's a billionaire. And beautiful. He's probably used to 'those' girls being at his beck and call. And I am bound and determined not to be one.

I pull my hand out of his and lean my head against the window. I'm determined not to look at his reflection, particularly because I can feel him staring at me.

I squeeze my eyes shut as the engine roars and we lift off the ground, shakily at first and then we soar across the sky like a motorized bird.

I think I might have a heart attack and this time, when Dante reaches over and squeezes my hand, I squeeze it back. To hell with trying to seem guarded. That had lasted all of three minutes. I'm a girl who wears her emotions on her sleeve. I'm not going to change that just to look cool.

Not for any boy, not for any reason.

The drone of the helicopter fades into my subconscious as I close my eyes and try to imagine that I am anywhere but 15,000 feet in the air.

I focus on my favorite daydream, the one where I return from London at the end of the summer and am all glamorous and drop-dead gorgeous and every girl in my school is completely jealous when Quinn McKeyan asks me to Fall Homecoming because he can't resist my charm.

Hey, it's my daydream. I can dream what I want to.

The thing is, Quinn's face keeps getting replaced in my head by Dante's.

Since I've had a mad crush on Quinn from the time we started kindergarten all the way through our junior year last year, that's saying something.

Every daydream I've had for eleven years has been of him. I'm a very loyal daydreamer. And I suddenly feel like I'm cheating on my imaginary boyfriend, a boy who happens to be real, but who has been dating my best friend Becca for the past two years.

And no. Becca has no idea that I'm secretly in love with her boyfriend. It's the one secret that I've kept from her.

I clear my head from cluttered thoughts and instead focus on emptying it. I focus on blackness and feel myself drift to sleep.

I'm not sure how long I sleep. But my eyes flutter open to find Dante watching me. I'm instantly self-conscious and seriously hope that I haven't done anything gross in my sleep.

"I like the name Reece," Dante says randomly, as though he'd been thinking about it.

Once again, everyone in the helicopter is listening since we're all on the same frequency. My blush comes back with a vengeance, fiery hot.

"Thank you," I answer, not looking at him, trying to will my cheeks to not be pink.

"How did your parents choose it?" he asks, staring at me with interest.

I straighten in my seat and once again look at him in the glass. I find it is safer to look at his reflection, rather than into his startlingly blue eyes. It helps me to keep my wits.

And I need every wit that I have.

"My father has always had a man-crush on the baseball hall of famer, Pee Wee Reese," I tell him. "He played for the Dodgers a long time ago. My father has a signed Pee Wee Reese baseball that his grandfather gave him. Do you watch baseball?"

He shakes his head. "No. But I played it when I was a kid."

"Well, it is one of the things that my dad lives and breathes for, when he isn't working," I explain. "So, naturally, he named me after his hero. But like I told you earlier, he was expecting a boy. I was quite the surprise."

Dante looks at me seriously and I can't help but turn to meet his gaze. As a result, my heart thumps so loudly that I'm afraid my mouthpiece will pick it up and give me away.

"Yes," he agrees. "You are quite the surprise."

What the hell does he mean by that?

But I don't have any time to ponder it because Dante looks out his window and begins giving me a blow-by-blow tour of the scene below us. And as I lean into the window and look, I gasp at the beauty below. It is so gorgeous that it effectively takes my mind off my fear of flying.

"Where are we?" I ask in awe. This is so much better than being in the dreary rain of London.

The landscape is beautiful.

There are so many white sandish-colored buildings and I can see, even from here, that they are ancient. Houses dot the countryside which is filled with green grass and rock. The ocean looms huge and blue around it and I've never seen such a lovely place.

"This is the land of the gods," Dante tells me. "Greece. Look there," he points. "That's the Acropolis. And that there? That's the Pantheon, a temple made for the goddess Athena a couple of thousand years ago."

"Wow," I breathe as I stare at the history sprawling beneath me. "The United States doesn't have such history. We're such a baby country compared to Greece."

Dante nods, apparently satisfied with my reverence.

"It's an amazing place," he agrees. "To walk here, among the buildings where the gods are said to have walked, it is the most incredible feeling in the world."

"How far are we from Caberra?" I ask. "Is it near here?"

"Very near," he confirms. "Less than twenty minutes by plane."

I settle back into my seat and stare absently at the turquoise water beneath us. It is almost hypnotic as we race above the glass-like water. And honestly, before I even know it, the helicopter descends for a landing.

We hover above a building for just a moment before we shudder to a stop.

I straighten in my seat and find that we'd just descended into paradise.

"Wow," I breathe again, as I stared at the bright blue sky, quaint old buildings and shops and lush greenery below the helipad. "It's beautiful here."

Dante nods again. "Yes. I'm blessed to call this my home."

"Where are we?" I ask as I stare around us in wonder. We're clearly on the roof of someplace, but beyond that I don't know.

Dante smiles.

"This is my home. They call it the Old Palace because that's exactly what it is. Once upon a time, hundreds of years ago, Caberra was a monarchal society with a royal family. This was their palace, but it has been turned into the prime minister's home now, as well as housing a few governmental agencies. Since its royal family days, Caberra has evolved into a parliamentary representative democratic government with my father currently serving as prime minister."

"Yikes. Say that three times quickly," I challenge him.

Dante smirks slightly. "You should try living it."

Turning to Buzz Cut, he asks, "Where is my father?"

"He's in London," the security guard tells him. "He decided to finish his meetings there and he will then depart for home in a day or two."

"Fine. We'll need to show Ms. Ellis to a room so that she can freshen up and she will need to call her parents."

Buzz Cut nods as he helps me out of the helicopter. "Very well. Your father has already been appraised of the situation. We're under instruction to give Ms. Ellis a proper welcome."

Dante stares at him. "You were already under that very same instruction," he points out. "From me."

Turning his back on the burly security guard, Dante guides me away from the helicopter and through the doors leading into the Old Palace.

Once inside, I suck in my breath, trying not to say something stupid or act like the country girl that I am. The interior of this ancient building is dazzling. Amazing. Like nothing I've ever seen.

Air the exact perfect temperature washes over my damp skin, bathing me in a cool breeze. Priceless antiquities surround me in the form of statues, artwork and heavy antique furniture. The marble floors glisten mutely in the sunlight and are covered with woven rugs. Beautiful vases adorn ornate tabletops and even the ceiling is gilded in what appears to be gold. Glittering chandeliers hang overhead and crystal doorknobs adorn the doors. Everything is beautiful, but so perfectly in place that it seems almost sterile. I feel like I should whisper from the reverence of it all.

"Your home is beautiful," I tell Dante politely and in a hushed voice. He grins.

"It is, isn't it?" he answers. "But it's not really my home. My family home is on the outskirts of Valese. Valese is the capital of Caberra, by the way, and we are in the very heart of it right now. My home is in the Giliberti olive groves, where it is beautiful and peaceful at all times. That sounds stupid, right?" He gestures around us. "But I always feel like I am in a museum here. It's too uptight."

It does feel as though I have stepped directly into the National Museum of History. I'm not surprised to find that some of these things, probably priceless relics, had actually been cordoned off with red velvet ropes.

"Well, at least there are no creepy suits of armor standing around," I tell him wryly.

And no lie, just as the words are out of my mouth, we round a corner and there stands a small suit of armor.

No. Lie.

And it is, in fact, creepy with its empty blank holes for eyes and dangling arms and legs.

"You were saying?" Dante asks, with a raised eyebrow.

"Um. Yes. You do seem to live in a home straight out of an old Scooby Doo episode," I laugh.

He chuckles as I step closer to look at the tiny suit of armor. It seems to be bronze and it is no more than five feet tall.

"It's so small! Were your ancestors dwarves?"

Dante's eyes twinkle.

"No. Caberra used to have armies made from children so that our strapping adult men didn't die in

43

battle." As my mouth drops open in horror, he laughs, a rich sound that sends goose bumps erupting down my arms.

"I'm kidding," he assures me. "People used to be much smaller hundreds of years ago," he explains. "Surely it was the same in the United States. People were simply littler. By way of evolution, we have grown bigger and bigger."

"How big are you?" I ask, sizing him up as I spoke.

"That's kind of personal, isn't it?" he answers impishly. My cheeks catch fire as I realize his implication.

"I'm sorry," he apologizes quickly. "That wasn't polite or appropriate. I hope I didn't offend you."

"Not at all," I assure him. "I grew up in a rural town full of cowboys and farm animals. Trust me, I seldom get offended."

"But still," Dante continues. "I'm sorry. It came out before I had thought about it. I'm 6'3", to answer your question. How tall are you?"

"I'm 5'8"," I answer. "Tall for a chick, I know."

"Yeah, but you were supposed to be a boy, so I would totally expect that out of you," he replies, his eyes sparkling again. I really like it. It is just so ornery, like he always knows an entertaining secret.

"Yeah, yeah," I answer with a sigh. "Keep it up, smarty."

He laughs as we step onto yet another landing and then start climbing our third flight of stairs.

There are So. Many. Stairs.

"Yikes, how many floors are in this building?" I'm practically panting.

"I know," he sighs. "It's too big to be a real home, right? There are three stories sprawled over two city blocks. First story is government offices, parliament, etc. Second story has the ball rooms and museums. And the third story is the personal living quarters of the Prime Minister. And me."

"There's *actually* a museum in your house?" I ask, trying not to laugh, although secretly I'm impressed.

He shakes his head. "Yeah, yeah. Keep it up, smarty."

I go ahead and laugh, at his embarrassment, at the way he threw my words back at me, at his cute dimple, at the absurdity of the situation. I shouldn't be standing in a Scooby Doo episode because I'm supposed to be in London having an uncomfortable dinner with my father right now.

That last thought is actually sobering.

Dad is probably having a steak so rare that there is blood in the plate and a finger of Pimm's, which is just a weird way of saying that the liquor is poured to the height of a finger held against the glass.

If I were there, he'd be trying to talk to me about baseball, horseracing and any other imaginable male topic of conversation and I would be attempting to act interested. But I'm not there. I'm here, standing in a beautiful old palace in the most beautiful country I've ever seen with the most beautiful boy I've ever laid eyes upon.

But all good and beautiful things must come to an end. I turn to Dante with a sigh.

"Do you have a phone…a landline? I really have to call my dad."

And if I'm really, really lucky, Alexander Ellis, NSA Agent Extraordinaire, won't kill me dead right on the spot.

Dante shows me to a phone and I settle into an ornate carved chair. I don't want to speculate on how antique and expensive it might be. My father answers on the first ring, a bad sign, but he isn't angry at all. I am pleasantly surprised when the conversation doesn't go badly at all.

In fact, he seems in awe of the fact that I am staying in the Prime Minister of Caberra's palace.

"Tell me again how you met this boy," he instructs me in his London accent.

Interesting fact: My dad doesn't actually have a London accent. He was born and raised in America. He says he's acquired it from living abroad for so long. Um, I haven't picked it up after spending every summer in London since I was small, so I know that he really just wants to seem sophisticated. But I've never called him out on it and I'm not going to start now.

Instead, I answer his question and he tells me that he's already up to speed on everything because Dante's father had personally called him and explained the situation. Since my father can't exactly be angry with the Prime Minister of a country, he seems perfectly okay with me being here.

Shocker number one.

It turns out that Dante's father has extended the generous invitation of letting me stay with them until the airports open back up and surprisingly, my father already accepted the gracious invitation. Apparently, he figures it would be educational for me to learn about another culture firsthand.

Shocker number two.

Dad's exact words are, "Surely, since you're being hosted by the Prime Minister himself, you won't get into any trouble."

Eyeing Dante from across the room, I suddenly sense that my stay here will be *very* educational. But I can make no promises about not getting into trouble.

Shocker number three.

Chapter Four

The next morning, I consider my options before I even get out of bed. And this is a bed that is surprisingly uncomfortable considering that Napoleon himself once slept in it during a visit to Valese. I lay still for a moment, my arm dangling over the side.

The bed is gigantic and I briefly wonder how little 'ol Napoleon even climbed into it at all. It's a gigantic carved mahogany monstrosity, really. But thinking about Napoleon and his size or lack of or even the ugliness of this bed isn't helping me decide what to do with my day.

I can tell from the cheerful sunlight streaming in my windows that it is beautiful outdoors. Although, I imagine that it's always beautiful here in Caberra. Because of that I should do something outside, like sight-see.

Maybe.

But my problem is, what do I do about Dante? I'm a guest in his home. Am I supposed to wait until I am summoned before I leave my bedroom? Or can I just get up and search him out? This is a Capitol building so I'm pretty sure that I'm not allowed to just go poking around.

The room phone ringing from my bed stand interrupts my quandary.

"Reece?"

Dante's voice fills my ear, husky and beautiful. Yes, beautiful. He's a boy and he's beautiful. It's a fact that I am constantly reconciling myself with.

"Good morning," I tell him. Why is my tongue instantly tied?

"Good morning." I hear him smile through the phone as he speaks and my heart picks up. "Did I wake you?"

"No," I answer. "I'm just laying here trying to decide what to do with my day."

"So you're still in bed?"

I look at the clock. It's only 9:00am. I don't need to lie so that I don't seem lazy.

"Yep. But I'm getting ready to get up."

"Perfect," he smiles again, I just know it. "Would you like to spend the day at the beach? It's going to be a beautiful day."

"Are all days beautiful here?" I ask.

He laughs. "Yes. You're not in Kansas anymore, Toto."

I cringe. "I've heard that one before, you know."

"I'm sure. So, how about it? Do you want to spend the day with me?"

More than anything, I think.

"Sounds good," I actually say.

"Then it's a date," he answers. "Wear shorts and I'll pick you up in thirty minutes."

A date.

The line goes dead and I sit limply for just a second before I leap from the bed and fly into def-con-five-hyper-speed. I have a lot to accomplish in thirty short minutes. I have to go from looking like a rumpled farm girl who just woke up to looking like an ultra-glam, sexy siren.

It's not happening.

It's impossible, in fact.

I decide this twenty-eight minutes later as I stare into the mirror.

I do, and always will until the end of time, look like the girl next door. It is my curse. My eternal fate. They're probably going to put it on my tombstone.

Here lies Reece Ellis, the cute little girl next door.

There's nothing I can do about it. I've tried a thousand times to be a bombshell, but it's just not going to work for me.

My blonde hair is a pretty color with high and low lights, but it's not sleek and sophisticated and doesn't even have sexy round curls by any stretch of the imagination. It's wavy. Just wavy. Like it couldn't make up its mind what it wanted to be. And for lack of something better or more creative, it's clipped back in a barrette right now. My hair straightener is in my checked luggage which is still being held at Schiphol airport. I only have what I was carrying in my carry-on.

And it's true that my eyes are a pretty blue. But they always seem to sparkle, which makes me seem young. And pair that trait with the smattering of light freckles on my nose, and I will forever be the dreaded girl next door, not a glamorous Marilyn Monroe type of girl. I sigh. Oh well. I'll just have to resign myself to being more like Doris Day. That's okay. There are worse things in the world, probably.

And why am I comparing myself to classic movie stars, anyway?

A knock on my door interrupts my ridiculous musings.

He's here. Right on time. Right outside my door, actually. My heart picks up again as I open my door and then I inhale deeply, trying not to hyperventilate.

Dante is more beautiful than he was before and he practically fills my doorframe. Was he this tall yesterday? He's wearing a pair of khaki shorts, a white t-shirt and a white button-up shirt with the sleeves rolled up.

He's casual and smooth and sophisticated, everything that I want to be but am not. I'm a farm girl, born and raised and I have never been more aware of that fact than I am right now. I fight the urge to stuff my hands in my pockets to hide my peeling purple nail polish.

"Good morning," Dante tells me again. His smile is radiant and dazzling and my knees literally grow weak from staring at it.

Trembly knees, much?

"Good morning," I smile what I hope is a confident smile.

"You look lovely," he announces, his blue eyes warm. "Did you sleep well?"

"Like a baby," I lie.

He cocks his head and the light catches the gold in his hair.

"Do you know that saying that would actually indicate that you slept horribly? Babies wake up a million times in the night. It's the same thing as when people say that they eat like a bird when they mean to convey that they don't eat much. It's not accurate. Birds actually eat half their body weight every day. They have such a high metabolism that they need all of those calories."

I stare at him.

"Thank you, Encyclopedia Brown," I tell him with a smile. He is a refreshing change. Where I come from, guys don't think it's cool to be that smart.

"Who?"

I'm astounded for a second, then remember that kids might not read the same books in Caberra as I did growing up.

"A fictional character," I answer. "He was a kid who was super smart and solved mysteries. Never mind."

Dante looks amused. "Do you think I'm super-smart, or are you making fun of me? American humor is sometimes lost on me."

"I wouldn't dream of making fun of you," I exaggerate as I grab my purse. "Unless you do something truly hilarious."

He looks amused again. "I'll take that under advisement." The corner of his lip twitches. "Just for clarification, though, how would you define 'truly hilarious'?"

I consider that.

"Um. If your drawers fell off while speaking to the Prime Minister of Britain, maybe. That would be pretty hilarious, especially if it was televised. Or if you accidentally texted your mom a *private* text meant for your girlfriend. That would be hi-lar-ious too."

Nice. I'm probing to see if he has a girlfriend and he won't even realize it. I'm the *definition* of smooth operator. Not.

He rolls his eyes.

"Well, there's a couple of problems. First, I don't wear drawers. I wear underwear. I wear trousers. I wear pants. But drawers? You Americans and your crazy-talk." He pauses to grin. "Second, I don't have a mom. Or not anymore, I mean. She died when I was a baby. But even still. You seriously think those things are funny? You're a mean-spirited little thing."

He smiles and nudges me, but I am appalled. His mother is dead and I made a joke about him accidentally sexting her? Did I say that I was a smooth operator?

Not hardly. More like WorldClassFreakingIdiot.

Before I can apologize or say anything at all, he continues.

"Now then. Are you ready for a day on the most beautiful beach in the world?"

He smiles his gorgeous smile and I nod mutely, like the WorldClassFreakingIdiot that I am.

Dante holds his elbow out for me to take and I realize once again that boys are different here. They have manners. Real manners. Not just the "I'll hold the obligatory door for you so that I can get into your pants later" manners like the boys do back home.

I grip his elbow lightly and we wind our way through the Old Palace. I try not to act overwhelmed at its size and fanciness again today.

I'm casually aloof.

I think.

As we spill out onto the cobblestone sidewalk in front of the palace, I look around for a car.

"Did you lose something?" Dante asks in concern.

I shake my head. "I was just wondering where your car is."

He stares at me for a second, then smiles. "We don't need a car today. The beach isn't far. But first, I thought we'd stop and get a gelato on the way. It's the best in the world here, better than even Italy. You're going to die."

"Gelato for breakfast?" I quickly scan my memory for what gelato actually is. It's clearly something Italian.

"Why not?" Dante shrugs. "I think we should always eat dessert first."

So gelato is dessert. Got it. I make a mental note.

We wind our way casually along the busy sidewalks of Valese. I can't help but notice that women literally stop what they are doing to gawk at Dante. Then they stare at me curiously, probably wondering who the heck I am. I can hear pictures being snapped and I realize that Dante is a celebrity here.

Gulp. I slightly tighten my hold on his arm.

So, to recap, Dante is a gorgeous, beautiful son of a Prime Minister who happens to be a billionaire. And these things combine to make him a local celebrity. He's like the Caberran version of Princess William or Harry.

Good Lord.

I am so over my head here.

Breathe, I silently instruct my lungs. I suck in a mouthful of sea air. It smells really good here. Like salt, sun and…something else. I can't put my finger on it.

"Have you ever been clam digging?" Dante asks conversationally as we cross the street. Traffic literally stops for him. We don't even have to watch where we're going. They are watching for us. I shake my head.

"No. I'm from the heartland of America. There are no oceans where I'm from, trust me. Just fields and fields of wheat and some sunflowers. They're the only things hearty enough to survive the soul-sucking heat."

"That sounds charming," Dante laughs. "You paint a lovely picture of your home." He speaks in Caberran to a street vendor, who scoops two scoops of fluorescent fuchsia-colored gelato into two bowls and hands them to us.

I study mine.

"I'm pretty sure ice cream isn't supposed to be this color," I announce to Dante.

He rolls his eyes again. "It's gelato, not ice cream. Try it. You might faint from the sheer deliciousness. Trust me. Prepare yourself."

He scoops a huge spoonful into his mouth and I hear more pictures being snapped of him. Dante seems oblivious to it as he stares at me, waiting for me to try the unnaturally colored ice cream.

I will never let it be said that I am a chicken so I take a tentative bite. And Dante was right. I almost swoon from the sheer deliciousness.

"Holy cow," I breathe as I stick another huge bite into my mouth and savor the explosion of cold flavor as it melts on my tongue. It's like a little frozen piece of fruity heaven. In my mouth.

"How have I lived seventeen years without gelato?"

Dante laughs and we continue walking, looking into quaint shop windows and dodging the people who keep stopping directly in our path to stare.

"Do you ever get tired of that?" I ask quietly as we round the side of a store and walk down a worn path toward the beautiful sandy beach. The ocean yawns huge and blue in front of us. I kneel for a quick second to pick up a perfect white seashell.

"Get tired of what?" Dante glances at me as he scrapes the bottom of his bowl with his spoon already, before tossing it into a nearby receptacle.

"That," I motion behind us at the people still clustered in groups watching our backs. "They watch you and take pictures of you."

"Oh, that," he shrugs. "It's been that way since my father was appointed PM. I guess it just comes with the territory."

I glance over my shoulder. "Do they follow you?"

He looks pained. "Sometimes."

But right now, they aren't. They are still staring though, as we descend into a sand dune and out of their sight. I breathe a sigh of relief. It's slightly unnerving to have so many people watching. I stoop down and slip my sandals off. Walking on the soft sand feels wonderful on my feet. Plus, it might exfoliate my rough soles. Bonus.

As I look around, I realize something. All of a sudden, we are alone. Truly alone. This beach is empty. It stretches out like a long, silvery ribbon and I turn to Dante.

"Where is everyone?" I ask curiously. "It's beautiful here. Shouldn't there be surfers out or something?"

"They don't use this beach," he tells me. "There are too many sharks out here by this coral reef. There are better surfing spots on the other side of the island."

Sharks?

I freeze and Dante notices the instant fear on my face, put there as a result of seeing *Jaws* at a very young age. He picks up my hand and holds it, letting our adjoined hands dangle loosely between us. The jolting sensation of his skin against mine is an effective distraction.

"Don't worry," he assures me. "I'll never let a shark get you. While you are here with me in Caberra, I give you my word that nothing bad will happen to you."

Not two minutes after his promise, I step on a jellyfish.

Chapter Five

Within five minutes, my calf has swollen to five times its normal size. Apparently, I'm very allergic to jellyfish. But seriously, how would I have known this before? Being from Kansas, it has never been on my list of life experiences until now.

And now I look like I have some strange version of Elephantiasis.

And the most beautiful boy in the world is carrying me back to a bench.

And I am mortified. Utterly mortified.

Omigosh. Just kill me now.

Right now.

"Are you feeling alright?" Dante asks and his breathing is only slightly labored even though he's been carrying me for five minutes already. I weigh 124 pounds. I am no feather. But he's not even breaking a sweat. Impressive.

"I feel fine. Except for my leg. Why do you ask?"

But even as the words exit my mouth, I feel the waves of nausea coming on. I am instantly overwhelmed by sickness, by the uncontrollable need to vomit. Saliva pools in my mouth and I know it is coming.

"Put me down. Oh my gosh. Put me down," I practically claw at his arms and he sets me quickly down. I drop onto my hands and knees and before I even know it, I am puking at his feet. Not on them, thankfully, but at them.

I retch until there's nothing left in my belly. A horrible, bright fuchsia-colored vomit. Even when there is nothing left to vomit, I dry-heave over and over until I am resting limply on the sand.

And now I really want to die.

Right here.

Right now.

I can't even bring myself to look up at Dante, but as my wits slowly return to me, I realize that he has been holding my hair back for me.

OhMyGosh.

JustLetMedie.

"I want to die," I moan, not looking at him. "I'm so sorry."

"Sorry for what?" Dante asks incredulously. "Sorry for getting sick after you got stung by a jellyfish? Um, that's a natural reaction. That's why I asked how you were feeling. Don't feel bad. I know that it hurts like a bitch. Come on," he pulls me to my feet. "We really need to have a doctor look at you, just to make sure you're okay. Are you having trouble breathing?"

Of course the second that he says that, I imagine my throat swelling closed and I clutch at it, sucking in air like a crazy person.

Dante's gaze flickers over me in concern and he strokes my back lightly.

"Calm down," he instructs softly. "Relax. I think you're fine. Just relax."

I realize that he's right as I take deep, slow breaths. I can breathe. I am just overreacting as I often do. My throat is not swelling closed. I am not dying, after all.

I take four more shaking breaths and then nod.

"I'm fine," I whisper.

Unless a person can die of embarrassment. And if that's the case, then I'm at death's door.

"This is so embarrassing," I groan.

Dante grins.

"Hmm. This is probably Karma's way of getting back at you for thinking that it would be hilarious if I lost my trousers in front of the PM of Britain. Just sayin'."

I feel too sick to smile, but he's funny. Really funny.

"And just for the record, I *don't* think it's hilarious that you're having an allergic reaction to a jellyfish."

He's sweet, too.

Dante wraps his arm around my shoulders and pulls me into his side so that I am leaning heavily on him as we walk. It's a protective gesture that instantly makes my heart go pitty-pat.

But my leg still hurts and I still look like the Elephant Man's long lost sister.

And I probably smell like vomit.

We slowly make our way back up the beach until we reach the quaint stretch of shops once again. People are still staring, even more so now that Dante is with such a freak.

I try not to look anyone in the eye. Maybe if I can't see them, they can't see me either. The click of cameras, though, lets me know that I'm delusional. Not only can they see me, but they are documenting my swollen and bloated look for posterity's sake. Fabulous.

And just when I think that this morning can't get any worse, a fake voice so sugary-sweet that it could practically be used to bake cookies with floats down the sidewalk.

"Dante Giliberti! You were supposed to call me the instant that you were back in town."

I know even before I turn to look that the owner of the voice is gorgeous. The level of confidence that it contains betrays that fact because only the beautiful sound so sure of themselves. Dante is grinning like he's just won the lottery so I reluctantly turn to see who we are dealing with.

It's Miss America.

Or, Miss Caberra, rather. I'm sure of it. She has to be.

Perfect russet colored hair, not red, but not quite brown, flows perfectly down her back. Her legs are two miles long, her skin lightly tanned to a golden sheen, her teeth are brilliantly white, and her face. Oh, her face. Michelangelo himself could have used her as a model. She is perfection personified, there's no doubt about that.

Her deep emerald green eyes assess me thoroughly and shrewdly for a moment, evaluating any threat that I might pose to her. After all, I'm clutching Dante's arm. Her eyes flicker down to my swollen, grotesque leg and then back up at my face. Is that amusement that I see in her face right before she dismisses me and turns back to speak with Dante?

Bitch.

Utter bitch. I can tell right now.

But Dante seems oblivious.

"Elena!" he smiles and releases my arm so that he can embrace Miss Perfect. She kisses him on both cheeks in what I have learned is a European custom. I try not to seethe with jealousy. He turns to me.

"Reece, this is Elena Kontou. We've known each other since we were toddlers. Her father is my father's best friend. They live on the estate just south of Giliberti Olives."

My stomach plummets into my toes. This is even worse than I had thought.

Miss Perfect has a long-standing claim to Dante. And I can see in her eyes that she's not relinquishing it any time soon. She extends a slender, well-bred hand toward me. Her rings cut into my hand as she shakes it.

"It's very nice to meet you, Reece. Are you here for an extended visit? Dante didn't tell me that he was expecting company."

She turns her beautiful green eyes toward Dante for an explanation which leaves me wondering how much they actually share with each other. Do they talk about everything?

Dante quickly gives her the run-down of what had happened in Amsterdam and I can see the instant she decides that I'm not a threat to her. Her face lightens right up.

"Oh!" she exclaims. "Then you've witnessed firsthand Dante's heroic tendencies. He saved my life once. I fell off of his father's yacht and I can't swim. Dante dove right in and pulled me out of the ocean."

"She should have been wearing a life-jacket," Dante interjects, "But she didn't want to mess up her tan." He rolls his eyes good-naturedly and Elena nudges him.

"Who needs a life jacket when I have you?" She smiles up at him and bats her eyelashes and I want to throw up. And this time, my nausea has nothing to do with the jellyfish that just tried to kill me.

Elena turns to me. "How long will you be here?" she asks innocently. "I'll have to show you around Valese. And what happened to your leg?"

"Apparently, I'm allergic to jellyfish," I answer. "And I would love to hang out with you while I'm here. I'll be staying until the airports open back up. They're closed right now due to the volcanic ash."

"I know!" she gushes as she returns her attention to Dante. "Did you know that Michel is stranded in London? He's furious because he'll probably miss the Regatta. He's got a new boat this year and everything."

She and Dante talk about that for a few minutes, about this important annual boat race that is apparently a big deal thing here in Caberra, and I have been forgotten. I stand there awkwardly with my freakish leg throbbing until finally Dante looks at me as if he suddenly remembers my presence.

"Oh, god. I'm sorry, Reece. I forgot my manners. We really need to get you back to the palace. I want you to lie down for awhile and I'll get the doctor to look at you." He turns to Elena. "We'll catch up soon, Leni."

He calls her *Leni*. I am instantly and ridiculously resentful of that.

"There's a bonfire tonight," *Leni* tells him as she watches him take my arm. "Will you be there?"

He glances at me, then back at *Leni*. "Maybe. We'll see how it goes."

"Don't keep me waiting, D," she warns playfully. "You know how I hate that."

And I hate that she calls him *D*.

I've known her all of five minutes and I already hate this girl because she's known Dante longer. He's *D* and she's *Leni*. Plus, she's perfect. I hate that too. And hating that makes me petty, which of course I hate also. I'm just downright hateful today, apparently.

Dante smiles at Elena and we walk away. I know that if I turn around, I'll see her watching us. I can feel her emerald green eyes staring a hole into my back. She is not one to be messed with. I know that, too.

Chapter Seven

"Mom, I swear to you, I'm fine," I insist once again into the phone. "It's just a jellyfish sting. It's not like my leg was amputated or anything. Apparently, it's a common thing around the ocean. I had a slight allergic reaction, but I'm all fixed up. The doctor gave me a shot of cortisone and it's not even swollen anymore, it just has red patches."

I look down at my splotch-covered legs and know that I look like I had been on the losing end of a jellyfish tentacle, which of course, is exactly the case.

Also, the cortisone shot hurt like a wench.

But I don't mention that part.

My mother is already wound up enough. She's not happy that I'm here. She's happy enough that I'm getting exposure to culture and all, but she wishes that I'd get that exposure in a country that she's actually heard of before. And somewhere that isn't thousands of miles from home.

I listen to her motherly concern and nagging for the next ten minutes as I stare absently out of my bedroom window. I am situated at the back of the house over the tennis courts. I can see a sparkling blue pool to my right and pristine gardens to my left. The tennis courts are in the center.

There are rose bushes everywhere. And peonies, which are my favorites. And lots of white marble statues of Greek gods. And one of Napoleon. Why in the world is this country so obsessed with Napoleon?

I am just wondering if the small statue is life-sized when Dante interrupts any coherent thought process that I might have by striding across the lawns with a racquet in hand and wearing short-short tennis shorts.

Sweet.

Baby.

Monkeys.

It's like a slow-motion scene from a movie. Dante shakes his blond bangs out of his eyes and the sun catches every glint of gold in his hair. His legs are long, lean, tanned and muscled and HolyCowThereIsAGod.

If I were a man, I would totally be wolf-whistling right now. But then again, if I were a man, I guess I wouldn't be wolf-whistling at Dante.

I'm such a weirdo.

"Reece Elizabeth Ellis, are you listening to me?" my mother demands from the other end of the phone.

Um, no. I hadn't been. I have no idea what she said. In fact, I had forgotten that she was even on the phone at all. Dante's short-short shorts are to blame.

"Of course I am," I answer as I push the curtains back so that I can see Dante better.

Stalk, much?

I ignore the voice in my head and the voice in the phone and concentrate on Dante. I don't know who he is playing with. It must be one of his friends, because the boy appears to be our age, too. But the strange boy doesn't hold my attention. He's totally eclipsed by Dante and I don't feel bad about that because the strange boy probably used to it.

Dante serves the ball and it whizzes past the other boy like a comet.

Dante laughs and the other boy scowls as he positions himself to return Dante's next serve. Dante fakes him out and laughs as the boy swings at the air. I am reminded of a Labrador when you throw a ball, then fake it and the dog still runs to get it.

Dante laughs again and then serves for real. It whizzes past the boy's head again. The boy throws his racquet and Dante rolls his eyes. As he does, he catches sight of me watching. I duck behind the curtain.

"I've gotta go mom," I say quietly. "I'll talk to you later. Love you, too."

After a moment, I peek carefully out the window again and Dante is waiting for me, standing in the middle of the tennis courts, waving cheerfully at me.

He totally knew that I was watching and he waited to catch me fair and square. Nice.

Dante: One. Reece: Zero.

I smile at him and wave, and he motions for me to come down.

My heart goes pitty-pat again and I glance down at myself.

I'm wearing the same shorts and shirt that I was wearing earlier because I have nothing else to wear. I'd only packed one extra outfit in my carryon. And I'm thankful for that much.

My mom insisted that I do so in case my flight was delayed or my bags were lost and I'd thought it was stupid, but apparently she knew what she was talking about. I make a mental note to thank her. But I'm definitely not pointing out that she was right. That would set a dangerous precedent.

But for now, I cautiously make my way down the stairs and toward the back doors of the Old Palace to find Dante. I am still amazed and in awe of this house. Palace. Mansion. Capitol. Whatever you want to call it. It's crazy big and crazy gorgeous. And it has a staff. One of them, a maid dressed in an honest-to-god black and white maid uniform looks at me and smiles.

"May I get you anything, miss?" she asks. I shake my head.

"I'm just hunting for the back doors," I admit to her. "I'm afraid I'm a little turned around."

She laughs and I realize that she's not much older than I am.

"That's okay," she tells me. "This is a big place. I couldn't find my way for weeks after I started working here. Go down that hallway there and then it will open up into a huge room. There will be a glass wall of windows and doors and just pick a door. They all open up to the outside."

"How old are you?" I ask curiously. She looks taken aback for a moment and I apologize. "I'm sorry. I'm American. I guess we don't have much tact. Or that's what I'm told anyway."

She laughs. "No, you're fine. I'm sixteen. I work here in the evenings during the school year and full-time during the summer."

That makes sense. A full-time summer job. That's perfectly normal for a teenager. It allays my fears that Caberra has hideous or non-existent child labor laws.

I stretch out a hand.

"I'm Reece," I offer. "I'm staying here for a little while until the airports open up."

"I know," she tells me as she shakes my hand. "I know who you are. I'm Heaven. I work here. And I'm probably not supposed to be socializing with you right now."

"Oh." I feel deflated. She had the potential of being a friend. And honestly, I could use a friend. I'm thousands of miles from home and my BFF Becca.

"It's okay," she assures me. "I'm not going to get into trouble. Don't worry about it."

"Hey, how did you know who I am?"

Because it just hits me what she said. *I know who you are.*

She smiles again. "Everyone knows who you are. Or, at least what you look like." She pulls her phone out of her pocket and punches at it, then turns it to me.

A picture of Dante and me from this morning, pre-jellyfish sting, stares at me from the screen. The caption screams, "Is Caberra's Favorite Prince in Love?"

"Prince?" I ask dumbly as I stare in shock at the picture. "This was from this morning. How did they get it posted so fast?" I look closer at the website. It looks to be a gossip website. Oh, sweet Lord.

"Oh, that's just how the media refers to Mr. Giliberti," Heaven answers. "And pretty much everyone else does too, I guess. He's not actually a prince, but he might as well be."

I gulp and take a moment to center myself.

I am in a beautiful place with a beautiful boy who just happens to almost be a prince. No big deal.

"Reece?"

Speak of the Princely Devil himself.

Dante's husky voice fills the room we're standing in and as I turn, I find him filling the doorway too. He's sweaty and hot, in more ways than one, and I smile weakly.

"I'm sorry," I tell him as he crosses the room. He's wearing a white tank top that perfectly shows off his bulging biceps. "I got turned around. Heaven here was just showing me the way outside."

Dante glances down at Heaven, who is hastily shoving her cell phone back into her apron pocket. He acts like he's never seen her before and he gives her a polite smile.

"Thank you, Heaven," he bows dramatically. She blushes and he stands upright again. "You might have saved poor Ms. Ellis' life. She isn't known for her directional prowess."

"What?" I demand in mock agitation. "You have no way of knowing that. It's an unfounded rumor."

He cocks a golden eyebrow.

"Really? You forget that I was on the beach with you this morning. After we got onto the beach, you couldn't tell north from south."

"That might be true," I acknowledged. "But I do know right from left. And you have to cut me some slack. I'm new here."

"True," he concedes. "But I have a feeling that it wouldn't be much better even if you weren't." He laughs as I swat at him.

"Would you like to come meet my friends?"

He has a hopeful tone in his voice that makes him seem like a little boy, which immediately penetrates my soft spot. I'm a sucker for big strong guys who have a gentle side.

"Sure," I nod. "I saw you playing tennis with one of them."

"Is that what you call it? Playing?" he grins cockily. "I call it annihilation."

"Really?" I laugh. "Pretty sure of yourself, aren't you?"

He laughs too as he holds the door open for me.

"I have to be," he confides to me softly as he passes by. "If I'm not, the public will sense it on me and descend like a pack of wild wolverines."

He winks and then leads me to where two boys and a girl are sitting by the pool sipping what looks to be lemonade. The dark haired boy who was playing tennis is here, as well as a black-haired girl and another blond boy. Neither boy is as good looking as Dante. But that's probably not a fair thing to say. No one is as good-looking as Dante. I've come to peace with that fact and they probably have too.

"Guys," Dante says easily. "I want you to meet Reece Ellis. She's my houseguest for a while."

The boys look up and the girl appraises me quietly. She seems friendly, not cat-like like Elena. Her face is sincere and open and I sense that she could be friend material.

"Reece," Dante continues. "This is Gavin, Nate and Mia. We've known each other since kindergarten. In a nutshell, Gavin is our resident Casanova, Nate is the smart-ass one and Mia is the sweet, talk-your-ear-off one."

"And which one are you?" Nate scowls mockingly.

"I'm the good looking and charming one, obviously," Dante jokes. Only it's not a joke. He really is.

I smile and wave at the group. "It's really nice to meet you."

Gavin leaps to his feet and circles the table, grabbing my hand and kissing it. "The pleasure is mine," he purrs. "You're every bit as beautiful as your pictures, mademoiselle."

He's not French so it's pretty funny. But my heart still plummets. Even they have seen the stupid pictures? Has everyone?

Dante sees my expression and rushes to assure me.

"Reece, seriously, I'm sorry. It's just a part of my life- the press loves to speculate. But it will blow over, I promise. And they didn't use your name."

76

"Yeah, because they don't have it yet," Mia mumbles. She stands up and leans over to hug me. "It will be fine," she assures me also. "Those stupid gossip sites are piranhas, but Dante is right. They have very short attentions spans. They'll forget about you soon enough- once you go home, for sure. It's nice to meet you."

"It's nice to meet you, too," I murmur. The last boy, Nate, stares unabashedly from the table. He doesn't stand up and his eyes seem sort of cold. He's got white blond hair and ice blue eyes. He doesn't seem friendly. At all.

"You're pretty skinny for an American," he observes. No smile.

"You're pretty rude for a Caberran," I answer. No smile. And that's hard for me because I'm usually pretty smiley.

"Oh, snap!" Gavin crows. He laughs and shoves Nate's arm, while Dante scowls.

"Behave yourself," Dante instructs Nate. "I mean it."

What the hell? What had I done to Nate? I hadn't even had time to offend him yet. Yet, apparently I had. Even I'm not fast enough to stick my foot in my mouth that quickly.

"It's alright," Dante tells me. "Nate had a bad experience in America when he was there last. He's not a fan."

"Oh?"I raise an eyebrow. "I thought you said Caberra loves Americans. Or, our tourist dollars, anyway."

Dante smiled graciously. "I said *I* love Americans. I think most Caberrans do. Nate just had a bad experience."

"Really?" I turn toward Nate, determined to try one more time. "What happened? Pick-pocket in New York? Rude people on the subway?"

"Girl problems," Mia told me. "He dated a true wench. She only wanted his money and a free vacation to Caberra."

"Oh." I felt red stain my cheeks. I should have known. Relationship troubles seem to be the root of all evil. "I'm sorry."

"Don't be," Nate says stiltedly as he pushed away from the table. "It's just been my experience that American girls are all the same: self-entitled, arrogant and complete bitches."

I stare at him, dumb-founded. "I don't know what to say to that," I admit.

"Say nothing," Gavin advises. "He's just being a dick."

Nate glares at him before stalking off. Dante follows him and I watch as they seem to have a few heated words by the edge of the pool. Dante sticks his finger in Nate's face and Nate's scowl seems glued into place.

"What's his deal?" I ask Mia. "Did he really get burned that badly?"

She nods. "Uh-huh. The girl was a cold-hearted wench. I know that all American girls aren't that way. But Nate can't seem to get it through his thick, pale head. And truly, he's just kind of a dick in general. He's never happy."

I watch as Nate stalks away and Dante returns to the group. He doesn't even seem flustered.

"Where were we?" he asks smoothly as he pours a glass of lemonade and offers it to me. It actually has mint leaves floating in it. Fancy.

"You were getting ready to tell us that you are bringing Reece to the bonfire tonight," Gavin answers fluidly without missing a beat.

Gavin turns to me and takes my arm, speaking conspiratorially.

"There will be fresh crab legs, oysters- and you know what those are good for- and clams. And all the fresh melted butter that any girl could ask for. Plus, of course, the fruity drinks with umbrellas that all females appear to worship." He bats his eyes in exaggeration. "Please say you'll come. I will die a slow, painful, horrible death if you don't."

"What are oysters good for?" I ask him innocently with a straight face. He stares at me as Mia hides a giggle.

"Seriously? You haven't heard this?" he asks. I shake my head even though I know dang good and well what they are good for.

"They're aphrodisiacs. Tried and proven," he thumps his chest proudly. "I'll make sure they have extras for you tonight, my lovely."

Gavin grins at me and I have to laugh. He's ridiculous. But I find that I like it. Charm, cockiness and an inflated sense of ego. What's not to like? The charm is the key. Without it, he'd just be an ass.

I grin. "Alright. I'll be there." But then I look at Dante. "I mean, will we?"

He smiles patiently. "Anything you'd like. You're a guest in my home. Your wish is my command."

Gavin looks at him, then at me. "You'd better study your list of commands," he advises me. "Ask for something good."

I laugh at his ridiculous expression, then turn to find Dante watching me.

His blue eyes are solemn and I wonder what he is thinking.

Laughingly, I ask, "I can ask for anything?"

Dante leans in, his lips so close to my cheek that I can feel his warm breath.

"Just say the word and it's yours."

I suck my breath in and stare at him. He's seems so serious all of a sudden and my heart starts skipping beats. His nearness is making me crazy. He smells delicious, like the earth, the sea, the sun and the woods.   I have to literally bite my lip from replying, *You. I want you.*

And I realize with a start, that I do.

I do want him.

I've known him all of two days and I want him completely, utterly and absolutely.

OhMyWord.

Chapter Eight

The sea here in Caberra is amazing.

During the day, it's turquoise and clear and smells like salt.

At night, right now, it is massive and black and mysterious. And smells like salt.

I guess that's the case with the sea anywhere, but it seems especially amazing here. So clean and huge and romantic. Maybe because this is Dante's home. Or maybe it's because I'm walking with him right now.

Next to the sea.

In the dark.

Under the stars.

Be still my heart.

"So, what do you think of my home?" Dante asks conversationally as we navigate our way over driftwood that has washed ashore. He gently guides my elbow and I feel my stomach tighten with warm and trembly feelings. He's just so...perfect. Too good to be true, almost.

"I think it's beautiful," I tell him honestly. "It seems so ancient and perfect."

He smiles in response. "Thank you. It is pretty ancient. Not perfect, though, but it's close. Tell me more about your home. You haven't said that much. What would you be doing right now if you were home in Kansas?"

I try to stare at him in the night, but it's hard because it's dark. He senses my gaze though and laughs. "Come on. It can't be that bad."

I glance again at the sea next to us.

"Coming from here, you can't begin to imagine a place where there isn't much natural beauty," I tell him. "Picture a place where pioneers used to work themselves into an early grave in the sun and dust. And that's Kansas."

Dante laughs again.

"But it's not pioneer days anymore," he reminds me. "Seriously. I want to picture where you come from. Tell me about it."

"Okay." I think on it for a second. "Right now, it is stiflingly hot there. I'm talking hell's kitchen hot, and not the cool New York City Hell's Kitchen. I'm talking suck-your-breath-right-out-of-your-body hot. And right now, I'd either be lying on my bed writing in my journal or on my phone with my best friend, Becca. Or I'd be sleeping over at her house. And we might be sneaking out of her window to hang out with our friends. We can't sneak out of mine- my bedroom is too high up."

"So, you're a rule-breaker, then. Noted," he says. I'm sure his eyes are twinkling again, although I can't see them to make sure.

"No, I'm really not," I answer. "We don't do anything bad. We just meet up with our friends down by the river. We light a little bonfire. Sometimes there's beer, although I'm not a beer drinker. Sometimes, we float down the river on innertubes, which is pretty cool under the stars. Although, we do have to watch out for Water Moccasins."

"Water moccasins?"

"Poisonous water snakes. They're black and look harmless, like a stick floating in the water almost, but when they open up their mouths, the inside is cotton white. That's why they are also called Cotton Mouths. And they can kill you in the time it takes for you to drive to the hospital."

Dante winces. "Sounds interesting. Tell me about Becca. How long have you known her?"

We climb a small sand dune and I find that we are really out in the middle of nowhere. Apparently, they come this far out so that Dante can have some privacy as he hangs out with his friends. I think it's nice that his friends are so understanding.

"Becca is…Becca."

I try to think of how to describe her.

"She's wild and crazy and funny. She's been my best friend since kindergarten. She lives about five minutes from me so we can walk to and fro if we like. She lives on a farm, too. She's got an older brother, Connor, who is a bull-rider. We go see him ride on Saturdays."

"Bull riding?" Dante sounds dubious, like he thinks I'm trying to pull one over on him. I have to admit, it does sound like a contrived sport. Who in their right mind would want to sit on a pissed off bull? I spend a second explaining it to him.

"Anyway," I continue. "Becca always hopes that Connor and I will end up together so that she and I will be related."

"And what do you hope? Do you like Connor?" Dante asks.

I can't read his tone. Is he interested in my answer for any other reason aside from idle curiosity?

"I do like Connor…like a brother. I've known him since we were kids and honestly, I can't *like* like someone who knows every single thing about me. There needs to be some mystery there. I only want the best for him, though. Connor is a really good guy. He's away at college right now. He comes home on the weekends."

"I see." Dante says. Does he see? "What does your farm look like? I want to picture it in my head."

"Well, it's an old farm house. Not old by Caberran standards, but old. Two story, with white siding. My mom and I live there with my grandparents. My grandma is a big fan of your olives, by the way. Sunflowers grow like crazy in Kansas and my mom has a small field of them behind one of our barns just because she likes them. We always seem to have a vase of them sitting on the kitchen table. We have horses, cows, goats. My horse's name is Mischief."

"I've always wanted to learn to ride," Dante muses.

"Then why haven't you?"

"There aren't any horses in Caberra," he tells me. "I suppose my father could have one shipped in for me, but I've never asked."

"Well, if you ever come to the States, you'll have to come visit me and I'll give you a riding lesson," I tell him.

"I'd like that," he answers. And he sounds really sincere. I try to picture him on a horse. But I keep picturing him in his suit, or a set of linen trousers and I just can't see him on a farm.

"Look," Dante points. "We're almost there."

A bonfire glows in the distance in what appears to be a little inlet.

"We're really out here," I observe. "Surely the media can't find you here."

"Even if they could," Dante says, "They would be trespassing. This is a private beach now. And in this particular spot, it's hidden from public view. Even with zoom lenses, they can't see us."

For a second, I ponder this. Dante has to live his entire life thinking about how he can go places without getting his picture taken, how to not get followed, how to not get hounded by photographers. It must get really tiring.

"Do you ever get tired of having to be so careful?" I ask. "Isn't it exhausting? I mean, you didn't ask for this. It's your father's job. Not yours."

"That's true," Dante answers thoughtfully. "But I would never ask him to not do it. Apparently, ever since my mother died, he hasn't been the same. This job gives him something to focus on. It makes him happy."

"How old were you when your mother died?" I ask. "Do you mind talking about it?"

He shakes his head. "No. I don't mind. She died giving birth to me, so I don't remember her at all. I have pictures of her so I know that I look like her. My father tells me that I act like her. But I never knew her."

"She died giving birth?" I'm appalled. "I didn't know that happened these days."

"It doesn't usually," he agrees. "But apparently, the placenta detached during the birthing process.

She hemorrhaged internally and there wasn't anything they could do. It happened very fast. My father was devastated. My grandmother helped him raise me until I was five and then she died, too."

"You grew up with your grandmother?" Then we have one thing in common, at least. My grandparents are a huge part of my life.

Dante nods. "Yes. She was like a mother to me."

My heart is happy that he had the experience of having a mother-like figure. I can't imagine growing up without a maternal influence of some sort. And his entire situation tugs at my heart strings. Here he is... so beautiful and the son of such an important person and a billionaire to boot, yet he experienced tragedy at such a young age. It just goes to show that money really can't buy everything.

I reach over and grab his hand. I find that I want to offer him comfort, even though his injury happened so long ago. He squeezes my fingers and then all of a sudden, we are at the party.

Kids are laughing and joking, the fire is blazing in a warm glow that reaches into the dark sky, and the moon hangs heavy overhead. The evening breeze is just slightly chilly, but in a good way.

"Cold?" Dante asks me as I shiver. He wraps his arm around my shoulders and his warmth makes me feel like I am home.

And then I feel stupid for thinking something so corny, but it doesn't make it any less true.

"Reece!" Mia shouts from the perimeter of the party. She's dressed in an off-the-shoulder dark purple sundress and is standing with Gavin. He grins from ear to ear when he sees me.

"Good luck with that," Dante murmurs into my ear. I smile. If the worst thing I have to deal with is a good-natured Casanova, I'm in pretty good shape.

I head over to Mia while Dante gets waylaid by a group of boys that I haven't met yet. They're wearing swim trunks and I can't imagine why they aren't shivering to death.

"Reece," Mia greets me, handing me a wine cooler.

I take it, even though I don't drink. It's not because I'm afraid to break the rules because I'm not. I just don't like the taste of alcohol. I figure it's an acquired taste and I simply haven't acquired it yet. I've put it on my list of things to do later.

"We're going to have to go shopping tomorrow," Mia tells me as she looks me up and down. "Dante said that your bags are still in Amsterdam."

"Yep," I answer, grimacing at my one outfit of clothes. "They'll be stuck there until the airports open. But when the airports open, I'll be going to my dad's anyway, so I guess my luggage will never make it to Caberra."

"Well, here's to an excuse to shop!" Mia toasts, clinking her bottle to mine. "I never need one, but it's always nice to have."

I laugh at her because it's apparent that she's buzzing. She was pretty reserved this afternoon and now she's practically exuberant. She's done a complete one-eighty.

"Thanks," I tell her. "My mom gave me her credit card to use in an emergency, and I think this probably qualifies."

"Dude, this totally qualifies," she agrees. "I'll come pick you up at 11:00 a.m. Will that work?"

"That will be perfect," I tell her gratefully.

Gavin chimes in, wrapping his arm around Mia's slender waist. "I'll tag along, too, if you don't mind. I don't have plans."

"Nope," Mia tells him, leaning heavily into him. "It's a girl's day. And you don't qualify. You don't have the right parts."

"It's better to have too many parts then not enough," he informs her and she laughs.

"Gavin, I love you. I really, really do."

He kisses her cheek and then behind her back, he mouths words to me.

She's REALLY drunk.

I nod. That much is obvious. I only hope that she remembers that we have a shopping date. If I have to wear these clothes one more time, I might die.

"Can you take her for a minute?" Gavin asks, slipping Mia to me like she's a child or something.

I put my arms around her shoulders so that she is leaning on me. Gavin saunters off, already mouthing off to Dante, who is across the fire from us. And then I realize that he totally just made an escape. And now I'm Mia's caretaker.

"I'm fine," Mia insists to me. She takes a step away from, stumbles, then slumps back into my side. "*Fine.*"

"Yes, you're fine," I agree with her, tightening my hold. I wonder if she will pass out, then tighten my hold even more. She winces, but doesn't shirk away.

"Dante likes you," she confides to me, in a not-so-quiet whisper. "I can tell."

I look around quickly to see who is within hearing distance. Thankfully, no one.

"What makes you say that?" I ask curiously, my heart starting to stutter. Dante doesn't *like* like me. There is no way.

Mia shrugs. "I can't explain it. I just know it because I know him."

Well, that's helpful. I want to know exactly how she knows so that I know if it is just drunken musing or if it actually has credibility. Which it doesn't, because there is no way on God's green earth that Dante likes me.

"But what about Elena?" I ask her.

I figure I might as well get as much information as I can tonight while Mia's still chatty. And by *chatty*, I just mean 'pump her for information while she's drunk'. I should feel guilty, but I don't. I like Mia and I'll never tell anyone anything that she says. It's for my info only.

Mia snorts. "Elena is a bitch. Utter and complete bitch."

Tell me something I don't know, I think.

"What makes you say that?" I actually say.

Mia stares at me incredulously, her eyes slightly unfocused. "Have you actually spoken with her? Utter bith."

Oh, great. And now she's slurring. And she's leaning more and more on me. For such a little thing, she's actually kind of heavy and my arm is going to sleep.

"Just because their fathers are friends, she thinks she's going to marry Dante. And connect their families and then they'll have wine *and* olives."

"She owns a winery?" I ask, appalled again.

I own cows. Elena owns wine. What's wrong with this picture?

"Her *father* owns a winery," Mia corrected. "But it will be hers someday. She wants to marry Dante and he probably will because he likes to please his father. Dante is a pleaser," she explains. "He always does what is expected of him. But that's a shame.

Because he likes you. Oh, look. Speak of the she-devil now."

I follow Mia's drunken gaze and my breath freezes in my throat. Even though it is cold out here on the water, colder than a witch's you-know-what, there stands Elena, draped on Dante's arm and wearing a miniscule, barely-there white bikini.

And she is beautiful.

And her boobs are hanging all over Dante.

And I hate her.

And as she turns and locks eyes with me, I can see that she hates me too.

Chapter Nine

I settle Mia on a folding lawn chair, making sure she has a bottle of water before I leave her. I turn back to look and she's curled around the bottle, her head slumped on the arm of the chair. She'll be passed out within the minute.

I look around and marvel at this party. They really know how to do a party up right here. Someone has lugged in countless folding chairs, tables, coolers, cookware. They are boiling seafood and heating what looks to be butter. I can't imagine how long it took to lug all of this stuff in. And I try to imagine kids from back home doing this, but there's no way. They wouldn't go to all of this trouble. We just sit on old logs at the river and drink from red plastic cups.

"Reece!"

Dante waves from a seat near the fire. He's holding what appears to be a giant claw and I gulp as I make my way to him.

"Do you like crab?" he asks.

"I don't know," I answer. "I've never had it."

He looks at me as though I've suddenly grown another head.

"You've never had it?" Elena asks disdainfully. I didn't even realize she was standing there. "How is that even possible?"

I stare at her coolly. "I grew up in the middle of the United States, a thousand miles from the nearest ocean. Fresh seafood isn't exactly easy to come by there."

"Ah, right," Elena pretends to remember. "You're a little farm girl. You've never experienced culture. Well, welcome to Caberra, sweetie."

She waves her arm in a sweeping, condescending gesture and I found that I would like to break it. Her arm, I mean.

"We've got plenty of culture," I reply through my teeth. "Just not an ocean nearby."

I turn my back on her and sit in the empty seat next to Dante. I'm surprised that Elena's not already sitting there, but I try to put her out of my mind as I kick my shoes off and scrunch my toes into the soft sand.

Dante glances at me while he sticks a crab leg in a nut cracker. He crunches it and I cringe at the horrid sound. Why would anyone want to eat that?

"You've really never had crab legs?" he asks doubtfully as though it couldn't possibly be true.

"Nope," I confirm. "Never."

"Well, then, my little Sunflower, you're in for a treat," he announces.

I freeze at the nickname. Is he making fun of me? I look at him and he doesn't seem to be. He's busy pulling stringy white meat from the broken crab legs. He was just being sweet.

It's an endearment, you idiot, I tell myself. So what does that mean? I'm starting to become endeared to him? And is endeared even a word?

"Here, try this," Dante instructs me, holding out a piece of crab dripping with melted butter on a small fork. I study it for a second and Dante rolls his eyes.

"Just try it," he tells me. "It's not going to bite."

I let him stick the fork in my mouth, expecting to taste a piece of Heaven, like I did when I tried the gelato.

But no.

That is most certainly not what I receive.

This isn't Heaven.

This tastes like a dead fish in my mouth, which is actually true.

I try to resist spitting it out, instead concentrating on chewing up the hateful piece of meat. Dante looks at my face and then dies laughing.

"Can I assume you don't like it?" he asks, his face lit up like a Christmas tree in his amusement. He hands me a napkin.

I spit my crab into it and fold it in half, then in half again. Dante holds out his hand and I reluctantly hand him the chewed-up crab carcass and he throws it into a trash can. They even thought to bring trash cans? What kind of teenagers are these, anyway?

"It's alright," he tells me. "I think maybe it is an acquired taste. Which would also probably rule out oysters for you. Those are also an acquired taste. Have you ever had them?"

I shake my head. "Not unless you count Mountain Oysters. Which I definitely do not."

"Mountain Oysters?" he looks confused.

I blush and Dante looks immediately interested.

"What? What's wrong? What are mountain oysters?"

I hesitate. Then decide to pull my big-girl panties up and explain. Holy crap. I'm not a child. I can totally do this without blushing. I can.

"Mountain Oysters are bull balls. Bull testicles, if you want to be technical. I accidentally tried them when Connor and Quinn tricked Becca and I into eating them at a rodeo."

I'm blushing. My cheeks are red-hot.

"A rodeo?" Dante looks both curious at that and appalled and disgusted at the notion of eating a bull's balls.

"It's a sporting event," I tell him. "I can explain it later. Is there anything else to eat here?"

Dante looks around and then shakes his head regretfully.

"I'm sorry. No. This is sort of a tradition. We cook fresh seafood on the beach at night. Our parents did it, our parents' parents did it. And so on. We're not civilized enough to bring bread or anything." He grins and touches my arm.

I feel the heat from his touch long after his hand is gone.

A perfect imprint of his hand is emblazoned on my arm.

It might be there forever for all that I know.

"Are you ready?" Dante asks, in a tone that suggests that he's repeating himself.

"What?" I look at him dumbly.

He stares back patiently.

"Are you ready to go? I'll get you something to eat in the Palace kitchens."

"Oh. We don't have to go so soon. We can just eat when we get back. No big deal."

Dante looks around and I follow his gaze.

There are two girls leaning into each other on the sand near us. It looks like they will pass out at any given moment. The group of boys in swim trunks have moved their party to the water and are rough-housing in the cold waves, shouting and hollering. Gavin is busy trying to score with a petite blonde who still seems a tiny bit sober and all around us, drunken laughter splits the night. It seems that we are the only two completely sober people here. I don't see Elena anywhere.

"I'm ready," Dante tells me. I realize then that I haven't seen him with a drink in his hand all evening.

"Do you not drink?"

He looks down at me, his face oh-so-handsome in the moonlight. The silvery light washes across his cheeks, illuminating his cut-cheek-bones and I find that I want to touch him. I want to run my fingertips across his skin and inhale his man smell. Oh, Lord. What is wrong with me?

"I don't," he tells me. "Not usually. Some champagne here and there at my father's functions, but not really anything else. The last thing I need is for pictures of *that* to hit the papers. I can see the headlines now: *Caberran Prince parties himself to an early grave.*"

"It must be hard to be you," I say softly. "You have to think about every little thing you do."

He stares down at me again, his eyes dark blue in the night.

"It's not so hard to be me," he tells me. "And sometimes, it's better than others."

He brushes against me then, his hand lingering slightly against my hip. It stays there for a second, then another. Did he mean to do that?

Surely he knows where his hand is.

I feel connected to him, like there is electricity jolting in the air, just like it felt on the plane. His eyes are staring into mine and my heart is taking off like a galloping race horse. He takes a step closer to me and now he's definitely in my personal space. But I like it. I can feel the heat emanating from his body and it's pulling me to him. If I wanted, I could take one little step and push myself against his chest.

If I wanted.

Which I do.

Want to.

And then, just when I start to move my foot, I hear my name.

A plaintive, pitiful mewl.

"Reece."

A whimper.

I turn, only to find Mia on her hands on knees next to the chair that I left her in. She stops whimpering and throws up gallons of purple wine-cooler. I wince. And she throws up more. Then she's crying.

"I'm sorry," I murmur to Dante and then I rush for Mia.

I feel him behind me, but I don't look. I just sink to the ground next to Mia and hold her short hair out of her face while she pukes.

Because this is what a friend does. They take care of their friends even when it is inconvenient or inopportune. Am I her only friend? I look around, but don't see anyone else coming to help. But to be fair, half of the people here are in her same condition.

"Reece, I feel so horrible," Mia whines.

"Of course you do," I soothe her, patting her back. "We should get you home."

She sits up and throws her arms around me. "Thank you, Reece. You're a really good friend."

I'm about to answer her with a sweet reply when she starts heaving again and before I can turn her around, she throws up on me. Her orangey-purplish vomit runs down the front of my shirt and the smell makes me want to throw up too.

"Oh, jeez," Dante cringes. "I'm sorry, Reece."

He scoots around me and picks up Mia gently by her arms. "Mia, sweetie, we've got to get you home."

He pulls his phone out of his pocket with one hand and murmurs something into it. Within two minutes, Buzz Cut and another security guard are at Dante's side. Were they out here on stand-by this whole time? The thought impresses me and creeps me out at the same time. Does Dante ever get any privacy?

"Mia, Russell is going to take you home," Dante tells her. "I'll talk to you tomorrow, okay?"

Mia nods in her barely cognizant state and then her head flops limply against Russell's chest. It looks like Russell glares at Dante before he stalks away, but I can't be sure.

Dante turns to me. "Let's go get that rinsed off."

I nod mutely and let Dante take me by the arm again. He leads me away from the party, down by the water, away from the splashing boys. We're in a quiet little inlet where my feet sink into the wet sand and I look around. Were the rest of his security detail close-by and watching?

I bend down and try to wash my shirt off.

It's not happening. It's too difficult while I'm still wearing it on my body.

"Okay," Dante assesses the situation. "You're going to have to take it off."

My gaze flies to his face in surprise.

"No."

Is he really just like every other boy?

He just wants to see my boobs?

I thought he was different.

Dante sighs patiently.

"I mean, I'll give you my shirt to wear and you can rinse yours out in the water before it stains. I've never actually seen it specifically mentioned on laundry detergent commercials, but I'm guessing that bright purple vomit will stain a shirt."

"You're probably right," I cringe as I feel the nasty stuff soaking through and touching my skin. "Okay. You're definitely right. I need to take it off."

The prospect of taking my shirt off in front of him both thrills me and terrifies me.

"Here," Dante says. He's already shrugging out of his button-up chambray shirt. He holds it up against me like a shield. "You stand behind my shirt and take yours off. No one will see you."

"Okay. Close your eyes," I instruct him. He instantly closes them tight.

I pull my shirt off quickly and drop it on the ground next to me. I feel odd standing here in just my bra and shorts when Dante is literally just a breath away. Just one breath. He could reach his hand out and my bare skin is right here for him to touch.

And I'm being ridiculous.

He is standing there with his eyes closed like the gentleman that he is.

He's not going to reach out and touch me.

I gulp and reach to take his shirt and I hear something.

Something quiet, non-descript... and something that shouldn't be there.

I turn, just in time to hear the clicking of a camera. The flash bulbs practically blind me as I yank Dante's shirt around me.

Dante yells and chases whoever is taking the pictures and I am left to quickly slip his shirt on and button it up. I glance toward the bluff and no one is there. Dante is gone and no one else even noticed that anything had happened.

Everyone else is too drunk to notice, apparently.

I take my shirt to the edge of the water and kneel down to wash it. Dante's shirt is soft against my skin, and it smells like him. I enjoy the feeling for a second and then roll the sleeves up so that they aren't dragging over my knuckles.

"I couldn't catch him," Dante's voice said from behind me. He was resigned and pissed off. "I'm really sorry, Reece."

I'm confused and I turn to him. "Why are *you* sorry?" I ask. "You didn't do it."

He shakes his head. "No. But it's because of me. My life will never be normal and I'm really sorry that it has affected you in such a way."

"If you hadn't sent Russell with Mia, this wouldn't have happened, would it?" I guessed. I can just tell that Russell's eyes never miss anything.

"Probably not," Dante admitted. "So, I'm sorry about that, too. She just needed to go home and I wasn't ready to leave you yet. I wanted a little bit of time alone with you. So, this is my fault."

I roll my eyes. "No, it wasn't. Not at all. You were trying to be a good friend."

But in my head, I'm singing. No, I'm screaming. In my head. Silently.

Dante wanted alone time with me? *With me??*

Dante turns his head and his eyes meet mine and for a moment I see something in his, something a little vulnerable and slightly sad and very beautiful all at the same time.

Just for a moment.

And then it is gone.

Chapter Ten

Dante cuts me the biggest slice of chocolate cake that I've ever seen, then pours a glass of milk. He pushes both things toward me.

"Is that goat's milk?" I ask hesitantly, eyeing the foaming white liquid. "Because I haven't seen one single cow since I got here."

"And you've seen a goat?" he raises an eyebrow. "Just because we don't let our cows run in the streets like they do in India doesn't mean that we don't have them. We have dairies like everyone else."

"Okay. Don't get all offended," I grin. "It was a valid question."

He shrugs good-naturedly. "I'll give you that. And I'm not offended."

Dante smiles and my heart races.

It's just that simple. When he does anything, smiles, laughs, looks at me, *breathes*... my heart reacts. He's definitely replaced Quinn in my daydreams.

I take a bite of the chocolate cake and all of a sudden, I feel like I'm a president's kid sneaking to the kitchens of the White House in the middle of the night for cake. The only difference is, I'm across the world from the White House and I'm not the President's Kid.

Dante is.

More or less.

"What?" he asks, studying my face. "What are you thinking about?"

His hand is splayed on the granite counter and I look at his fingers. They're long, like he is. I wish I had the guts to pick his hand up and hold it. I know that we had a moment back on the beach earlier. I know it. But we hadn't said anything the whole way back and now here we are talking about goat's milk.

Romantic.

"Nothing," I answer. "I just can't believe I'm here. That's all. It seems too surreal. I'm a normal girl from small-town America. This kind of thing doesn't happen to me."

"Yet it did," Dante points out. He has a cleft in his chin. I'm in love with the cleft in his chin. It's masculine and perfect and I find that I want to place my thumb in it to see if it fits. But I don't.

"True," I acknowledge. "But only because of a crazy accident at the airport."

"Some might say it was a *lucky* accident," Dante points out.

"Well, that probably depends on your perspective," I answer. "The families of the people on that crashed plane wouldn't agree. But for me, yes. It was lucky. I'm in a beautiful country instead of having uncomfortable silences with my father right now. So, thank you for that."

"Oh, that reminds me," Dante says. Is that a slight flush in his cheeks? "I spoke with *my* father. He will be back here in the morning and would like for you to join us for dinner tomorrow evening. Would you like to?"

I stare at him. Dinner with a Prime Minister?

"It depends," I answer slowly. "Will we be having crab legs?"

Dante laughs and shakes his head.

"You have no idea what's good," he chuckles. "We can have whatever you'd like to have. Do you like steak? Steak from a cow, not steak from a goat?"

I crack up and we laugh together and start talking about fathers and goats and life and before I know it, we've been talking for over an hour.

"Holy cow," I breathe, looking at the clock on the wall. "It's 2:00 a.m."

"You should definitely go to bed, little Sunflower," Dante says. "You've got an 11:00 shopping date. That is, if Mia remembers."

I stare at him again. "How did you even hear that? You must have ears like a bat."

He rolls his eyes. "Either way, you should get some sleep."

We put our dishes in the sink and creep through the dark, quiet mausoleum-like house. At night, it seems even less like a real home.

"Do you think the airports will open up soon?" I ask as we climb the stairs.

"I have no idea," Dante answers. "But they can't stay closed forever."

That's sort of what I'm afraid of.

He walks me to my bedroom door and pauses. And I almost think that he might kiss me. Because we did have a moment back on the beach, dang it. But he doesn't. Instead, he pushes my hair behind one ear and then leans forward ever so slightly as he tells me to have sweet dreams.

Of course I will, I think. *They'll be about you.*

"Thank you," I actually say. "You too."

He smiles a tired smile and starts to walk away and as I stare at his bare back, I remember his shirt.

"Wait!" I cry. "What about your shirt?"

He smiles again.

"You can just send it to the laundry," he answers. "They know where I live. They'll get it back to me."

I shake my head and close my bedroom door.

And then I sit on my bed and inhale his shirt. As in, I literally bury my face into it and breathe. It smells just like him. And I love it. I wonder if he would notice if I *don't* send it to the laundry? Being the rule-follower that I am, though, I know that I will.

I'm not going to steal his shirt. But I go ahead and do the next best thing.

I sleep in it.

Scratch that.

I *over*-sleep in it.

When I open my eyes, the clock says 10:30 a.m. And the clock has no reason to lie.

With a yelp, I scramble out of bed and find that my shirt has been laundered and is wrapped in tissue-paper on the end of my bed. A member of housekeeping had crept in as I slept, which is a little unnerving, but I put it out of my mind as I rush to brush my teeth and get dressed.

And then as I fumble around for my shoes, I notice my cell phone.

12 missed calls, 8 voicemails. What the eff?

Grabbing it, I see that I have it set to silent, which would explain why I didn't hear it ring. Did something happen? Did grandma or grandpa have a heart attack? It's the only thing I can think of until I see that all of the calls are from Becca's number.

Weird.

I hold it to my ear and listen.

And then I want to die as I hear the messages.

Becca had been rummaging through my clothes to borrow my favorite yellow halter-top and came across my journal. And of course, she read it.

And I had written all about how I'm secretly in love with Quinn.

Because my journal is supposed to be secret.

But now she knows.

And she wants to kill me.

OhMyGosh.

Not only does Becca know, but she thinks that I'm secretly plotting to break them up. Because awhile back, she and Quinn had had a fight and I'd advised her that I didn't know if I'd believe him when he said that he hadn't been flirting with a strange girl at our track meet. And I'd meant it. I didn't have any ulterior motives. I'd simply seen Quinn's face as he was talking with the girl. He was flirting.

And Becca busted him. Period. It was pretty cut and dried, I thought. But I guess it wasn't.

I drop my face into my hands. This isn't good.

But it is 10:56 a.m. and Mia will be here any minute to go shopping.

So I can't call Becca back right now.

And honestly, it might be good to give her a little space anyway.

Just a little.

Just until I have built up enough courage to face her, because Becca's right. I totally betrayed her by falling in love with her boyfriend. She has no idea that my crush on Quinn has totally been eclipsed by my crush on Dante.

It doesn't take away the fact that I'd kept it a secret from her. And that's the most hurtful thing. We don't keep secrets from each other. Not ever. Not until now.

I sigh. Why is life so complicated sometimes?

10:58.

The phone rings beside the bed and I pick it up, hesitantly.

"Hello?"

It's someone from downstairs. Mia's here. Apparently, they can't just send her up without permission from someone, so I give my permission and wait. She arrives just a minute or two later.

She raps on my bedroom door and I answer and am surprised to see that she looks no worse for the wear. She laughs at my expression.

"Expecting someone else?" she asks, stepping into my room.

"No," I stammer. "I just thought you'd be… hung over."

She laughs again. "I hide it well," she confides. "My head is splitting."

Mia is dressed in a micro-mini layered with two black tank tops and about five rhinestone encrusted belts. Her short black hair is held back from her face by rhinestone headbands and overall, she looks like a sparkly rock star. She's even wearing five inch heels.

"You're so dressed up," I say tactfully.

She actually looks like she is going out to a club. Not exactly the outfit I would have worn for a day of shopping. But then, I have one outfit to my name at the moment, so who am I to judge?

"If you're going to do something," she advises, "Do it all the way."

Good point.

"Are you ready?" she asks, looking me up and down. "Never mind. You're ready. For some new clothes, that is."

"Snot," I nudge her. Mia already feels like an old friend and it is a really good feeling at the moment when I know that Becca would just as soon poke my eyes out as to look at me.

I grab my purse and we head out my door, down the steps and out the front. No one tries to stop me, and I realize that I expect someone to. I don't know why. We walk down the cobblestone sidewalks and this time, no one stops to look at me. They don't realize who I am, I guess.

Mia heads into a nearby shop, dragging me by the arm. We step inside and we are instantly surrounded by a teenage girl's paradise: racks and racks of clothing. I sigh a happy little sigh, pat my mother's credit card which is in my back pocket and start sifting through racks of clothing.

Four pair of shorts, two pairs of strappy sandals, two t-shirts, two pheasant-style blouses, one swimsuit and seven pairs of underwear later, Mia and I stand out on the sidewalk with our bags. I peer into Mia's.

Everything she bought is black.

I look back up at her. She just doesn't seem like the goth kind of girl.

"Trying to change your image?" I ask curiously. She smiles broadly.

"How did you know?"

"Just a guess. Why?"

She shrugs. "I don't know. Mix it up a little bit, I guess. Keep my parents on their toes."

I nod. That's as good a reason as any, I guess."

Mia starts to answer, then rolls her eyes.

"Ugh. Total bitch at 9:00."

"What?" I stare at her and she tugs my arm back into the shop. I turn and find Elena and two other girls, strolling down the sidewalk.

"Oh."

I can hear them chattering from here, cat-like remarks that are designed to be hateful. I don't see what Dante sees in her and I ask Mia that very thing.

"I don't know," she answers thoughtfully, chewing on her bottom lip. "I don't know that he sees anything in her, to be honest. They are together sometimes, and sometimes they aren't. I think it's a convenience thing. Their families are practically joined together. And then of course, their fathers sort of expect it so that someday, their families really will be joined together."

"What year is this?"I demand. "1623? People don't get married anymore to join families together."

"Maybe not in America," Mia levels a glance at me. "But you're not in America."

"Don't I know it," I mutter.

And then, when Elena and her two meanies are just steps away, my phone rings. I look at it and the screen says Becca Cline and her heart-shaped face is smiling at me. And my heart stops because I know that I have to answer it, but now isn't the time. Or the place.

But I have to.

I pick it up.

"Hello?"

"So." Becca's voice is as cold as ice. As cold as I've ever heard it. Ever. "You're in love with my boyfriend. You've *been* in love with my boyfriend for years. And you haven't told me. What kind of friend are you?"

"Becca, it's not what you think," I offer. "Really. Have I had a crush on Quinn for awhile? Yes. Have I ever acted in any way that would be inappropriate for your best friend to act? No. Not on my life, not ever. I wouldn't do that."

"If it was such an innocent crush, you would have told me," Becca accuses, and her voice is so…accusatory. And mad. And I have no defense.

"I know," I admit. "It's true. I've had a huge crush on him forever. But I didn't want to tell you because how in the world would I say something like that? I never intended to act on it or ever let anyone know about it. If you hadn't read my journal, you wouldn't know either."

"Don't start pointing fingers," she snaps, icicles forming through the phone line from her tone. "I came across your journal by accident. Should I have read it? No. But I never expected to read that. Not ever. You've always been the one thing in my entire life that I can count on. And I think that's what hurts the most. I know now that I can't count on you. I can't count on anyone."

She starts crying and my heart breaks a little.

"Becca, please. Don't cry. I didn't mean to hurt you. I promise. I would rather die than hurt you. You're my best friend and that's why I didn't tell you. It's *because* I didn't want to hurt you. I promise, I don't even like Quinn anymore so you don't have anything to worry about. I met someone here and he's amazing. And so you don't have to worry about me and Quinn. I promise."

"Your promises don't mean much," she snaps. "And I'm not worried about you and Quinn. There is no *you and Quinn*. Just like there's no you and me. Not anymore."

I start to answer but realize that the line is dead. For the first time ever, in the history of our relationship, Becca has hung up on me. I think she probably hates me. And I can hardly bear it.

"Are you okay?" Mia asks in concern.

Mia's thick black eyeliner is smearing in the heat and I realize that she's been standing there all along. I was so caught up in my dramatic phone call that I hadn't even realized it. Just like I hadn't realized that Elena and her cronies had stopped and were staring at me. And listening to me. Elena's emerald green eyes glimmered dangerously as they met mine and I know that she heard every word.

"So," Elena says icily, flipping her perfect hair over her perfect shoulder. "Just who did you meet here in Caberra, Reece? I know you're not talking about Dante. Because I will happily claw your pathetic, hick-a-billy eyes out before you ever dream of making a move on Dante. Do you understand me? Dante is mine. He will always be mine. You don't stand a chance, farm girl."

I nod silently because I'm not sure what else to do. Because I don't have it in me to argue or fight. My best friend had just yanked my guts out through my cell phone.

"I'm glad we understand each other," Elena says, then turns a perfect high heel on me and walks away.

Complete. And utter. Bitch.

Chapter Eleven

"Come on," Mia tells me, yanking my arm and dragging me behind her. I follow limply. I don't really care where we go. My insides feel smashed.

She leads me to a little coffee vendor on the sidewalk where she speaks fast Caberran and the dark-haired barista (Is that what they call them here?) quickly makes two dark, foaming cups of something. He hands one to me and Mia pays and I sniff at it. It smells strong.

"Drink it," Mia advises. "You need it."

"Is there alcohol in here?" I ask suspiciously, because Mia is in the midst of a full-blown rebellion against her parents and I wouldn't put it past her to drink a coffee-tini for breakfast. She laughs and shakes her head.

"No, but there should be. You need it. But this will have to do."

I sip at it and it burns my lip, but in a very delicious way. "What is it?"

"It's our version of Italian Espresso," she tells me as she closes her eyes and takes a long gulp. "It's my version of heaven."

She looks around. "You need one more thing," she muses. "Follow me."

She leads me to another vendor- they have so many here with cute little fold-up carts- and this time, she buys chocolates from an ancient white haired lady with cloudy, scary eyes. The old lady has a bright red silk scarf wrapped around her head and even though it looks like she is blind, she still looks at people straight in the eye. It's unnerving.

"All will work out for you, young one," she tells me, looking at me with her creepy eyes. Her fingers are gnarled and they dart out to grab my hand. She feels my palm and slides her wrinkled fingers up to my wrist, where they press against my pulse-point.

"You are strong," she says, closing her eyes. "Strong enough."

Mia and I look at each other wide-eyed and I pull my hand away as politely as I can. I can still feel exactly where the old woman's claw-like fingers were grasping me and I rub at the spot.

"Strong enough for what?" I ask hesitantly as Mia hands me the chocolate that she had just bought from the old woman.

The old lady nods. "Strong enough to protect your heart."

She closes her eyes and begins humming, oblivious to us now.

Mia looks at me and makes a circle next to her temples with her fingers.

Cuckoo, she mouths to me.

I nod. That's the only thing that makes any sense. This old lady has lost her marbles. If she ever had them in the first place, which is highly, highly debatable.

We sit on a nearby bench underneath a tree with weeping branches and I decide that it's the perfect place for me to sit. Poetically perfect because I feel like weeping too.

"Get your chin up," Mia demands. "I'm serious. Did you screw over your friend? Maybe. But can you do anything about it from thousands of miles away? No. You've got to live in the here and now. You'll fix it when you are able to. You're a nice person, I can tell. You didn't purposely hurt anyone. Your friend is being a dumbass."

I stare at her.

"Was that supposed to be a pep talk?"

Mia laughs. "I'm not that good at pep talks," she admits with a shrug. "I'm more of a 'walk it off' type of person. I don't dwell on things. Especially things I can't change."

"I didn't screw over Becca," I tell her. "I had a crush on her boyfriend. I can't help that, can I? I never acted on it. I never told him. And I don't have a crush on him anymore. That means something, right?"

Mia nods in agreement as she takes a bite out of her little chocolate mountain. I'm not sure exactly what our candies are, but they look like tiny volcanoes.

"No. You can't help that. And as far as I'm concerned, you didn't do anything wrong. Americans are so uptight," she observes. "You get your panties in a wad over the slightest little thing."

"You wouldn't be mad if your best friend had a crush on your boyfriend?" I ask dubiously. Because I don't believe it. Anyone would be mad, American, British, Caberran, whatever.

She shrugs again. "I don't know. I don't have a boyfriend *or* a best friend. So I can't reply to that with any amount of accuracy."

I stare at her as a bite of the sent-from-heaven chocolate volcano lava melts in my mouth.

"You don't have a best friend?" I ask, dubious once more. Everyone has a best friend.

"Nope." She shakes her head and honestly doesn't seem bothered by it. "My father has always been very picky about who I can hang around with. He's the Minister of Defense for Dante's father. He's very picky about image and public relations and being politically correct and all of that ridiculousness. He won't let me hang out with just anyone. And the people that he will allow, aside from Dante, are all douche-bags. So I would rather be alone."

And now her slight rebellious act of dressing like a goth made total sense, I decide as I stare at her jet-black fingernail polish. Her dad is a complete control freak. He deserves it.

"What does he think about you hanging out with an American?" I ask with a grin.

She smiles.

"What he doesn't know won't hurt him."

"Agreed." I smile back, feeling like we're co-conspirators and oddly enough, not feeling offended at the thought that being American was a crime.

"What are your plans for the rest of the day?" Mia asks as she licks the chocolate lava from her fingers. I shrug.

"I don't have any."

"Well, that's a crime," she announces. "A true crime. Look around you! The day is young, the sky is blue, the sun is out. How do you like scuba-diving?"

I freeze, with vivid images of JAWS stuck in my head. In my mind, his gigantic jaws are swallowing me whole.

No, scratch that.

He's biting me in half and blood is turning the water red.

Yeah, that's it.

That's exactly what will happen if I step one foot into the ocean here.

I'll die a bloody death as shark food and my mom will never see me again. Mia laughs at the look on my face.

"It's amazing," she tells me. "You've got to try it. We'll start you out snorkeling because you probably won't be here long enough for a scuba-diving course."

"Nope. No way," I answer adamantly, shaking my head. "Dante told me about your little shark problem. You'll never get me to do it."

Thirty minutes later, I'm in the water with a rubber mask strapped to my face. It can never be said that I'm not adventurous when forced to be.

Mia shows me how to get water out of the tube when it leaks in by blowing it out sharply. She tells me that the most common problem is when new divers get flustered when water gets into their tubes. I'm supposed to keep calm and simply blow the water out. That's a little difficult to do when I'm so completely focused on watching for sharks.

We swim and after a few minutes, more like thirty, I start to feel more at ease.

Every once in a while, Mia reaches out and grabs my hand and pulls me to a different place where we watch tropical fish leisurely swim in their little schools. Or a sea turtle gliding gracefully by. Or colorful tropical plants waving in the current.

Under the surface, the water is perfect and aqua and silent. There is no drama, there are no mean girls and best friends and boys that I shouldn't have crushes on but do anyway.

I sort of love it.

I kick my legs, letting the water flow fluidly over me. I am weightless here. I am relaxed and I haven't been this comfortable in a long time.

Just as I am thinking about how wrong I had been to be terrified of sharks and about how wonderful this is and how I have never been this comfortable or relaxed in my whole entire life, I spot something out of the corner of my eye that makes me freeze.

A gray bump slowly coming toward me.

I pull my head out of the water so that I can see better and find that Mia is nowhere near. But the gray sleek bump is only a hundred yards away and getting closer by the minute. I flail and splash, then remember from watching Shark Week on TV that you definitely *don't* want to splash.

Sweet Holy Monkeys. What the eff do I do??

I yell for Mia, but don't see her. Has she been eaten?

I look around frantically, but we've drifted to an isolated location and there isn't anyone else here.

Except for me and the shark.

And the shark is certainly taking his time to reach me.

Oh my gosh.

Oh my gosh.

Oh. My. Gosh.

My breathing comes in pants as I try to slowly and calmly paddle backward, away from the shark, toward land, away from the shark. Toward Land. Away. From. The. Shark.

Then, a fin emerges. *A fin.* And I scream. And scream. And forget about not splashing. I am splashing so much that every shark and sea creature in a hundred mile radius will know that I'm here. And I don't care. All I care about it surviving this shark attack. Because it is going to attack me. It's stalking me right now like the prey that I am. And very soon that water around me will be red because I'm going to die a bloody death.

And then I notice that the fin is made from hands. A pair of hands.

I freeze.

What the eff?

Dante bursts from the water, wearing gray swim trunks and shaking droplets from his hair as he lunges to grab me with a roar.

I scream again because it's happened so fast and my brain hasn't had a chance to truly realize that it is Dante and not a shark.

I'm not going to die.

I'm not going to die.

I'm not going to die.

I'm not going to become breakfast for JAWS.

But I'm going to kill Dante.

I'm so mad that I smack him on the arm. And smack him again.

"Dante, what the hell?" I demand angrily, so mad that I'm seeing spots. "Not funny! So not funny!"

He looks confused, then startled as it registers with him that I am truly pissed off. Severely and completely pissed off. Both with him for pulling the stupidest and oldest prank ever and with myself for falling for it.

Oh-my-gosh-I'm-such-an-idiot.

I try to force my heart rate to slow down before I become the first seventeen-year old in the history of the world to die from heart failure in the middle of a fake shark attack. I definitely don't want that on my tombstone.

Here lies Reece Ellis: Dumbass.

"I'm sorry," Dante tells me quickly, reaching for me. I kick away from him, still furious.

"I'm really sorry," he tells me again, swimming toward me.

Even soaking wet, he is gorgeous. Maybe even more so than when he is dry, if that is even possible. The water runs over his defined muscles, the sun catches the highlights in his hair. His blue eyes are contrite, his expression apologetic. His jawline chiseled, his chest rock hard. Wait. I don't want to notice those things right now.

I'm pissed, I remind myself. Seriously pissed.

He reaches out for my arm and this time, his long fingers wrap around my wrist and pull me to him. He folds me into a hug, a sincere hug, and holds me tight.

And I'm not pissed anymore.

Dante's body is long and lean, his arms strong and bulging and wrapped around me right now. He's wet and slippery and so am I and I'm going to internally combust. He smells like soap and salt and sun and I can't breathe.

Sweet baby monkeys.

We tread water and Dante tells me again how sorry he is. He's cold and I'm cold and my lip starts to quiver because I'm freezing. And also nervous because the most beautiful boy in the world has his arms around me.

Dante looks down into my eyes, his arms still wrapped around my shoulders, pulling me tightly to his chest. I feel every inch of him pressed against me- *every inch*- and I might die. Seriously die.

"I'm stupid," he tells me with his super-sexy accent. "Reece, I didn't realize how afraid you are of sharks. That was a stupid prank and I will make it up to you, okay?"

He looks seriously into my eyes, his face so sweet and gorgeous and sincere. How can I stay mad at him when he is so unbelievably sweet and gorgeous and sincere?

I can't.

I nod instead.

"It's okay," I whisper. He tightens his hold on me as we kick to tread water and I enjoy the hardness of his body and how every plane of his chest ripples when he moves.

He bends his head and I think… I'm pretty sure… I know… he's going to kiss me.

But he flicks his fingers out and adjusts the strap of my mask instead, straightening it up from where it was crooked from leaning against him.

I exhale shakily and swim away from him a little ways, like a normal person, like I'm not someone whose wits were just addled from being so close to Dante Giliberti.

"Why aren't you wearing a mask?" I ask.

My voice sounds a little nasally from my stupid face mask. I decide that I don't want to look like Darth Vader and pull it off. I'm not going to be snorkeling anymore, anyway.

Dante smiles. "I'm not here to snorkel," he tells me. "I came to find you."

"How did you know where to look?" I ask.

He looks amused. "Really?" he asks wryly. "It's one of the few perks of my dad's job. I know everything that happens in Caberra."

I narrow my eyes. "Do you have someone watching me?"

He looks guilty. "Um. I may have assigned one of my security guards to you. Just while you're here, of course. I mean, you're my responsibility and I can't let anything happen to you."

"Because the crime rate here in paradise is so high?" I ask, sarcasm dripping from my voice. Dante looks properly chastised and I have to admit, in a weird stalker way, it was a sweet thing that he did. I feel protected, anyway.

"It's alright," I add. "I'm not mad. But can you not do it again? I don't want to be followed around."

He smiles lazily, as he flips onto his back to float. "Then in order for you to stay safe, you'll have to stay with me constantly," he tells me. "I mean, in the interest of keeping you safe."

And there it was again, the electricity in the air between us. It practically crackles and my heart flutters.

"Do you agree to my terms?" Dante asks, jokingly, but not. "If you don't want a security guard, you'll have to allow me to escort you. Everywhere. At all times."

There are definitely worse things in the world. I'm not sure if he is exaggerating or kidding but I nod anyway and fight the urge to launch myself into his arms.

But I resist the impulse and instead, we start joking about sharks and he does the JAWS theme song and chases me through the water with his stupid fin made from his hands. This time it is funny.

Mia finally reappears and after a proper lecture on leaving me alone, the three of us float in a lazy circle and I decide that I am in love with Caberra. And I am rather fond of its 'prince.'

Very fond.

And I definitely doubt the sanity of the crazy old lady who sold us the chocolates now.

Because I am seriously doubting my ability to protect my heart.

I am not strong enough.

Chapter Twelve

Dante's father is home.

I know this because the royal flags with the ancient royal crest are flying outside of the Old Palace. Heaven told me this morning that when the Prime Minister isn't home, the normal country flag flies. I hadn't even noticed.

Caberra is weird. It voted out a royal family hundreds of years ago, but everyone still acts like the Prime Minister and his family are royals and they still have a palace and they still have a palace guard. It's very, very odd. It's like they want all of the old traditions, but they want modern government.

Another way that I know Dimitri Giliberti is home is because a hush has fallen over the Old Palace. The servants are quieter than normal, everyone creeps around and even Dante is subdued. I dread meeting the man who instills so much reverence and anxiety.

Besides educating me on some of the Caberran traditions, Heaven had also brought me a laptop earlier from the Old Palace library and had given me the wireless password.

And now I'm truly in heaven, courtesy of Heaven. Yes, I'm just corny enough to think of such a goofy phrase.

I cruise the internet and browse through all of the social sites that I've missed over the past week. But honestly, I find that I haven't really missed them, particularly after I see Becca's many, many status updates that involve me.

Best friends forever?? More like Best Friends Never Again.

@ReeceLEllis: Lie Much?

I can't stop crying. Betrayal hurts.

@ReeceLEllis: I'll never forgive you.

And what's worse than her status updates are the outpouring of comments in reply. It looks like everyone we know has rushed out to support Becca, without even talking to me about it. Am I such a horrible person that it's so easy for them to believe that I screwed Becca over?

A knife plunges into my heart and twists this way and that. I feel instantly numb and shocked and horrified. But I'm also puzzled. Why is Becca taking this so hard? Yes, I have a crush on her boyfriend. Make that *had*. But she's acting like Quinn and I had cheated on her and we didn't. I wouldn't. Not ever in four million years.

But she won't pick up the phone. I try, then I try texting her. Then I try to call her again. I leave her four voicemails and four texts.

Silence.

I sigh.

Mia was right. I can't fix it from here. If Becca isn't going to pick up the phone, then I'm going to have to put this out of my mind until I can march up to her door and make her listen to me. But I can't do that until I'm back in Kansas.

There's no place like home, Dorothy. If only I could click my heels together three times and make it happen.

There's a knock at my door and then Heaven pokes her head in.

"Can I come in?" she asks politely.

"Of course," I answer, closing the laptop. I make a conscious decision to put Becca out of my mind as I turn my attention to Heaven.

She's so small – heavens, are all Caberrans so tiny? They make me feel like a giant or an Amazon- and she's carrying a white box that seems almost as big as she is. And that's only a slight exaggeration.

"Whatcha got?" I ask curiously, as she lays it on the bed and beams.

"It's a gift for you from Dante," she answers with a grin. "It's for dinner tonight. I take it that you'll be dining with them."

My heart sort of stutters before it begins beating again.

A special white box to prepare me for dinner? This can't be good. It's instantly apparent to me that dinner tonight will be a big deal thing. No simple barbeque or cookout or goulash or spaghetti. Of course not. They literally change flags when the Prime Minister is in. They aren't going to serve him meat loaf.

With nervous fingers, I lift off the lid and gasp.

A gown, as in, *a ball gown*, is folded neatly inside the box inside of elegantly folded tissue. A white card is lying on top.

I pick it up and read, *Reece, I hope this isn't presumptuous, but dinner tonight will be formal. I assumed that you didn't buy anything formal this morning, so I thought this might work. If it doesn't fit or if you don't like it, just let me know and I'll have it replaced. D.G.G.*

His writing was bold and scrawling and it took me a moment to decipher it.

"D.G.G.?" I looked at Heaven.

"Dante Griffen Giliberti," she answered. She looked surprised, as though she thought I should have known that. Of course I don't. The subject of his middle name has never come up and I've only known him for a matter of days. Nevermind the fact that it feels like weeks already.

I lift the gown out of the box and gasp again.

Made from deep blue stretchy velveteen, it is floor length and strapless. The material is so soft and light that I know it will feel like I am wearing nothing at all. It's gorgeous and I know that it will look nice with my eyes and skin color. This whole situation is so Pretty Woman or My Fair Lady. No man other than my father had ever bought me clothing before.

And the things I'm feeling for Dante are far from daughterly.

"It's beautiful," I announce to Heaven, because it's clear she is waiting for a response. "But can you tell me… where can I find a strapless bra?"

She points impishly to the box and I find a strapless bra folded neatly in the bottom of the box. 34B. Just my size. My cheeks flare and I want to die. Just knowing that Dante had even pondered the size of my boobs makes me want to curl up and expire.

"He knows my bra size?" I utter in humiliation. Seriously? Oh. My. Gosh.

Heaven grins. "No. He asked me to guess your size and then pick up a bra that would fit under the dress. He was a little helpless about that. And very uncomfortable, I might add."

Thank goodness. I no longer want to die as much, but still. It's still a little humiliating.

Next to the bra, there is a pair of silver shoes, size 8. Strappy three-inch heels.

"I guess I'm all set then," I tell her. "That is, if I don't break my neck trying to walk in those stilts. At prom last year, Becca and I took flip-flops to change into. I only wore heels for about an hour. And trust me. I'm not very good at it."

I'm slightly anxious, if *slightly anxious* can be defined as me banging my foot against the bed like a lunatic. I've never had dinner with anyone more important than my sophomore track coach after a track meet.

"You'll be fine," Heaven tells me assuredly. I stare at her.

"Easy for you to say," I answer. "You are around these people all of the time. Do you know who I'm usually around? Cows. And trust me, creatures of the bovine variety are not exactly up to the highest social standards. I may need to brush up on my fancy party etiquette. Do you happen to have a Miss Manners book in your pocket?"

Heaven giggles, then stands up. "I've gotta go," she tells me. "I'll tell Dante that you love the dress."

"Leave out the part where I'm terrified, okay? I don't want to ruin my chic and sophisticated image."

She rolls her eyes and nods. "Yeah, I don't want to let *that* cat out of the bag."

"What time is dinner?" I ask.

"It's at 8:00," she answers. "And Dante is with his father now. I don't know how long they'll be, but I'm guessing he won't have time to hang out."

"How did you know that would be my next question?" I stare at her blankly. "Hmm. What will I do to kill time this afternoon? You've got to work and Dante is tied up." I force my mind out of the gutter after uttering those last four words.

Heaven shrugs with a smile. "You could practice walking in your heels," she suggests with an ornery grin.

She looks around my room. It's completely neat. I have two lone shopping bags from yesterday sitting on the desk, and two pairs of sandals peeking out from beneath the bed. Other than that, everything is immaculate and untouched.

"There's nothing to clean in here, so you can't clean your room," she observes and then eyes my new shoes. "You should just practice walking."

With that bit of advice, she slips back out my door and I'm alone. I look at the clock. It's only 3:00. What in the world am I going to do for five hours?

I decide that practicing the whole walking-without-breaking-my-leg-thing is actually a good idea, so I slip on the high-heeled-stilts-of-death and toddle round my room.

Okay. That killed five minutes.

I sit on a chair and look peacefully out the window. Another three minutes.

I situate myself on the floor and meditate. Three more minutes go by before my thoughts are muddled by visions of Dante's face and smile and toned arms and then by anxious thoughts about dinner tonight.

I sigh. This isn't going to work.

I climb carefully to my feet, still wearing my strappy silver stilts, and decide to go for a walk. Who cares if I look ridiculous wearing fancy shoes and running shorts? Dante is tied up with his dad and won't see me, anyway.

I try to walk quietly down the hall, but apparently, it's impossible to walk quietly in heels on a marble floor. It practically sounds like I am playing the drums. I pick up my phone and try to call Mia, but it goes straight to voicemail. I find that I miss her already and ponder the sad fact that she doesn't have a best friend. Since I recently lost my own, I might as well apply for the job.

I text my mother, then get three rapid fire responses back from her. She's pissed that I haven't called her today. But I'm not in the mood to talk. I'm too nervous about a State dinner tonight. Or whatever a dinner is called when a Prime Minister is present.

I text Mia.

I even text my grandmother who hates to text on her big-buttoned-old-person's-phone.

And that's when I realize that I've hit rock bottom.

I'm pathetic.

What kind of person can't entertain herself for a few hours? Who cares if it is a foreign country and I don't know the language?

I march back to my room as gracefully as I can in my stilts and change into tennis shoes. I'm going to see the city if it kills me. And it might. Because I don't know anyone. And I don't speak the language. But so what?

I stroll out of the Old Palace without anyone questioning me, not that they would because they aren't my keepers, but I always expect someone to ask me what the heck I think I'm doing in such a fancy place. But they don't. I look behind me. It doesn't appear that I'm being followed by a security guard. But that doesn't surprise me. Dante promised that he wouldn't do that again.

I'm alone.

Truly alone.

And suddenly, I feel very *very* lonely.

I find myself in a random shop that sells knick-knacks…blown glass figurines and whatnot. I stroll through as though I am perfectly at home here because attitude is everything. If I act confident, I *will* be confident, right?

And then I see a tiny green glass sea turtle. And I know that Becca would love to have it in her collection. She's collected turtles since we were in kindergarten. At last count, she had 453 of them. Her dad built her an entire wall of shelves in her room for them.

And this one would be perfect for her. It's nibbling on an olive branch. How perfect is that? I could buy it and send it to her as my own personal olive-branch-peace- offering. Unless she interprets it as the turtle EATING my peace offering, which wouldn't be so cool. But I could include a note. And apologize once again and surely this time, when she sees the turtle's cute little face, she will forgive me.

Surely.

I pay for the tiny trinket with my mom's credit card. I mean, surely this classifies as an emergency too. And it's only a few Euros. I'm not exactly sure how much that converts into for US dollars. But surely mom won't care.

Surely.

And I've got to stop saying surely.

I stroll down quaint little cobblestone boardwalk again, and browse through the windows and look at all of the little carts. The crazy old gypsy-looking woman isn't here today, which is almost a relief. I'm not sure that I'm brave enough to walk past her without Mia.

I buy a little bag of hot sugared almonds, again with my mom's credit card. And no, this isn't an emergency, but surely she wouldn't want me to go hungry.

Crap. I said surely again. What is wrong with me?

I decide that I'd better leave my mom's credit card back in my room until I go home, just so I'm not tempted to use it again.

Excellent idea.

I stroll down to the beach and stand at the edge of the water, munching on my nuts and watching the majestic sea roll in and slide back out. It's hypnotic and mesmerizing. And beautiful.

It's so serene here, so quiet. And it makes me realize once again how alone I am. I would love to take a picture and send it to Becca, but I can't. So instead, I take one and text it to my mom.

It's beautiful, honey. Are you wearing sunscreen?

She's such a mom.

I tuck my phone back into my pocket and then perk up my ears when I hear someone talking.

I look around and don't see anyone. But I'm nosy. And lonely. So I turn around and walk a ways to see if I can see them.

I round the corner of an old, unused lifeguard shed and see Nate, arrogant-rude-as-hell Nate, talking into his cell phone. He's pale as ever and his nose is stuck in the air even though no one is around to be snobby for. I decide that it's just his natural way of being. And then I scoot forward a little bit just to hear what he's saying. I'm nosy. And his face is wrinkled, like he's pissed or upset. And since I don't like him, I'd like to know what has ticked him off.

Because I'm nosy.

He doesn't see me, so I freeze at the edge of the building and listen. His voice is cold and I don't like it any more than I like him. And that's not saying much. The breeze shifts towards me and suddenly I can hear him better.

"No. I told you that I haven't found anything yet. Dante is very protective of him. No. I'll keep trying. I'm sure there's something to find. I just have to look harder. Don't worry. Okay. We'll talk soon."

What the hell is he talking about?

Nate sticks his phone in his pocket and glances up. His ice blue eyes meet mine and I'm totally busted. He absolutely knows that I was eavesdropping and he doesn't like it. His expression turns thunderous and he stalks immediately over to me.

I gulp and glance around. I'm here alone.

Just perfect.

I gulp again.

"Is it polite in America to listen to private conversations?" he demands when he reaches me. "Because here in Caberra, or any polite society for that matter, it is considered rude."

"Well, that's something that you would know a lot about," I zing back, my feathers ruffled. How dare he think he can lecture me on being rude? Really? He's the rudest person I've ever met. Ever.

And that includes crusty old farmers who have been out in harvest trucks in the sun all day. And that's saying a lot because they can get really grumpy.

Nate levels a glare at me and if looks could kill, I'd be deader than a doornail.

"I know that you're an American heathen," he begins. "So, I'll educate you. Don't eavesdrop again. It's rude. And it's unacceptable."

I stare at him incredulously.

"Unacceptable? I don't know a lot about Caberra, I will admit," I say as icily as I can with my heart thumping in my throat. "But I'm pretty sure there is no law against standing on the beach. If you don't want to be overheard, don't talk so loudly. Have a good day."

I spin on my heel and do my best stalking imitation.

And then I'm grabbed by the elbow and spun harshly around. I gasp and yank away.

Nate is staring at me again, and he thumps his finger on my chest.

"Mind your own business," he says. "And leave me alone."

He pivots and walks away before I can even say anything. I'm so shocked at his behavior and by the fact that he grabbed me-he actually freaking grabbed me- that I can't even speak. I watch him retreat as I rub at my arm.

What the eff just happened?

Chapter Thirteen

To: Becca Cline <l.am.a.B@bluejupiter.net
From: Reece Ellis <ReeciPiecie@thecloud.com
Subject: A package

Becca,
I know that you're really, really pissed at me. And I'm really, really sorry for never telling you that I had a crush on Quinn. I thought I was doing the right thing. I mean, it's not cool to crush on your best friend's boyfriend and I felt guilty about it. But I couldn't help it. The feelings were always there. But they aren't anymore. I don't have a crush on him anymore, I promise.
Having you mad is KILLING ME. I hate it.
I found a little gift for you here. I just sent it down to be mailed. I hope you like it. I don't know- I might arrive back at home before the package does. It's hard to say. If only this stupid ash would clear up then the airports would open. They say it might be a few more days.
Please forgive me for being stupid.
Xoxo,
Reece

I close the lid of the laptop again and rub at my elbow. I know there's going to be a bruise. I can feel the black and blue forming already. Nate had grabbed me hard. Really hard. Way harder than was necessary for the context of our conversation. Not that physical violence was ever necessary *at all*.

Why had he gotten so angry? I replay his words in my head and I can't help but wonder at them.

Dante is very protective of him, he had said.

Who is Dante protective of?

I'm sure there's something to find. I'll just have to look harder.

What is Nate trying to find? It is clearly something very important since he had gotten so angry with me. But his anger was senseless. I have no clue what he was talking about, other than it somehow concerns Dante. But Dante is Nate's friend. So whatever it is can't be a threat to Dante, right? I mean, they're friends. But the tone of Nate's voice hadn't been so friendly. And even now, I'm getting goose bumps just thinking about it.

I look at the clock. It's 7:00. Only an hour until the dinner, so I'd better start getting ready. My phone dings and I look.

Is it okay if I pick you up at your room at 7:45?

Dante.

I fight the urge to sigh out loud. Even a simple text message from him sets my heart loose on a 100-yard sprint. Just the sight of his name or the sound of it on my tongue makes the breath catch in my throat. I feel paralyzed. And excited. And a little like a seventh-grader.

I text back.

Sure. I'll be the one in the long blue dress.

I send it and then roll my eyes. I'm such a cornball.

Dante answers within a few seconds.

Thanks! I was wondering how I'd know it was you.

My heart smiles and the warmth spreads throughout my body. There is nothing hotter in the whole entire world than a great sense of humor. And Dante can make me smile almost without even speaking. He's just that funny. I adore that. A-Dore.

7:10. I'd better get a move on it.

I shower.

I shave my legs.

I shave my legs a second time for good measure.

I moan about a small zit in the crease of my nose.

I put some makeup on and then moan about the fact that I'm not Marilyn Monroe.

Then I moan about the fact that Marilyn Monroe has been dead for umpteen years.

Then I moan about the fact that I'm a lunatic who does not look glamorous at all.

At. All.

Even though I'm wearing as floor length strapless gown bought for me by a beautiful boy.

There's clearly something wrong with me. Anyone else would look ah-may-zing.

I stare into the mirror.

I had gotten some sun while I was out and about and my nose is a little pink. My eyes are pretty, like they always are, but I just look so little-girl-like, like I have an inner seventh-grader who is busting to get out. My hair falls over my shoulders in limp waves. And I decide that won't do. I've got to pin it up.

I dig through my makeup case and find a handful of bobby pins. I vaguely remember how to do a chignon from my ballet years a long time ago. I also hope that I haven't used the pins to clean out my toe-nails or something equally gross. I twist my hair into a bun at my neck and stick the pins through it.

I examine myself again.

Okay. I look better. More elegant, anyway, more grown-up, more polished. More like I am attending a State Dinner instead of prom. I hitch up the front of my dress and pray that it doesn't slip down during dinner. I am not what you might call *overly endowed* in the chestal region. Underly endowed is more like it, if there is such a word. Which I'm sure there's not, but still.

Time check.

7:37.

My heart pitty-pats and I slip my feet into the high-heeled-stilts-of-death. I practice walking, walking quickly, then jogging. Then I walk again, because who am I kidding? I'll never be running in these things.

There's a quick knock on the door.

Time check. 7:40.

Dante is five minutes early, the rascal.

I rush to the door.

I throw it open.

And my heart drops into my feet and practically cries.

Because it isn't Dante in my doorway. It's Gavin, Casanova himself, standing there with a goofy grin and a red rose. He holds the flower out to me, smiling, and I can't help but smile back.

"Hi Gavin," I tell him, taking the rose and burying my face in it. Its sweet smell fills my nose and I inhale again, trying to hide my disappointment. It's not Gavin's fault that he's not Dante. "What are you doing here?"

Gavin is wearing a tux and his dark hair is freshly washed. I can tell because it's still wet and I can see the comb tracks. I can also smell the soap from here.

He bows low. He's not as tall as Dante, but he's tall enough, maybe six feet or so. While his head is down, he reaches blindly and clownishly for my hand to kiss it. I smile and shake my head because he's so idiotic sometimes that it is impossible not to like him.

"I'm here to escort you to dinner," he tells me with a grin. "Dante sent me. Something came up and he can't so I've been delegated. Are you honored by my presence?"

My disappointment was temporarily clouded with my amusement at Gavin's gall. "Honored? Um. Yeah. That's exactly what I am."

Gavin knowingly shakes his head and holds out his arm. "I thought you would be. Are you ready to dine with the most stuck-up and stuck-on-themselves group in all of Caberra?"

He cocks his head and waits thoughtfully for my answer, as though I actually have a choice in the matter. I'm a guest here. If they want me at their dinner, that's where I'll be.

"Well, if you put it that way, how can I say no?" I answer. It's hard to stay disappointed with Gavin for long.

He leads me down the long hallway leading away from my rooms. I can see that the Old Palace has been spruced up for the dinner tonight. Fresh flowers and lit candles adorn practically every available surface and it looks beautiful. The soft candlelight is exactly perfect to hide the freckles on my nose and it creates the perfect intimate ambience... one that I would love to be sharing with Dante right now, rather than Gavin.

But, that's not how it is. My hand is carefully tucked inside of Gavin's black-jacketed arm. Not Dante's.

"So, why are you here?" I ask curiously as we descend the stairs. "I mean, at the dinner."

He waggles his slender eyebrows. Does he get them waxed??

"Because my father is Dante's Minister of Interior."

I stare at him, dumb-founded. Or maybe just plain dumb. I'm not sure.

"Your father is a member of Mr. Giliberti's cabinet too?" A light goes on. "Do all of you have important fathers? Is that why you and Dante are friends?"

Gavin's typically playful face goes all serious for a minute. I know that I won't see this very often, so I pay close attention while it lasts.

"Pretty much," he says. "Mine is the MoI. Mia's is the MoD. Elena's mom is the Minister of Foreign Affairs. And her dad is Dimitri's best friend." Yeah, I knew that part. But I didn't know her mom was important, too. I gulp.

"And Nate?"

"Nate's father is the Deputy Prime Minister, Dimitri's second-in-command. He travels a lot in Dimitri's stead for public relations purposes. That might be one reason for Nate's constant bad mood. His dad is always gone. From the time we were small- his dad has always had to travel. Nate hates it."

"Well, he's certainly always in a bad mood," I agree. I absently rub the bruise on my elbow. "Do you think he'll be here tonight?"

Gavin shrugs. "We usually try to avoid these things like the plague. I came tonight because Dante asked me to. I think he asked Mia, too. He wanted to make sure you have friends to talk to."

Warmth rushes through me at Dante's thoughtfulness. He might be tied up elsewhere, but he's still thinking about me.

"I don't know if he asked Elena," Gavin adds. He might as well have tossed a bucket of cold water on me. His words are just as dousing. Ugh. I could have done without hearing that. Because now I'm doubting Dante's motives. Is he trying to be sweet because he *like* likes me, or is he just being cordial and friendly because I'm his guest and he is nothing if not polite?

That's the new question of the year.

"Are you ready for this?" Gavin asks as we pause outside of a large set of ornate double doors. I eye the doors, then eye him.

Hell no, I'm not, I think.

"I think so," I actually say.

I fidget with my dress, fighting the urge to hike up the front of it again. It hasn't actually slipped down yet, but I'm sure it will. My chestal region is a hilly plains, not a mountainous terrain.

Gavin smiles.

"You're ready. These are the things to remember: Smile. Look pretty, act polite. People will probably ask you a million questions about America. Just smile and answer and laugh. You'll be fine."

"Will I?" I scrunch up my face. "I don't know."

"You will," Gavin assures me. "I promise."

"But everyone hates Americans," I practically whimper.

Gavin rolls his eyes. "We do not. We love you *and* your money." He grins. "Seriously. Be likeable and they'll like you. It's that simple."

Well. Once he put it that way, it did seem simple. And I suddenly felt a new responsibility to represent America accurately to these foreigners. We're not all the obese selfish pigs that people seem to think we are. I square my shoulders, which I might add, are not obese shoulders.

Gavin nods at the guards guarding the doors. Each man is dressed in a blue and white uniform with a leather band criss-crossing his chest and a sword in a sheath at his side. Each has the ancient Giliberti family crest on his uniform, as well.

Mia had informed me earlier that with each Prime Minister, the royal guard changes their crest to match the incoming PM. And they are still called the Royal Guard even though there is no royal family anymore.

Caberra is weird.

But steeped in tradition and I have to respect that.

The guards open the doors and I suppress a gasp when I see the ballroom inside.

First, a ball room??

Second, there are so many people.   So. Many. People.

They are all sparkling and glittering and dressed to the nines and holy-freaking-ballgown, Dante was not exaggerating when he said that it would be formal.

It is *so* formal.

Silver bows adorn each banquet table, along with mounds of flowers and flickering candles. Chandeliers hang overhead, *so* many of them, and each crystal-encrusted-string on each crystal-encrusted-arm sparkles like diamonds. For all I know, maybe they *are* actually diamonds. Every person here is immaculately attired and standing on a gleaming floor that is waxed to a shine so brilliant and bright that I can practically see up women's dresses.

I am suddenly thankful for both my high-heeled-stilts-of-death and the fact that I twisted my hair into a chignon. I would have looked horribly out of place with plain hair and ballet flats.

But who am I kidding? I'm horribly out of place anyway.

I gulp and clutch frantically at Gavin's arm. He seems so comfortable and relaxed as he smiles at the people who turn to look at us. I can see the curiosity on people's faces as they stare at me. And it makes me blush. I only pray that they haven't seen the stupid pictures on the stupid gossip websites. I think I hate Caberra. I suddenly wish that I could be at home, safe and sound in my bedroom.

I ignore the stares and search the room for the most important person.

No, not the Prime Minister.

The Prime Minister's son.

I don't see him and my heart plummets.

Where is Dante?

There is no way that he would send me to this dinner and then not even show up himself. He wouldn't do that, would he? Would he? I could be safely and happily ensconced in my room right now eating pizza straight out of the box and in my pajamas. But no. Here I am, trussed up in a strapless ball gown and ready to fall down in my heels at any slight misstep.

And Dante isn't here.

I definitely hate Caberra.

I've looked at every inch of the room.

He definitely isn't here.

"Where is he?" I hiss under my breath at Gavin.

He stares at me sideways.

"He'll be here," Gavin assures me. "What? Are you bored with me already?"

I'm in the middle of rolling my eyes at Gavin, when I sense *his* presence.

Dante.

I can feel him just as sure as I am living, breathing and miserable in my strapless bra.

I turn slowly, trying to be casual, trying not to break my neck as I hurry to find him.

And there he is, filling up the doorway with his own special golden awesomeness.

Breathe, Reece, I tell myself.

I am reminded once again that Dante is devastatingly handsome. Freaking hot, to tell the truth. He's wearing a tuxedo with a deep purple tie and a smile and I want to melt into the highly waxed floor.

He steps down into the ballroom and makes his way through the throngs of people, nodding and smiling at everyone who greets him.

And then he is standing in front of me.

"Reece," he says, his voice husky and sexy. "You look beautiful."

My tongue is tied and I can't speak. I stare at him like an idiot. All of a sudden, I am overcome with feeling inadequate and excited and spellbound. All at once.

"Reece?" Dante asks in his oh-so-charming accent. And I shake my head, snapping myself out of it.

"Yes. I'm sorry. Thank you. And thank you for the dress. It's absolutely lovely."

He eyes it, then pulls his eyes back to mine.

"Not as lovely as you are wearing it," he tells me seriously.

Not one of the boys back home could get away with that line without sounding ridiculous and out of place. But Dante pulls it off effortlessly. He's got old world charm and modern good looks and I am finding more and more every day that it is futile to resist that particular combination.

And honestly, why would I want to? He's practically perfect.

I realize then that Gavin is still holding onto my arm, only because he's making gagging sounds and rolling his eyes.

I pull away from him before I even realize what I'm doing. With Dante in front of me, I simply want to gravitate towards him. And unconsciously, I take a step forward.

"Why didn't you wait for me?" Dante asks, his eyebrows slightly furrowed. "I was right on time."

I could listen to his accent all day long.

He's so tall and graceful. Yes, graceful.

Have his eyelashes always been that long?

Wait. What?

His words break through my reverie.

Why didn't I wait for him?

I stare blankly at him, then at Gavin, who immediately looks guilty.

"Didn't you send Gavin to pick me up?" I ask Dante, shooting daggers at Gavin.

Dante rolls his eyes and then punches Gavin good-naturedly on the arm.

"No, I didn't," he answers. He turns to Gavin. "Again? Really? There are thousands of girls on this island," he says. "Do you really have to trick *my* date? Go bother someone else."

He shoves Gavin slightly, and definitely not as hard as *I'd* like to shove him.

Gavin grins and bows to me.

"It appears that I've been caught red-handed," he says without once ounce of chagrin. "But it has been lovely escorting you. I hope you have a wonderful evening."

And with that, he melts into the crowd and I turn to Dante in bewilderment.

"What just happened?"

He shakes his head. "Gavin happened. Don't worry about it. He's been this way since we were kindergarteners. He likes to compete with me. He doesn't mean anything by it." Dante steps closer to me and my heart automatically picks up.

"Now, where were we?"

Chapter Fourteen

"Well, I don't know about you," I answer. "But I was just escorted to a really fancy party by deceptive means. That's where I was. Where were you?"

Dante laughs, an honest, happy sound and I find myself wishing that I could bathe in it. He's tan and handsome and self-assured. He's so different from the boys that I know from back home. Did I say that I hate Caberra? I meant that I love it.

I love Caberra. I'm sure of it now.

"I was looking for you," Dante admits, ducking his head and grasping my hand. He brings it to his lips and kisses it. Holy-freaking-monkey-balls. Are all boys in Caberra this swoon-worthy or is it just Dante?

I study him as he straightens up, scanning over his broad shoulders, golden hair, sparkling deeper-than-the-ocean eyes and healthy, bronzed skin.

It's just Dante.

Of that, I am sure.

"Well, you've found me," I answer when I finally can.

He grins. "That I have. Now what should I do with you?"

Holy-loaded-question. I know exactly what I'd like for him to do with me. But obviously I can't answer that. My mama raised me to be a lady. Or she thinks she did, anyway.

I shrug nonchalantly, as though I don't care, as though he isn't the first thing I thought of this morning when I woke up or the last thing I thought of before I went to sleep last night.

Dante Giliberti has certainly made himself at home in my thoughts. And I don't think he's going anywhere any time soon.

He holds out his arm and I slide my fingers into the crook of his elbow.

"Come with me," he tells me. "You should meet my father."

For some reason, I have to force my feet to move. I don't want to meet his father because if I haven't met him yet, then I haven't said anything stupid yet. And that's just fine with me. I'd rather just be a faceless house-guest in his mind.

Dante chuckles when he looks at my face.

"Don't worry," he tells me gently. "He's just a normal person. He'll love you."

"Yeah," I answer. "A normal person who happens to have a royal guard and his very own family crest. Normal people in Kansas have those things, too."

Dante laughs again as he navigates our way through the crowded room. Everyone is looking at us and I focus hard on not getting my heels tangled in my dress. The last thing I need is to trip and fall in front of everyone.

On the way, Dante pauses and stops a waiter who is wearing black tails and white gloves and is walking like he has a broom taped to his spine. Dante takes two elegant flute glasses from the waiter's tray and hands me one. I sniff at the bubbling liquid.

"For courage," Dante says, and clinks his glass to mine.

Champagne.

I look around quizzically and somewhat frantically. I'm so not a rule-breaker. Are we seriously going to drink this in front of all of these adults and law-enforcement figures?

Dante laughs at my expression.

"I forgot," he chuckles. "You're American. You have a ridiculously repressed drinking age. Here, we can legally drink at 15 if we are in private homes or private parties. We can't buy it until we are 18, though."

As I think about the many drinking and driving accidents back home with teenagers who aren't supposed to be drinking, I wonder at the wisdom of such a ridiculously young drinking age.

But then again, there's always the theory that if society condones an activity, then it won't be as appealing for teenagers as it is to break a law. Either way. I'm holding a glass of what is probably very expensive champagne and it is not illegal for me to drink it here. And Dante is right. I need some courage.

So I sip at the bravery-in-a-glass.

And immediately snort as the bubbles well up in my nose.

Then I cough.

And I turn red in the face as I continue to cough.

Oh. My. Word. Can I not do anything right? I need to look graceful and cool as I grasp the elegant champagne glass and drink it. Instead, I am hacking like a drunk donkey and I've only had one little sip.

Dante gently pats my back, trying to help.

I want to melt into the ballroom floor and die. Everyone is looking at me. Including Dimitri Giliberti.

The Prime Minister stops what he is doing and heads in our direction. He is wearing a very authentic and important looking military uniform. He has a band across his chest like the guards, but his is more of a satin sash. It's blue and his jacket is dark red. I picture that same outfit on Napoleon

Bonaparte. Only Dimitri is a lot taller. And Napoleon was French.

Dimitri Giliberti doesn't look very much like Dante. Dante is blond, Dimitri is rather dark. But they have the same tall build with broad shoulders and slim hips. And they have the same eyes.

Dimitri draws to a stop in front of us and extends his hand.

"Good evening, young lady. I'm Dimitri Giliberti and I hear that you've had some travel problems. I do hope that your stay in my home has been pleasant."

He's so formal and adult, but his eyes are warm. I instantly like him. I can't help it. I nod.

"Yes. Thank you so much for hosting me. I can't believe that all of the airports are closed. What a freak thing."

I just used the word *freak* in a conversation with the Prime Minister of a country. I'm the freak.

He smiles and I see that he and Dante share the same gorgeous, nerve-raveling smile, as well. That smile should be illegal.

"It is certainly a freak thing," he answers with a smile.

He holds out his arm, and I stare at him. Am I supposed to take it? If I touch him will his guards throw me to the ground and subdue me? I see Buzz Cut in the distance, watching our interaction with his hawk-like eyes and I'm sure that he'd love to manhandle me. Jerk.

Dante helps me by gently undoing my hold on his arm and subtly stepping away. He's silently giving me permission, I can tell. I shoot him a look of gratitude. I'm such a fish out of water here.

I grasp Dimitri's arm as lightly as I can, while trying not to spill the champagne that I am holding in my other hand all over him. I also have to try and not trip on my skirt in my stilts-from-hell. I'm so screwed. I've never been a great multi-tasker.

Dimitri guides me through the crowd and introduces me to various VIP's, including Elena's mother and Gavin's father. They are both very friendly and social. I expected it out of Gavin's family, but not Elena's. But her mother is perfectly friendly. Perfect manners. Perfect face, just like Elena.

Once we have made the rounds, Dimitri guides me to a nearby elegant table where he slides a chair out for me, then slides it back in after I have taken a seat. He sits beside me and I watch Dante mingle across the room. He checks on me every once in awhile. I see him look at me. Our eyes meet and he smiles, then he continues his conversation.

I wish he is the one sitting with me.

But he's not.

I'm sitting with the Prime Minister.

Of a country.

Dimitri watches me. "You like my son, yes?" he asks. He and Dante have the same accent.

"Your son is extremely nice," I tell him. "He has the most perfect manners that I've ever seen. You should be very proud. He puts all of the boys from back home to shame."

"Ah, America," Dimitri muses thoughtfully. "Tell me of your home, Miss Ellis. I do love hearing about other countries. America is particularly fascinating."

He takes a sip of champagne and motions for me to do the same. So I do. It's fruity and bubbly and not as sweet as you would think. I decide that it must be an acquired taste. And I haven't acquired it yet. But at least I don't choke on it this time. Baby steps, I guess.

I start talking about home. I tell him about the farms, the sunflowers, the wretched summer heat, the storms, the tornadoes, the friendly people. Before I even realize it, I've been talking for fifteen minutes and my champagne glass is empty. Mr. Giliberti motions for a waiter, who arrives with a fresh glass within seconds.

He's the Prime Minister. He obviously doesn't have to wait.

"Your home sounds lovely," he tells me in his charming accent. "Especially the people. I have heard that the people from America's heartland are truly some of the friendliest in the world."

I nod. "I agree with that. It's certainly true of Kansans."

He sips at his champagne and I notice a huge glittering Onyx ring on his ring finger. It looks like a black eye. I sip at my fresh glass of champagne.

"Tell me more about you," he encourages me. "You are entering your last secondary school, yes?"

It takes me a second to realize that he means high school and I nod.

"Yes. I'll be a senior this year, like Dante."

"Where will you be going to University after that?" he asks politely.

I shake my head. "I don't know yet. All I know is that I want to get into marketing. I think that sounds fun. So I suppose I'll have to find out which schools are best for that."

Dimitri's eyes light up. "Ah, marketing. Such an interesting field," he says and I can tell that he means it. "Has Dante mentioned that we own an olive business? We have to dabble in marketing strategy ourselves. It's quite interesting. We employ a marketing team, of course, but I do enjoy working with them. What are your plans for this summer? Perhaps you would like to intern with them."

I stare at him, speechless.

Did he just invite me to stay for the summer? Dante's voice interrupts my fog.

"Reece! That's a brilliant idea! You could stay and work for Giliberti Olives. It would look great on your college applications. Do you think your parents would let you?"

I'm dumbfounded.

I could stay in Caberra with the most beautiful boy in the world, working in his beautiful olive groves.

I find myself nodding. "I'm sure they would be flattered that you think that I am able," I stammer.

Dimitri laughs. "Of course you are able," he tells me. "You'll be an intern. It's an entry level position and you will learn quite a bit, I am sure. I can tell that you are a quick study. I will personally call your parents in the morning to gain their permission. It will be a wonderful opportunity for you."

I stare at Dante in shock. He looks pleased.

A wonderful opportunity? Try amazingly-awesome-I'm going to wet my pants-opportunity. That's how awesome it is.

"Thank you, sir," I tell Dimitri. "This is so nice of you. I'm speechless. I don't even know what to say."

"Well, I can think of one thing you shouldn't say," he answers with a twinkle in his eye. "Sir. Don't call me sir. You are a family friend. Please, call me Dimitri."

I feel shocked again. I'm on a first name basis with the leader of a country?

Surely this is a dream. It has to be.

Numbly, I nod. "Okay. Thank you. Dimitri."

He looks satisfied and takes his leave.

I'm left alone with Dante, which to be honest, I am ecstatic about.

"Will your parents say yes?" Dante asks me. He sits down beside me and hands me another glass of champagne. This will be my third glass. I take it with amazingly agile fingers. I've got this. I've so got this.

And then I realize that the liquid courage has worked. I feel invincible. I'm not even nervous anymore. About anything. My mind is a little foggy but I can deal with that. It makes me a little detached…takes the worry away. I find that I quite like it. And then I giggle because it makes me think words like *quite.*

"What's funny?" Dante asks curiously, his fingers resting on my arm. Every nerve ending immediately explodes into flame, as every cell in my body is aware of his fingers. I like the weight of it on my skin. I hope that he never moves it.

But he does. And I feel its absence immediately.

"Nothing," I answer. "This just feels surreal. And I'm sure that my parents will say yes. How in the world could they tell your father no?"

"Not many people do," Dante agrees. "It's a hard thing to do, trust me."

He looks regretful, which makes me instantly curious.

"Why do you look sad?" I ask. "You live in a beautiful country with the world at your fingertips. Your dad is amazing and nice and you're a billionaire. What could possibly make you sad?"

Dante studies me, his cobalt eyes serious, his expression unreadable.

"Let's go for a walk," he finally says. "Someplace quieter."

A quiet place with Dante? Yes, Please!

I scramble to my feet and walk with him through the crowd again, this time oblivious to the stares. He has a huge stride and I find myself hurrying to keep up, two steps for every one of his. He weaves us through the people and out the doors in record time.

Before I know it, we are on a terrace. In the dark. Under the stars.

With Dante.

This may as well be Heaven.

In fact, it might actually be.

Have I died and didn't realize it?

I flex my fingers and poke at my thigh.

My mind is fuzzy and I feel like I am moving slower than I actually am. Is life in slow motion right now or is it me? I blink hard then poke myself again.

"Are you alright?" Dante asks, watching me curiously. I nod.

"Yep. I've just never had three glasses of champagne before. In fact, I've never even had one. Until now."

I giggle at the thought and Dante smiles.

"Okay, drunk girl. Let's sit you down."

He guides me to a lounger and eases me onto it. I clutch at his arm, not wanting to let him go. He stares down at me.

"You really have had too much to drink, haven't you, little sunflower?"

The name warms my heart and I decide that he is the handsomest person in the world.

"Is handsomest a word?" I ask him.

He looks at me blankly.

"I don't know," he answers slowly. "Why?"

"You're the handsomest person in the world," I announce. "I don't care if it's a word or not. You are it, one way or another."

Dante smiles and runs a hand through his hair, as though he's trying to decide what to do. "Oh. Okay. Um, thanks? What am I going to do with you? You're adorable when you are drunk. But I made you drunk, even if it was an accident. How was I supposed to know that you're such a lightweight?"

He sounds like he is waging some sort of battle with himself.

"Who exactly are you arguing with?" I ask, the champagne clouding my thoughts in a very thorough way. "You will get no arguments from me tonight. No matter what."

He sighs, a husky and ragged sound.

It's sexy.

I scoot closer to him and drag him down until he is sitting on the lounger with me. His warmth feels nice out here because the air has turned cool. It's dark and I feel like we're in our own little world. I run my fingers over his arm, then grip at his shoulders.

"You're so strong," I tell him. "And your fingers are so long."

I don't know what that has to do with anything, I just feel like pointing it out. Because his fingers *are* long. I pick up his hand and slide my own against it. His hand is at least a full inch longer than mine. Probably more. I curl my fingers around his and hold tight to his hand.

I look up at him.

He is so devastatingly beautiful in the moonlight.

I tell him so.

He stares at me, his dark gaze unwavering. Except for my knees. It definitely wavers my knees, if that is possible. I know I wouldn't be able to stand up if I tried. Which I'm not going to. I'm staying right here…with Dante.

"Kiss me," I whisper. "Please."

Dante is silent, his blue eyes frozen on me.

And then he lowers his head and his soft lips are upon mine.

And I might seriously die this time.

For real.

I'm kissing Dante.

Kissing.

Dante.

The thoughts won't stop running through my head as Dante kisses me in the most romantic and soft kiss I've ever experienced. My thoughts blur together and all I can do now is immerse myself in the moment. The world actually seems to explode for a second. This is the most amazing kiss in the history of the world.

Dante smells so good, and his arms are so strong and his tuxedo jacket is so soft against my skin and this is the most romantic terrace I've ever seen. So, so romantic. I am clutching at him, trying to get closer and closer. The flowers that surround us throw their luscious scents into the breeze and I never want this moment to end. Not ever.

Not.

Ever.

But it does.

Exactly one moment later, actually.

Dante's phone rings in his pocket and the loud noise brings us both back to reality. I stop clutching at him and he reluctantly reaches into his pocket and answers his phone.

"I'm sorry. I didn't hear it earlier." Long pause. "No, I'm not there at the moment. I didn't realize you were coming." Longer pause. "I'll be there in a few minutes." Pause. "Yes. See you then."

He hangs up and my heart falters for a moment because I know who he was speaking with even before I ask.

"Elena?"

My voice seems small and suddenly the terrace seems like it is moving. I steady myself with my hands on the lounger and I blink hard to clear my fuzzy vision.

Dante nods without saying anything.

But I have liquid courage raging through my veins and I'm suddenly not afraid to ask the question that I've been wondering all along. It's burning within me and I have to know.

"Is she your girlfriend?"

There is utter silence on the terrace and I am afraid to look at him. I'm afraid of the answer. I'm afraid of the expression that might be on his face. I'm suddenly afraid of everything.

"Never mind," I stammer quickly. "Don't answer that."

"It's complicated, Reece," he tells me. "I'm sorry. It's just really complicated."

And apparently, liquid courage is also sort of like liquid fire-starter because my temper flares right up.

"It's not complicated," I tell him icily. "Either Elena is your girlfriend or she's not. It's pretty simple, actually."

"You don't understand," he sighs. "My world isn't the same as yours."

And suddenly, the fire in my veins is doused with ice cold water.

Because he's right. We're from different worlds and I've known that from the beginning. I shouldn't have asked him to kiss me because he can never be with me. I know that. I'm not in his league at all. And I suddenly realize that I'm not sure that I even want to be in it. His world is so *complicated*, after all.

"This was a mistake," I mutter as I try to get up from the lounger.

I stumble and fall back down, directly into Dante's lap. His legs are strong beneath me and I fight the urge to linger there. He holds me for a second, his eyes glued to mine. His are clouded with regret and I 'm not sure why. Does he regret kissing me? Or does he regret that he can't kiss me again? Either way, it's enough. I bolt from his arms and run.

And I'd thought that I wouldn't have to run in my heels.

My footsteps are loud on the marble floors and anyone in a hundred yard vicinity can hear me coming. Guards are stationed at periodic intervals in the Old Palace and although they look at me curiously, they don't interfere. I can hear Dante behind me and I can hear him calling my name. But he never asks the guards to stop me.

I almost make it to my room before my left heel tangles in my gown and I fall to the ground in a heap. My dress is spread around me and my hands don't quite break my fall. My shoulder scrapes the floor. I should be humiliated since this is exactly what I was afraid of from the moment I put the high-heeled-stilts-from-hell on, but surprisingly, I don't care. I lay there for a moment and compose myself. I can hear Dante next to me.

"Are you alright?" he asks softly.

I don't say anything.

I stay still and he bends down and scoops me into his arms.

He holds me with one arm and opens the door with his other and then carries me inside, placing me gently on the bed. He doesn't sit down.

"Are you alright?" he asks again, staring seriously at me. He picks up one of my hands and examines it, but I pull it away from him. I want nothing more than for him to touch me, hold my hand, hold *me*, but that can't happen.

I steel my heart and nod silently, then I look away.

"Goodnight, Dante."

I am dismissing him. It is clear.

"Can we talk tomorrow?" he asks. He is almost pleading. He's so polite. So… Caberran.

"I don't know."

"Please, Reece. Let's talk tomorrow. You'll feel better in the morning."

I nod silently. I can't talk right now. I just can't.

"Sleep well."

He turns and leaves and I bury my face into my pillow and cry.

It's what any normal girl would do.

Chapter Fifteen

If I've ever, at any point in my life, thought I was dying, I was wrong. I wasn't even close then. I know that, because I'm dying now. So now I know what it feels like.

I groan and shove a pillow over my face as the morning light assaults my eyes with a cold-blooded vengeance. My head is splitting apart. Someone is crushing my skull with a hammer. And poking my eyes with a sharp stick. And banging my head into the wall. And then stomping on my forehead.

I squint one eye open. Who am I kidding? I'm alone. And I'm hung-over.

And I am not enjoying it.

I groan again. This is so not worth it. Why would anyone in their right mind do this to themselves?

My phone buzzes and I realize that it is what woke me in the first place. I have no idea how long it has been vibrating, but I throw out an arm to clumsily grab it. I peer at the screen.

Quinn McKeyan.

Oh, perfect.

Just who I need to talk to.

Not.

I drop the phone back onto the bed and then throw my arm back over my eyes. I'm not answering it. And no one can make me. I'm hung-over and grumpy.

My phone is silent for a scant minute before it starts ringing again. I let it go to voicemail. It starts ringing again. We go through this process two more times before I realize that Quinn is not going to give up. He's bound and determined to talk to me.

Eff.

I growl into the phone.

"What?"

Brief silence.

"Reecie?" Quinn is taken off guard because I'm not usually bitchy, even during "that" time of the month. Even-keeled, girl-next-door. That's me. It's my eternal curse. "Are you alright?"

And he actually sounds concerned, so I feel bad about biting his head off. Sort of.

I swallow the build-up of saliva that is pooling in my mouth. Oh, the joys of hangovers. Again- really- why do people do this to themselves?

"I'm fine," I assure him and I even sound somewhat convincing. "I just have a massive headache. Why are you calling me a hundred times? Is something wrong?"

"Everything is wrong," he groans into the phone and I can hear the pain in his voice and I am instantly alarmed, sitting straight up in bed even though my head might explode from the contact with the light.

"Is Becca alright?" I ask quickly. A hundred different scenarios roll through my head, none of them good and most of them involving blood. Car accident. Horse-back riding incident. Drowning. Sickness. Surgery?

"No," Quinn answers. "She's not. She won't listen to me and I don't know what to do."

I start to feel calmer. No accident. Why am I such a paranoid freak?

"So, nothing has happened to her?" I just have to clarify.

Short pause.

"No, nothing bad has happened to her. It's just that everything is a mess. And it's all your fault, you know."

"Oh, great. Not you too," I snap. "Listen. Becca read *my* diary. Doesn't anyone care about that? She went into *my* house to borrow *my* clothes and she snooped through *my* stuff. But no one cares about that part. No, everyone just wants to act like you and I cheated. And we didn't."

"You don't have to tell me that," he sounds hurt. "I realize that we didn't cheat."

"So, why is Becca mad at you?" I'm curious about this and since Becca won't talk to me, Quinn is my only source of information.

He sniffs. Is he freaking crying? Really? Oh-my-word. It must be bad.

"When Becca called and told me about your journal, somewhere in that conversation I mentioned that once upon a time, years ago, I had a crush on you too. I thought it was funny because of the bad timing and all. But Becca didn't think it was funny."

The world grinds to a stop and freezes.

Or at least, my world does.

"You had a crush on me?" I whisper. I find that anything above a soft whisper drives nails into my skull. Long, three-inch nails.

This information should be earth-shattering. Mind-blowing. Amazing. And a scant week ago, before Dante Giliberti effectively took control of the full-on crush that I had on Quinn, it would have been.

But now, it only seems sad.

Or funny.

The bad timing is slightly hilarious. Especially given all the drama that the whole incident has incited.

"Yes, I had a crush on you. But that's not that surprising. Most of our junior high had a crush on you."

Our age at the time took a little of the impact out of the revelation.

"It was in junior high?"

"Why are you whispering? Yes, it was in junior high. And I think our freshman year, too. And then it was Becca. It's been Becca ever since. But now she thinks that I'm only with her because you didn't like me back- even though that was years ago. And she's worried that since I found out that you are crushing on me now –bad timing, by the way- that I'm going to break up with her and get with you."

Silence.

More silence.

"Are you going to say anything?" he asks. I can't read his tone. Is he actually hopeful? No. Freaking. Way.

"Quinn," I begin carefully. "You aren't hoping that I will say that we should get together, are you?"

Silence.

"Of course not," he finally answers. Thank God he possesses enough perception skills to read my tone.

I sigh. "Good. Because I'm not crushing on you anymore. And even if I were, we couldn't do that to Becca. I firmly believe that she will get over this as soon as she realizes that you are not breaking up with her to date me. Because that's not happening."

"No?" he asks and I can't even believe that he asks. Are all guys this dense?

"No," I answer firmly. "Quinn, you and I have been friends a long, long time. I value our friendship. I value Becca's friendship even more. Please, let's all just be friends."

"Alright," he agrees. "Good idea. As long as you can get Becca to talk to us again."

"Well, you're on your own with that," I tell him. "But personally, I'm going to give her some space. Then I'll talk to her when I get back."

"Reecie, why are you whispering?" he asks again.

"Because I have a headache," I answer quietly.

"Are you hung-over?" he crows. "Little Reecie-Piecie is hung-over? Miss Rule Follower herself? No freaking way!"

I hang up on him.

His voice is just too loud and too crowing.

My phone instantly rings again but I ignore it this time.

I lay still for a minute, remembering everything that happened last night.

Dante kissed me.

Dante's life is *complicated.*

I ran, I fell and Dante carried me to bed.

And then he left me here.

I.

Just.

Want.

To.

Die.

Not really.

Well, sort of.

I crawl out of bed and drag myself to the shower. I lean my head against the shower tiles and let the cool water run over my body for at least twenty minutes. I don't even feel guilty about wasting the water. I need it more than people in the Gobi desert right now, I am sure.

When I finally feel a teench more human, I step back out of the shower. And instantly get light-headed and instantly drop onto all-fours on the bathroom rug. My head might fall off and roll away. That's what it feels like, anyway. And part of me wishes that it would. It would at least solve the headache problem.

I crawl back out to my bedroom. My head feels better if I'm not upright. I slump against my bed as I pull on some clothes. And then there's a knock at the door.

Oh, no.

It can't be Dante.

Not right now.

Because I'm on the verge of death.

I slowly get to my feet and creep toward the door. And open it.

And there's no one there.

But there is a small white box with a navy blue velvet bow atop it sitting prettily at my feet. And a card.

I stare at it for a moment before I pick it up and head back inside, dropping into a heap on the bed.

I tear off the bow and the box lid, and find a woven leather cuff bracelet with a big silver sunflower on it. It's got pretty Mediterranean beads woven in the leather strands and it's beautiful and I love it. And I know, even before I open the card, that it is from Dante. His little Sunflower. That's what he called me last night.

My breath freezes in my throat as my fingers automatically snap it onto my wrist. It looks beautiful there, I have to admit. It suits me.

I open the card.

Reece,

I'm so sorry about last night. Please accept this as a ThankYouForComingToDinner and SorryThatIGotYouDrunkAndKissedYou gift. I'm really sorry that my life is complicated. But I'm really glad that I have met you.

DGG

I can't decide if I am angry or touched. My heart sort of melts at his last

I'mReallyGladThatIHaveMetYou line, but the fact that he thinks a gift will just wash away any hurt feelings is annoying.

He simply can't answer the Elena question with *It's Complicated.* Not cool.

I notice something else nestled in the cotton of the box and pull out a little packet of aspirin. Nice.

I can't help but smile.

But I do need to find Dante and give him this gift back. I don't want him to think that he can do anything at all and a trinket will fix it. I slip it off and regretfully put it back into the box. I keep the aspirin, though.

I set off to find him, but it is difficult. The Old Palace is huge and I'm not that familiar with it. I find myself wandering the halls with the little white box in my hands. I slip quietly in and out of cordoned-off areas and I don't see anyone familiar. Heaven is nowhere to be found and I don't know any of the other staff. I realize that I should call or text Dante and then realize that I left my phone in my room.

Dummy.

I stumble into a long quiet corridor. There is no one here and there aren't even that many windows. It's quiet in a disturbing, unnerving way. I can't explain it and I want to turn around and go back the other way, but I don't.

I open the first door to my right and take a step inside.

And gasp.

It's a huge studio.

And it's filled with a hundred different pictures of me.

Chapter Sixteen

I take a trembling step inside and stop dead in my tracks as I look around in wonder.

Oh.

My.

Word.

Pictures of me, in black and white, hang from various clips, wires and easels around the room. There are dozens of other pictures too, older pictures of scenery and pictures of another woman, but at least half of all of these prints are of me.

Light slants in from a wall of windows. There is a desk, several easels, a wall of art supplies. Overall, it's a cheerful room. But that doesn't take away from the fact that my face is plastered all over it.

"I see you found my lair," Dante murmurs from behind me.

I whirl around.

"Your lair? What is this?" I demand. "Why are there so many pictures of me?"

He looks abashed. Guilty. Caught. My heart flutters a little. Why does he look so guilty?

"I'm sorry," he answers quietly, his face impassive. Guarded. "I know it seems strange."

"Strange doesn't begin to cover it," I tell him. "More like criminally insane. Please tell me that you don't have a cat-suit made from human skin in one of these closets."

Dante smiles slightly as he skirts around me and enters the room. He picks up a camera lying on a nearby table.

"It's a guilty pleasure," he shrugs his shoulders. "I love photography. I always have. Life is so interesting from behind the lens. People seem more real, somehow. I take pictures of pretty much everything. See those cabinets over there?"

He motions toward the opposite wall filled with shelves and cabinets. "Those are filled with stacks of photos that I have taken over the years."

He aims the camera at me and I hear it snap a picture. I stride across the room and yank it from his hands. I want to throw it, but I don't.

"What are you doing?" I hiss, ignoring the pain in my temple. "I'm trying to ascertain that you are, in fact, sane. And you're just standing there taking a picture of me. Which, I might add, is not helping your cause. I think you've got quite enough pictures of me already. Who is the other woman in the pictures?"

"That's my mother," he answers softly. "She loved photography too or so I'm told. I found those old pictures in a box that my father had packed away. I didn't think they should be hidden, so I've kept them in my studio. My father hates this hobby. He thinks it's a waste of time. But it also just reminds him of my mom. So I never have to worry about him coming in here, into my space."

I felt instantly bad for snapping at him.

Honestly, sometimes he seems like a vulnerable little boy. A vulnerable little boy without a mother. My heart breaks a little bit and I look at him.

"Your mother was very beautiful. Look, I'm sorry for being angry. But I don't feel well, there are enough pictures of me here to wallpaper a room with and I'm grumpy. What happened last night, well, it was embarrassing."

Dante nods, takes the camera from my hands and puts it back on the table.

"I know. I'm really sorry."

He motions to a loveseat on the far wall. "Would you like to sit down? Can we talk now?"

A boy who actually wants to talk? Dante is definitely different from most.

I walk woodenly across the room and take a seat.

Dante slides the desk chair over and situates it next to me. So, he doesn't want to share the loveseat. Interesting.

190

I thrust the white box into his hands.

"The bracelet is beautiful," I tell him. "But I can't accept it. I'm upset with you for not being straight with me about Elena. I can't take gifts from you."

He all but smiles.

"That makes no sense," he tells me. "I want you to have it as an apology. I feel horribly about last night. And I saw the bracelet and thought immediately of you. Please keep it. It shouldn't be on anyone else's arm but yours."

Lord, but Dante has a way with words.

"I want to be mad at you right now," I announce. "You're playing with my emotions. And that's not cool."

He looks shocked. "I'm definitely not playing with your emotions," he says. "Not on purpose. Look, Reece. My life-"

"Is complicated," I interrupt. "Yeah, I know. You told me already."

I start to get up but he reaches over and puts his hand on my arm.

"No. That's not what I was going to say. My life has been planned out from the moment that I was born. My family owns Giliberti Olives. That's what we do. My dad wants me to get an MBA and run the business and then maybe enter politics like him. But that's not me. I don't want anything to do with politics. And I love the olive groves. It's not that. It's just that I'd like to be given a choice, for once in my life. Just the choice to do what I want. And be who I want. And to like who I want."

Pregnant pause.

"Like me?" I ask, my breath hitching in my throat.

"Like you," he confirms. "I can't stop thinking about you. Every minute, every day. I even see you when I'm sleeping. My dreams are about you—we're in the ocean, we're on the beach, we're under the stars at night, we're dancing at dinner. I know this sounds stupid and corny and dumb. But you've taken over every thought that I have. And I don't know what to do about that, because you're not in my plan."

I stare at him incredulously.

"What am I supposed to do with that? Was that speech supposed to make me feel better? You like me but you can't be with me?"

I feel suddenly hollow inside. Like I'd lost my heart along the way somewhere. But that can't be right because it's throbbing right now- worse than my head, even.

"No. You don't understand. I'm just trying to figure out what to do. How to handle all of this. Americans are different. Here in Caberra, we... well, we don't exercise our freedom to choose as often as you do. My father wants a particular life for me. I don't know how to go against that. It will devastate him and he's been devastated enough already. Our culture is polite to a fault, I think."

Oh, sweet Heavens. I can't even be thoroughly disgusted with him because he's so bleeding thoughtful even when he's being frustrating. He doesn't want to hurt his father. But that means he'll have to hurt me instead.

"Should I just make it easy on you?" I ask, trying to swallow my heart. "I'll just leave. As soon as the airports open back up, I'll go back home. You can go back to your life with Elena and back to doing things that are in your plan."

"No!"

Dante cries out sharply, almost like he's in pain. And he grabs my arm. I look at him, then look at his hand. He removes it sheepishly.

"I'm sorry," he says. "Please don't go home. I feel like I have this chance—this chance to do what I'd really like to do with someone who I really like. I don't know how to go about it, but I'd really like for you to show me."

I stare at him again.

"And how can I show you that? You'll have to learn to make up your mind on your own. That's not something that I can do for you."

"You're American," he explains. "You're already good at doing what you'd like to do. I can learn a lot just from being around you." He smiles and I try to decide if he's joking.

"Are you saying that Americans are good at being self-involved?" I ask, one eye-brow raised. Does he really think insulting me is going to help the situation?

Dante rolls his eyes.

"I'm trying to be sweet here and bare my soul to you. Seriously, Reece. I feel like I've got an honest to God chance at finding my own path in life. I've never felt the urge to deviate from my father's plan before. Not until I met you. And now everything feels different. Everything has changed."

He sits quietly, his hands clasped in his lap, his eyes down. His shoulders are even slumped.

I take pity on him. I can't help it.

"All you have to do is talk to your father," I tell him. "Just tell him that you don't want to go into politics and you aren't even that thrilled with being in the family business."

"It's not the business so much," Dante says. "It's the fact that he wants me to go to England to college to learn how to run the business. And trust me, it isn't so easy as simply talking to him. This isn't America. Kids here aren't just given free will over their own lives when we are teenagers. Our lives are planned out from the beginning. And we stick to those plans. Usually."

Dante looks miserable. And I find that I can't really relate so I tell him that.

"You're almost an adult," I point out. "You are almost of legal age to go to war and fight for your country. Shouldn't that make you old enough to plan out your own life? I know that I'm not familiar with Caberran law, but you are free to make your own decisions, right?"

"Theoretically," Dante admits. "But it's more difficult in practice than it is in theory."

I look at him, at how the light glints off the honeyed streaks in his hair and how his dark blue eyes are glittering. His mouth is drawn and tight and I know he is upset. And a part of me, deep down, wants to cradle him in my arms and make everything better. It's like a piece of him, the little boy in him, is broken and I just want to fix it.

But the little girl in me learned a long time ago that kisses don't make things better.

"I wish I could fix this for you," I tell him gently. "I truly do. But this is something that only you can do. Standing up for yourself... that's just a life skill that you have to learn. We all do. It's part of growing up."

He nods silently, his gaze meeting mine.

"I know," he says finally. "But it would be so much easier if my mom was still alive. I wouldn't worry so much about disappointing my dad. I'm all he has now. And that's a lot of pressure. He's got so many dreams for me."

"But so do you," I remind him. "And you've only got one life."

"Would it sound stupid if I told you that I think I met you for a reason?" Dante asks. "Okay. It does sound stupid. But I still think it's true. I don't want you to go home yet. Please tell me that you'll stay. Please be an intern for my father and we'll see what happens. I'm going to do my best to figure it out."

"All you need to do is be true to yourself, Dante," I tell him. "It really is that simple. You're right. I don't know the culture here. But I do know that your father is a good man. I can tell. And I know that as a good man, he'll want his only son to be happy in life. Whether that means being with someone other than Elena or not becoming Prime Minister in twenty years or even if that means that you want to work on a commercial fishing boat."

Dante smiles wryly. "I haven't lost my mind," he tells me. "So let's not go overboard."

"Okay. So you don't want to be a fisherman," I smile. "But if you just talk to your father, I'm sure he'll understand."

"Maybe," Dante shrugs. "But I have to work him up to it. I can't just drop it on him."

"Fair enough," I agree. "I suppose you can't change decades worth of tradition in one moment.

But be patient and no matter what, stay true to yourself. If you don't, who will?"

He looks at me, his gaze lucid and clear and nods. "You're right. And that's an excellent point. It's so simple that it's brilliant."

I suddenly find it funny that I am sitting here in an old palace giving out life advice when my own life is sort of in a shambles. I laugh and Dante looks at me quizzically.

"What?"

I tell him. I tell him all about Becca and my journal and Quinn.

"So you're not as pulled together as you seem, then," he observes when I am finished. He smiles at me now and I feel good because it's his first real smile this morning. My heart seems to have forgotten that I was angry with him because now all I feel is protective of him.

Weird.

"I guess not," I tell him. "But in all fairness, that journal was private. She didn't ask to be in my room, in my clothes *or* in my journal."

Dante holds up his hands. "Hey, I didn't say anything," he yelps as I swat at him. "I'm in full agreement with you. Becca is clearly to blame for your crush on Quinn. Not you."

I squint my eyes and glare at him.

"I don't have a crush on Quinn anymore."

He raises a golden eyebrow.

"No?"

I shake my head. "No."

"Why is that?"

I stare at him long and hard, trying to decide what to say. Should I be downright, painfully honest? I've always found that the best way to be, so I nod.

"Two words."

He waits.

"Dante. Giliberti."

I hear him suck in his breath and I smile. Sometimes, honesty is refreshing and so very worth it.

"Me?" He sounds so surprised, as though he doesn't know that he is practically a living breathing Adonis. I nod.

"You."

He studies me again and I fight the need to fidget as I wait for his reaction.

After a minute of nerve-wracking silence, he finally answers.

"So, will you keep the bracelet?"

I nod.

"Can I kiss you again?"

I nod.

So he does.

Chapter Seventeen

My parents said yes.

I'm not surprised, I knew that they would if Dimitri called them himself. And he did. And they said that I could stay in Caberra for the summer to work for Giliberti Olives. Dimitri decided that it would be best if I started out in the actual Giliberti olive groves somewhere, to learn the business from the ground up. He does the same for all of his important employees, he says. Including Dante. Dante will be shadowing the foreman in the groves this summer.

It doesn't matter to me that I won't be with the marketing team. In fact, as soon as Dimitri lumped me in with "important employees," I was putty in his hands. Dante clearly gets his charm from his father.

I decide that I'm probably the luckiest girl on the planet as I sip a lemonade by the sparkling infinity pool. My lemonade has mint leaves floating in it again which makes me feel fancy.

Make that extra fancy.

Because when I got out of the shower this morning, there were beach towels twisted into sea animal shapes on my bed along with a note from Dante to meet him at the pool.

We're not working today because it's Saturday. But Dante did tell me that we would make a trip out to the olive groves this afternoon so that I could look around.

He grins from the lounger next to me.

"I like having you here, Kansas," he tells me. "My father likes you. And you put him in a good mood. He says it's refreshing to have a young person so interested in business."

"You're just happy that he's focused on me instead of you," I tell him without opening my eyes. The sun feels so good here. Better than it feels in Kansas, I think. Of course that might be because I'm thousands of miles from my problems.

Or because Dante is lying next to me.

That's probably it, actually.

He reaches out and grasps my hand, holding it next to him. My heart beat stutters and I take a deep breath. He's so gorgeous. Ever since our talk yesterday, we've had sort of an easy-breezy-attitude about our relationship. Like, I know he likes me even though his life is *complicated*. And he knows I like him. And my life *isn't* complicated. We haven't exactly defined what our relationship is, but I think that's probably because of all the kinks.

Kinks like his father.

And Elena.

Life is full of kinks.

And the great thing about kinks? They eventually work themselves out.

But at least we know that we're on the right track. And we're working toward something. Something really great. I can feel it.

My phone buzzes. I glance at it and see Mia's name on a text.

Do U want to go shopping?

I consider that for one brief moment as I look at Dante's inert, beautiful form next to me. His brow is glistening slightly in the heat and he brushes one long hand against it to wipe the sweat away. He could practically be a swimsuit model. Do I want to leave here where I am laying with him in Nirvana and go shopping in a place where I might run into the creepy gypsy woman with Mia?

Um. Negatory.

I text back.

Can't. Want to come swimming?

She answers.

Can't. I need a new bra. My girls got a little bigger. My old bras pinch my nipples.

I answer.

Gross. TMI. :)

Then I add a P.S.

Girls are bigger? Are you pg??

Immediate response.

Bite me, Kansas.

I smile.

"What's funny?" Dante asks as he sits up to take a lazy sip of water.

I shake my head. "Nothing. Mia's just funny."

He raises an eyebrow. "Is she coming over?"

"No. She wanted me to come shopping. But I'm busy right now, so..."

My voice trails off as I lean forward to put my phone on the table. Dante sucks in his breath. "What the heck happened to your arm?"

I freeze.

My arm.

The huge, nasty bruise that Nate put on my arm.

I subconsciously cover it with my other hand while I frantically think of something to say. Honesty is always best, right? I wasn't so sure that it was this time. But it's not my place to protect Nate. I don't owe him anything.

Except a bruise.

"Um. I bumped into Nate on the beach the other day."

Dante stares at me in confusion. "You bumped into Nate the other day and got a bruise?"

I sigh. "No. I bumped into Nate the other day on the beach while he was on the phone. He thought I was eavesdropping and he got a little mad."

Dante freezes, his eyes boring into mine.

"Nate got a little mad at you?"

Each word is carefully enunciated and chillingly calm and I feel a storm coming. In fact, the hair stands up on my arms. I feel a sense of foreboding, actually. Dante is pissed and Nate is not someone to mess with. I sense that from a mile away. In telling Dante this bit of info, I'm essentially signing my Enemies-Are-Forever agreement with Nate.

But the truth is always best.

Right?

I nod. "He thought I was eavesdropping."

And I had been.

"What was he saying that was so very important?" Dante asks, his voice still icily calm. He sits up. "Matters of national security, I'm sure."

He's getting to his feet, wiping off with a towel and reaching for a shirt. This can't be good. Besides the fact that I'd rather he stay shirtless, I don't want him going after Nate. I know from these types of situations with farm boys in Kansas that they seldom end well. Bones get broken, eyes get blackened, blood gets spattered.

"No. I'm not sure what he was talking about. He was trying to find something, he said. And he mentioned your name. But honestly, I couldn't tell what the conversation was about. It might have been nothing at all."

"That's neither here nor there," Dante announces. "Because he laid a hand on you. And that was a mistake."

I sigh again.

"Dante, please. It's over with now. It's not going to do any good to confront him. He was just having a bad day, I think."

"Well, he's about to have another one today." Dante stalks away.

I sit frozen for a moment before I scramble up and trail after him.

He's on his phone already, leaving livid voicemails for Nate. I presume it's Nate, anyway.

"Call me, you bastard. Now."

I sincerely hope it's Nate.

Dante shoves his phone in his pocket and keeps walking.

"Where are we going?" I ask as I trail at his heels like a puppy. It's all I can do to keep up. He's moving very fast. And his legs are very long.

We wind through the Old Palace and come out on the other side, bursting through the main doors just in time to bump into... Nate. And Nate's father, Nathaniel. And Dimitri.

Gulp.

The three of them stare at us in surprise and Dante takes no time for pleasantries or explanations. He shoves Nate hard, causing him to stumble backward down the white marble steps.

"What the hell?" Nate looks bewildered and Dimitri grabs Dante's arm.

"What were you thinking?" Dante demands, struggling against his father. Dimitri holds him fast.

"What are *you* thinking?"Dimitri hisses, yanking at Dante. "Stop this."

Dante pulls his arm away.

"Do you enjoy roughing up women?" he asks icily, stepping directly into Nate's personal space. Nate is calm, unworried. He looks directly into Dante's eyes.

"I don't know what you're talking about, Dante," he says. My hand automatically fingers the tender bruise on my arm. Nate's gaze flickers to me and I can see in his eyes that he knows *exactly* what Dante is talking about.

But he's a very good liar.

Nate immediately puts on an innocent, puzzled expression. I can practically feel his father's breath on my neck as we all close in to listen. This is the first time I've seen Nate's father. He looks nothing like Nate. He is shorter, darker. He seems kinder and like the rest of us, he is waiting for Nate's explanation. And that is forthcoming, but it is full of shit.

"Dante, is this about Reece? I'm sorry, dude. I didn't mean to hurt her. She stumbled on the beach and I reached out to make sure she didn't fall. I certainly didn't intend to man-handle her."

Nate looks to me.

"Did you think I was purposely hurting you, Reece? My apologies. That certainly wasn't the case. Can you forgive me?"

His face is icy, his eyes cold. But the words he is speaking are the right ones. How can we argue with them in front of Dimitri and Nathaniel?

"I don't believe you," Dante says calmly. I guess that's how. We just lay it out there. I suck in my breath as Nathaniel steps forward.

"Come now, Dante," Nathaniel says quietly. "Nate says it was unintentional. Surely you can't believe that he'd harm a girl that he barely knows. For what purpose? Let's not be rash. Let us calm down and be adults. Is it possible that your judgment might be clouded because you're jealous that Nate was with Reece at the beach in the first place?"

"I'm not jealous of Nate," Dante answers. "I just know Nate better than you do, sir."

"Dante!" Dimitri snaps, his face a thunderous storm cloud. "Apologize at once. This is ridiculous. Nate has apologized. It was an accident." He turns to me. "My dear, I sincerely apologize that you have been injured here in Caberra under my watch. I will make it up to you. I do hope you won't hold Nate liable. I believe his intentions were true."

No, they weren't.

But Dimitri is waiting for me to speak, to agree, so I nod.

"It's fine. It's just a little bruise."

"It's not fine," Dante interjects, but his father grabs his arm.

"Dante," he hisses into Dante's ear. "Enough. We're in public."

Dante goes still.

"Now apologize," Dimitri instructs. Dante clenches his jaw so tightly that a little muscle ticks by his mouth. His beautiful mouth. I cringe inside at the thought that Dante has to apologize to this beast.

"Apologize," Dimitri says again.

Dante sighs, squaring his shoulders reluctantly as pulls his arm away from Dimitri. He is resigned to doing his duty. I can see it on his face. It's a role that he has played in his life many, many times. And once again, I don't envy him for it.

"I apologize," he says icily to Nate the beast. He takes two steps towards me to walk past Nate and as he passes him, he leans in and says, "For nothing," in Nate's ear.

I'm not sure if anyone but Nate and I hear, but the look on Nate's face is priceless. He's pissed and he can't say anything.

Dimitri and Nathaniel are already nodding and walking back inside as if the matter is closed. I doubt they truly care as long as public image isn't harmed. They are good people, I am sure. But they are public figures. They have been conditioned to always think about public perception. I can't blame them for that.

Nathaniel turns when they reach the doors.

"Are you coming, Nate?"

I realize that he doesn't want to leave Nate out here. He doesn't want to take the chance that Nate will do something regrettable. I can see that on his face. He knows his son. And he probably knows that Nate purposely bruised my arm. I stare at him. His gaze flickers to me and it almost seems apologetic. And then the expression is gone. He patiently waits until Nate joins him and then he nods at Dante.

Then they're gone.

Dante and I stare at each other.

"I'm sorry, Reece," he tells me. "Nate will get his. Trust me."

His voice is assured and calm with a promise in it.

"I don't want Nate 'to get his'," I tell him honestly. "I don't want conflict. I just want to go on with life, okay? Thank you for standing up for me. No one has ever done that for me before. And I'll never be alone with Nate again. I know he's your friend, but there's something about him…"

Dante nods. "I know."

We start to walk back into the palace, but Dante stops and looks at me.

"I don't want to go in there. Not right now. Want to take that tour of the groves?"

Do I ever. I don't even want to be in the same building as Nate Geraris.

"That would be lovely," I smile. I'm so grateful that I can't even see straight.

Dante leads me into a different direction. And before I even know it, we are descending on wide concrete stairs into a basement of some sort.

"The garage," Dante tells me when he sees the question on my face. "Come on. Let's get out of here."

He gets no arguments from me.

There are so many cars in this garage. There are gleaming luxury cars. Shining sports cars. Aggressive looking military trucks, even. And nestled next to a shiny blue Jaguar, there is a sleek black convertible. I have no idea what kind of car it is, but it is so sexy that it absolutely has to be Dante's. *Has to be.*

And sure enough, he walks right to it and opens the passenger door for me. I slip into the luxurious butter-soft leather of the seat and it immediately engulfs me in cushioned luxury. Dante gets into the driver's seat, shoves a key into the ignition and revs the engine before he punches at a button and the top slides soundlessly down.

Dante revs the engines again and it roars, then purrs quietly. I don't know a thing about cars but even I can tell that there is a lot of power under this shiny black hood.

"What kind of car is this?" I ask curiously. There is a fancy trident on the glove-box, but I've never seen that emblem before.

"It's a Maserati," Dante tells me as we glide out of the parking space.

"It's beautiful," I tell him. And it really is.

It feels like we are floating on air. That's how smooth the ride is. This car is perfect for Dante. It's classy, expensive, powerful. Back home, the boys drive Jeeps with jacked-up tires or pickups with rifle racks in the windows. My own car is a little used Honda Civic. My parents and grandparents had all gone in together and bought it for me for my sixteenth birthday. This is just another glaring reminder of how different we are.

"It's a car," Dante shrugs.

He's oblivious to the incredible things that he is blessed with. He's used to them. He's not arrogant or stuck-up. But you can't grow up in a family like his and not become accustomed to it. It's just human nature.

But still.

A little piece of me is panicked by this.

My heart feels fluttery about his car, by his attitude to his car.

By the fact that his father is a Prime Minister.

By the fact that his world is so glaringly different from mine. Just when I think I've got a handle on it, that I'm used to it, something jumps out at me that reminds me all over again.

Our differences are striking and real and this isn't a fairy tale. And sometimes, in real life, differences sometimes can't be overcome.

Chapter Eighteen

The countryside is beautiful. I can hardly take my eyes from it as we wind our way through the smooth country roads. Being from Kansas, it is hard for me to believe that there are no dirt roads here. But even the country roads are paved and immaculate, perfect like everything else.

The landscape is rugged and green, with rocks dotting the hills and tall grass waving. The highway that we are on winds above the ocean and below us, the blue sea crashes against the rocks. Above us, the sky is just as blue. It's truly breathtaking.

The wind blows my hair and the air smells like the sea. It's salty, vast and earthy. I know that I will never forget this smell. It smells like Dante.

He looks over at me.

"What do you think?" he asks with a smile.

He is happy now, now that we are racing away from the Old Palace. I can see it on his face, by the way he is relaxed in the driver's seat.

And I've not been out of Valese, so this is the first time I've seen the country here in Caberra. He knows what I think. I can see it in his smile.

"I think it's beautiful," I confirm. "You are so lucky to live here. It's so pretty. It's perfect."

"It's only perfect when you are here," he tells me seriously. And I laugh. Dante has the ability to say so many corny things without seeming corny at all. It's a true gift. He reaches over and grabs my hand, nestling it within his on his leg.

I suck my air in.

My fingers are on Dante's thigh.

It seems so intimate.

It *is* so intimate. OhMyWord.

My lungs have a spasm and I practically choke.

Have I mentioned to him that I'm a virgin?

Breathe.

Breathe.

Why am I such an idiot?

We're simply holding hands.

On his thigh.

He looks over at me and grins an ornery grin. And then he guns the engine. We whirl down the winding road and my hair twirls above my head, whipped by the wind. I clutch the handle on the door, but I don't say a word. The car hugs the ground and Dante drives it expertly.

"If you think you're scaring me, you're crazy!" I call above the wind. "I grew up sliding around dirt corners in farm trucks."

Dante laughs and shifts gears and we race even faster along the silvery road. I clutch the door handle harder, but I'm really not afraid. I just don't want to slide around in my seat. I trust him. He's too responsible to get out of control with the car.

We breeze onto a side road and the landscape around us became twisted and viney and even more rugged, but still gorgeous. It looks like orchards line the road. But I look closer and see that tiny olives are on the tree branches. They look almost like pebbles from here.

"Are these yours?" I ask, motioning around us.

Dante nods and I realize that the car is slowing down. I futilely mess with my hair but it's a lost cause. So I give up, wrapping it up in a ponytail holder. I'll deal with the tangles later.

We pull up to two massive wrought-iron gates that are standing wide open. There are G's on each gate.

Giliberti.

I look at this majestic arched iron gate and then picture the old faded white wooden fence that lines our property back home and sigh. The only gates that we have are to keep the cows and horses in. They are fastened together with a thick chain and the cows chew at the fence, so there are bite marks everywhere.

There are no bite marks here, of that I am certain. What I am looking at is surely a scene straight from a painting. A four feet high stone wall frames in the property and even though it is probably very old, it is in immaculate condition.

As we pass under the arch, trees line each side of the shady lane now, but not olive trees. These are trees with white blossoms of some sort. The blossoms drift peacefully down and flutter along the road, beautiful and tranquil.

"Callery Pear trees," Dante tells me before I have a chance to ask.

I can smell the sweet scent all around me. It's in the air, permeating my clothes, soaking into my hair. Combined with the cool breeze that brings in the scents of the ocean, it's amazing. The leaves on the trees above us rustle soothingly and I reach over and grasp Dante's hand again.

"Your home is beautiful," I tell him. "It's like paradise."

"I know," he answers. His golden hair is fluttering in the breeze and his face is so happy, so perfectly serene. I can truly see that this is where he belongs. Not in the Old Place in Valese. But here. In the cool, calming olive groves. He even looks at home here. He might say that he wants a choice in his future, but I know right here and now, that his choice will always involve this estate.

A house looms massively ahead of us on the left. It looks like something you would find on an old

Southern plantation, except it is made from white stucco. And it's bigger. It's beautiful, like everything else here. It sprawls far and wide and has tons of windows facing us. It looks warm and welcoming.

It looks like Dante's home.

I look at him and he's practically glowing as he noses the car into a parking slot in a semi-circular parking area in front of the house. The tires crunch on gravel and the car comes to a smooth stop.

Dante leaps from the car and flies around to open my door in two seconds flat. He's anxious for me to see his home and I think that's sweet. And honestly, I'm sort of anxious to see it too. I want to learn more about Dante and I have a feeling this is where I will learn it.

It sounds stupid to say, but I can feel him here. In everything around me, I feel Dante. And while I know it sounds stupid to say, it's the truth.

We walk up to the house and the white stone steps are wide. The porch wraps around most of the front of the house, which is unusual for this type of home. There is wicker furniture here with white silk cushions and large antique looking rugs. The front doors are huge and heavy and mahogany, also unusual for this type of home. It's clear that this home was personally designed by someone and it has an eclectic, unique feel.

Dante pushes the front doors open, bows slightly and gives an "After you" motion with his arm.

I step ahead and pause inside, looking around.

And I stare, practically wonderstruck.

It's beautiful here. Warmth and sunlight swirl around and it feels like I'm wrapped in a cozy, peaceful blanket. The feeling around me is serene and soft, like I've stepped into a beautiful painting or an enchanted place. I feel instantly at home, instantly at peace.

"Welcome to Giliberti House," Dante says with a proud grin. "This is the foyer. The wood on the banister there," and he points to a huge staircase spilling into the foyer, "Is made from six hundred year old trees. The marble that you are stepping on right now was brought in by hand hundreds of years ago by Gilibertis. Gilibertis built this house and there has been a Giliberti in it ever since."

The pride in his voice makes me feel warm all over. It's so refreshing. I want to reach over and brush the hair out of his eyes, but I don't.

A tiny elderly woman with gray hair walks in and Dante greets her with a hug and a kiss on each cheek.

"Marionette," he grins. "It's been too long, mami." He turns to me. "Marionette is French. She moved to Caberra long ago to marry her young groom. And they are still happily married today.

Her husband, Darius, is the foreman here. He's worked for us for a very long time."

Marionette nods, her wrinkles crinkling around smiling blue eyes.

"Oui," she nods. "My husband worked for Dante's grandfather. That is how long my Darius has been with the Giliberti's. Me and him, we're like family." She reaches a tiny arm around Dante's shoulders and squeezes him. "I knew his grandmere before she died." With this last statement, Marionette makes the sign of the cross on her chest. "May she rest in peace, God bless her kind soul."

"Also, you should know that Marionette knows fluent English," Dante tells me. "She may pretend not to from time to time, but don't let her fool you."

Marionette slaps at his arm and she looks so funny because she's so small and Dante is so big.

"You are not too big for me to beat, Mr. Giliberti," she tells him. "But tell me, who is this pretty girl that you are showing off for?"

"Where are my manners? I'm sorry, Mami. This is Reece Ellis. She will be working for Giliberti Olives for the summer. Reece, this is Marionette Papou. She runs this entire estate with a steel fist. Don't cross her. She's as mean as they get."

She slaps at him again and I have to laugh. She's ancient and tiny and adorable. And it's clear that she loves Dante. And he loves her too. Does Mami mean mom in French? I'm so clueless. But I decide that it is safe to assume. He must be very close with her. I make a mental note.

They show me the rest of the main floor and it is apparent that they are both very proud of Giliberti House. As well they should be. It's beautiful. And perfect. Just like its owner. Well, owner-to-be. I'm assuming that it will all be Dante's someday. After the tour, Marionette leaves to get us fresh lemonade. And I stand still, soaking in the atmosphere here. It is truly peaceful and refreshing.

It's beautiful and silent.

Almost reverent.

Dante is standing directly inside huge double glass doors leading out to one of the numerous porches. The sun shines onto him, illuminating him with golden, brilliant light. As he turns to smile at me, with his broad shoulders and slip hips, he truly seems otherworldly. He's just that beautiful. And suddenly, I feel speechless and tongue-tied again. This all seems so unreal again.

You don't belong here, a tiny voice whispers in my head.

Shut the hell up, I silently whisper to my stupid inner voice. *What do you know anyway?*

"What do you think?" Dante asks, walking to my side. I can't help but stare at him as a million thoughts speed through my head.

"It's lovely. Absolutely lovely. I never want to leave here. And I can't believe you do! If I were you, I'd stay here all of the time."

He grins ruefully. "I'd like to, to be honest. Should I tell you a secret?"

He steps closer to me and talks even quieter, low and husky in my ear.

"I feel my mom here," he says. "I feel her all around me. She decorated many of the rooms and my dad hasn't changed them. It's one of the reasons that I love being here so much, because I know that she is here, too."

I look at him and my insides melt. How could anyone's insides stay intact after hearing someone say such a sweet thing? It's impossible. I've heard other girls complain that their boyfriends are Mama's Boys and how annoying it can be. But this boy, this beautiful boy, never had a chance to be a mama's boy. It breaks my heart.

And this time, I do reach up and brush the hair out of his eyes. He leans into my hand and his face is cool under my fingers. I can feel the slight stubble on his cheekbone and the flutter of his eyelashes as he closes his eyes.

I want to kiss him.

I want him to kiss me.

Something.

Anything.

But his impossibly blue eyes pop open.

"Hey, would you like to stay here instead of the Old Palace?" he asks, excitement apparent on his face. He's animated now, energetic. Hopeful. "We'd have to drive out here every day anyway."

He looks at me and there's no way I could ever say no.

"Of course," I tell him. "I'd love to stay here. Who wouldn't?"

Dante grins happily and reaches for a nearby cordless phone handset. He calls his father and asks for permission and while he is talking, I wander around the large room looking at the various wall-hangings and paintings. Two minutes later, Dante is by my elbow.

"My father approves," he tells me. "We'll stay here for the summer. It will be perfectly respectable, I promise," he says. "Darius and Marionette sleep here in the house, so we won't be alone."

That was the furthest worry from my mind.

In fact, as he leads me upstairs to show me the bedrooms, I'm silently hoping that mine is close to his. And then I feel scandalous for thinking such a thing, but it's the truth. I want to know that he is sleeping somewhere close to me. I just like the thought, the idea, that his bed is close to mine.

It seems so intimate.

He leads me down a wide hallway with portraits of Giliberti ancestors hanging on each side. They all seem to frown at me, like they know that I am thinking impure thoughts about their descendent.

And I am.

As we continue down the hall, I feel like there are a hundred pairs of eyes staring a hole between my shoulder blades. I glance behind me and there *are* a hundred pairs of painted eyes.

And they all seem to be looking at me.

Because they are.

It's creepy.

"I should probably mention, there isn't much cell reception out here," Dante says apologetically. "Do you still want to stay?"

Again, there's no way that I can tell him no. Not when the idea of staying here makes him so happy. And honestly, not having cell reception isn't that much of a deal breaker anyway. Becca and I are fighting, so I won't need to text anyone two times a minute.

"Of course I do," I assure him. "There's a house phone. And there's a wireless connection for internet, right?" He nods. "So, I'll be fine. As long as I can email my parents so they don't worry."

"I think you're going to love it here," he tells me knowingly.

"I think you're right," I answer.

And then he opens up the door to what will be my bedroom.

And OhMyWord.

It's a girl's paradise.

A dreamy four-poster bed stands in the center of the room with white gauzy drapes surrounding it. Fluffy white bedding sits atop the bed and heavy furniture is artfully placed in the perfectly decorated room. And I have a balcony.

I cross the room and open the glass French-doors.

"My word," I breathe.

My bedroom overlooks the back of the estate and I can see olive trees for miles and miles. They line rolling hills and everything is green and shady and beautiful.

"That's my balcony," Dante points right next to me. "So we can stare at each other when we're having our morning coffee."

And that's when I notice that there is a small bistro table in the corner of each of the balconies. I can sit out here in the serene solitude and have coffee, breakfast, scribble in a journal, or think about Dante.

I'll probably be thinking about Dante a lot.

Especially now that I know that his room is literally right next door to mine.

I love him.

I make that realization with a start.

Because it's startling.

Is it possible to love someone that you've only known for a couple of weeks?

It has to be possible. Because I love him.

I love thinking his name.

I love saying his name.

I love looking at him.

I love everything about him.

"Dante," I whisper.

He turns to me, beautiful in the sunlight.

"Yes?"

Holy crap. Did I say that out loud? I scramble to think of something to say.

"I love your house."

He smiles.

"Me too. I'm glad you're here."

Me too.

Chapter Nineteen

To: Reece Ellis <ReeciePiecie@thecloud.com
From: Becca Cline <I.am.a.B@bluejupiter.net
Subject: A package

Reecie,
Thank you for the turtle. I love him and he's adorable. Question, though. Don't olive branches mean a peace offering? Um, did you notice that the turtle is eating your peace offering? Just an observation.

I hate fighting with you too. I love you like a sister. And I know that you don't want Quinn anymore. So, let's make up, okay? I'm sorry I freaked out. It wasn't all your fault.

I actually decided to take a break from Quinn. That's why I've been so upset. For a long time I've felt him slipping away. We're young and he needs to experience other things- other than me. Other girls. I'm not that upset now—I'd rather this happen now than later.

Your mom told me that you're staying there for the entire summer. What the eff?? What about senior pictures?
Xoxo,
Becks

PS. Who were you talking about when you said that you might like someone else? Details please. And pictures.

Holy cow.

I stare at the laptop and then sigh a huge sigh of relief. It's like a weight has been taken off of my shoulders and I didn't even realize that it was there.

But what a relief.

Becca and I have never had a fight as big as this one was. And I seriously thought that she might never talk to me again.

But she and Quinn have broken up? That thought makes it feel like the earth is a little off its axis or something. They've dated for years. Becca-and-Quinn. It's like a staple back home. It's the way it is. Becca-and-Quinn.

But things change, I guess.

Oh, how they change.

I'm sitting on my own personal balcony right now using the laptop that Dante had brought for me. My things have already been moved here and this will officially be my home all summer long. And I hadn't thought of senior pictures until Becca mentioned them. I briefly wonder if there is photographer here that I could use because OhMyWord it would be awesome to have senior pictures taken here in paradise. I make a mental note to ask Dante.

I stare absently over the olive groves and watch the various workers tending to the trees. I think they are pruning them, but I can't be sure. They are out there with sharp cutters and they are so very gentle, as though the trees are made from gold. And as much money as the Giliberti's make from the olives and olive oils, I guess they might as well be.

I watch as Darius, the foreman, visits random trees and inspects the budding olives. It's barely past breakfast. The sun hasn't even been up that long. But Darius lives for his job. Or so Marionette tells me.

I watch Dante out there, too. He's up early and working with Darius. He's wearing a short-sleeved dark blue tee and khaki shorts. Even at work, he's sort of dressed up. Boys back home would probably be wearing cut-offs. And I've got to stop comparing him to boys back home. There is no comparison.

Dante looks up and meets my gaze and grins. His smile is like a hundred suns and I smile back, waving. And then Darius calls him and Dante returns to work.

I sigh and close my laptop.

And then there's a knock at my bedroom door.

I tighten the thick robe that Marionette gave me and open the door.

Mia stands there with a hot croissant, a coffee and a folded-up shirt.

"Here you go," she tosses the shirt at me without any other greeting. And that's slightly odd since I haven't seen her since I left the Old Palace a couple of days ago.

"Well, good morning to you too," I raise my eyebrows and look at the shirt. And then I realize that she is wearing a matching one. A forest green polo shirt with a gold G embroidered on the lapel. "What's this?"

"Your uniform," she tells me as she sets the food on my dresser. "And I brought you breakfast too. You're welcome."

I smile and thank her. And then I notice that she now has bright green streaks in her jet black hair.

"I like the hair," I tell her. She nods.

"My dad didn't," she smirks.

"Isn't that the point?"

She grins. "I love how you get me."

I laugh and bite into the croissant. And then I want to die. Right after I eat a hundred more rolls.

"OhMyGosh. This is the best croissant I've ever had," I tell her in all seriousness. She nods.

"Marionette is French and she makes them from scratch. I honestly think it's the best thing about Giliberti House. I'll probably gain ten pounds this summer."

Wait. What?

I just realize that her shirt matches mine. And she'll gain ten pounds this summer?

"Are you working here too?" I ask. "No one mentioned this to me."

"Yep," she nods. "I worked for them last year. It's the easiest job in the world and it will look good on the college applications. We'll both be in the gift shop."

I look at her questioningly and she explains that there are tours of the olive groves and the estate and that at the end, the tour groups are brought into the gift shop. The tourists get samples of the olives and snacks made from the olive oil.

"They sell wine in there from Miss Bitch's family winery too," Mia adds.

Ugh. Elena. The thought of Miss Perfect puts an immediate bad taste in my mouth.

"But it's fun," Mia continues. "Dante is here all summer and he'll be in and out of the shop and there are tons of kids our age that are hired for summer help in the groves. You'll like it. But put your shirt on. It's time for us to go to work."

It actually does sound like fun.

Particularly the part where Dante will be in and out of the shop.

I smile and turn to strip off my pajama shirt and as I do, I see that Dante is standing with Elena on the edge of the groves.

I freeze and my shirt falls to the floor.

I am rooted to the spot as I watch them.

Elena is close to him, way too close, and Dante is talking. Her hand is on his chest and he doesn't push it away. After a few minutes, she leans up on her toes and kisses him on the mouth. It's a soft kiss, not long but way too long at the same time. Because he doesn't push her away. They talk for another brief minute and then he turns around and walks away.

Elena watches him for a second, then she turns to walk away in my direction. And as she walks, her green eyes find me, focusing in on me with laser precision and she glares with the most malice and hatred that I've ever seen.

I gulp.

"What's wrong?" Mia asks from behind me.

She marches over and sees Elena and before I can even think, she gives Elena the bird. Elena rolls her eyes and stalks away.

"What's she doing here?" Mia asks me.

As if I know.

"A better question is why is she kissing Dante?" I ask miserably.

"What?" Mia asks, her mouth open. "Not possible. I've seen him lately. He lights up like a neon sign at the mere mention of you. He's got it seriously bad."

I feel like a thousand rocks are sitting on my chest. Or someone kicked me in the stomach. Or someone punched me in the face. I sink onto my bed. I'm numb and I can't think straight. I can't think at all, actually.

"He didn't push her away," I practically whimper. I want to curl up into a ball, but that would be pathetic and I'm being pathetic enough. Strong girls don't freak out about stuff like this. And I'm a strong girl. Corn-fed-meat-eating-Kansas-girl-strong.

But still.

This took me so off-guard.

My heart has apparently forgotten my supposed strength for the time being.

Mia sits next to me and is uncharacteristically sympathetic. She wraps a thin arm around my shoulders and sits silently.

"Wanna go slash her tires?" she suggests evilly. I shake my head.

"No. I want to sit here and be miserable."

"Sorry," she says. "You can't. We've got to work." She stoops down and picks up my shirt and hands it to me. "You can be miserable at work."

I sigh and put my shirt on, then pull my hair into a ponytail.

"K. I'm ready."

Mia looks at me doubtfully. "Are you? I don't want to see you moping around in front of Dante. You're going to totally look like you couldn't care less. Alright?"

I return her doubtful look. "I don't know."

"*I* know," she says firmly. "This is what you need to do. Trust me. You are strong and confident and you don't need him. He needs to know that."

And with that, she takes my arm and leads me out of my room and out of the house. We hop into a little golf cart and she drives us across the property to a quaint little building next to what looks like a factory. A very clean, very large factory.

"This,"Mia says as she gets out of the cart, "is the gift shop. Yes, I know that it looks like Snow White's cottage. That," and she points to the factory, "is where they process the olives. And that," she points at another large building, "Is where they make the olive oil. Any questions?"

"Not yet," I tell her as we crunch across the gravel and she unlocks the gift shop. It's clear that she's done this many times before. She's very comfortable and knows where everything is. She flips on the light switches and immediately counts the money in the cash drawer. As she does, she explains the various processes and procedures. It sounds simple enough.

The entire time, I keep one eye looking through the window, hoping to see Dante.

And then I feel pathetic.

I've got to remember that I'm pissed at him.

And then I feel pathetic because I still secretly hope to see him.

What is *wrong* with me?

"Are you listening?" Mia asks as she hands me a green apron with the Giliberti G on it. I snap back to reality.

"Yes," I answer.

"No, you're not," she says, shaking her head. "In a little bit, Marionette will bring us homemade treats to give out as samples. The tourists love them. We open the door at 9:00 a.m. And you'd better perk up. I'm sure Dante will pop in here before then. Also, I just noticed that there is a case of Kontou wine by the back door. Maybe Elena was here to deliver it?"

I have a brief spark of hope and then I'm deflated.

"It doesn't matter if that's the case," I say sadly. "Because she was kissing him. He didn't have to let her."

Mia shakes her head. She knows, I can tell, that she can't say anything that is going to stick right now. I want to dwell on it for the time being.

So I do.

For hours.

The shop door opens at 9:00 like Mia said and it wasn't long before our first group of tourists comes through. My job is to hand out the samples and smile while Mia takes care of the cash register.

Everyone is very nice and friendly and hungry. I hand out more samples than I ever thought possible. And I conceal my mopiness with a blank smile and so no one is the wiser.

And then, when I don't expect it, the pair of hands that reach for a sample are Dante's.

And I freeze.

And then Mia catches my eye from across the room and gives me a look, so I smile at him. The same polite smile that I have given everyone else all morning.

Polite, sterile, matter-of-fact.

And it is so hard to stay blasé and casual because he looks so very good.

Sweet baby monkeys.

He is slightly sweaty, but just enough so that he looks manly and rugged. I want to wrap myself around him and kiss him hard, but then I remember that his lips have just been on Elena's and so I manage to restrain myself.

"Hi," he says quietly, his voice husky as he reaches for a cracker spread with olive oil and cheese.

"Hello," I say politely.

"You look nice in your shirt," he tells me solemnly as he pops the cracker in his mouth, his eyes glued to mine. Why do his have to be so freaking blue?

"Thank you," I say, as casually as I can. Am I supposed to act like nothing happened? Is that what being strong means?

I swallow.

Then swallow again.

Okay. My plan is to act normal and see what happens. Because I'm strong. I'm not needy and I don't need for him to explain. I'll keep an eye out and see how he acts, and see what happens with Elena. And see what happens with me.

I'm strong.

I'm strong.

I'm strong.

I'm freaking strong.

I repeat this over and over in my head.

"Why were you kissing Elena?" I blurt out quickly and Dante looks at me, startled.

I guess I'm not so strong.

He is hesitant and stands still. He isn't looking me in the eye so my heart drops. I don't know what I expected. A miracle? He was kissing a perfect, beautiful girl. Of course he liked it.

"You don't understand," he tells me quietly. "Everything is comp—"

"Yeah, I know," I snap. "Complicated. I'm tired of hearing about how *complicated* your life is. Life is not that complicated. Either you like someone or you don't. Either you are true to them and your heart or you aren't. Pretty simple, actually."

I glare at him and he is staring at me, unsure of what to say, probably surprised by my outburst or amused that I actually said the words *True to them and your heart.* What a goofy thing to say, but I don't focus on it because it's the truth.

I take my tray and stalk away into the back room of the shop.

He's either going to be true to me or we're not going to happen. I love him, but I deserve to be loved back. When you love someone and they love you, you deserve to be the most important thing to them, as important as breathing.

Dante doesn't follow me, but that's okay. I need a second to compose myself alone.

I stand still in the quiet back room, allowing my ragged breathing to slow and even out.

I feel a little shattered, but I feel good about one thing, too.

I'm strong after all.

Chapter Twenty

Strength is overrated.

I decide this as I soak in the bathtub of my massive bathroom.

It's the bathroom of a dignitary or a millionaire or a princess. And I am none of these things. I know this because a dignitary or millionaire or princess probably wouldn't be depressed and crying over Dante Giliberti.

But I am.

I've been mopey since yesterday. Since I stalked away from the most beautiful boy in the world and cried about him in the back room of his father's gift shop. I had dinner alone in my room and I haven't spoken with Dante since, even though he texted me and asked if we could talk.

I told him no.

Then he said please.

And then I considered it.

But then I didn't have to answer because he was called away to meet his father at the Old Palace. So I was granted a reprieve. But it won't last forever.

Why is being strong so freaking hard?

I rest my head against the stone tiles behind me and add more water to the huge, deep tub. And then more bubbles. Because a sad girl deserves bubbles, dang it. And my bubbles keep popping. And isn't that a great analogy for life right now? My bubbles keep getting popped.

Sigh.

I look at the clock on the counter.

8:45.

I have fifteen minutes to get to work. But I'm exhausted and sluggish. I barely slept last night and my eyes feel heavy and dark. They *are* heavy and dark, I realize as I stare at the bags under them in the mirror as I step out of the tub. Oh, well. I'm not Elena Kontou. I am not perfect at every given moment.

I yank my clothes on and then yank my hair into a limp ponytail.

My ponytail might as well match my spirits.

Limp as hell.

I walk woodenly through the house and say good morning to Marionette, who looks at me with concern and then I meet Mia outside the doors just as she's coming up the stairs.

"You look like hell," she observes.

"Thanks," I answer.

"You didn't talk to him?"

I shake my head.

"You're going to have to," she tells me.

"I know. But I don't have to right now."

"Okay."

We get into the golf cart and ride the rest of the way to the shop in silence and I am grateful that she lets me mope, at least for the time being.

The tourists come in, smiling and happy. So I pretend to be smiling. I can't quite muster happy, though. But that's okay. They don't know me well enough to tell the difference.

I hand out cheese.

I pour wine samples.

I give out crackers smeared with gourmet olive oil.

And every time I see the name Giliberti on the freaking olive oil bottles, I want to cry again. The most beautiful boy in the world was in my grasp for a scant second and I wasn't strong enough to hold onto him. *What is wrong with me?*

The shop phone rings and Mia answers it as I speak with some tourists. I don't even know what they are saying to me because I'm not paying attention. All I know is that they are happy to be here and they are happy to be eating free samples. But honestly, I don't care about any of it. My thoughts are only on my own misery. I hope that I am hiding it well enough. But at the moment, I don't care if I'm not.

And then Mia turns to me, hanging up the phone and her face is grave and scary.

"Reece," she starts out hesitantly and takes a step toward me.

My heart stops.

Something bad has happened.

I don't know how I know, but *I just know.*

"What?" I whisper.

She's scaring me.

But she's scared, too. I can see it on her face.

"There was an accident," she whispers. "Dante."

And then she can't speak anymore. Because we are both moving.

We usher out the tourists, we flip the closed sign and we jump into the golf cart, flying toward the house.

"What kind of accident?" I demand from her as we speed as fast as the little cart will go. I almost feel like I could jump out and run faster than it is going.

"He brought his father's car back here this morning. Apparently, he wasn't used to it and it went out of control on a curve. It rolled."

I can't breathe.

I can only stare at her.

"He's okay," she tells me quietly. "He's in the hospital. We'll go there right now. It will be okay, Reece. And he's asking for you. That's why they called."

They.

He.

Okay.

I'm hearing words in fragments and spurts and my thoughts are coming in blurs.

Dante's car rolled. Rolled where? Down one of those jagged hills? OhMyGosh. I can't think straight. My heart, which was broken and shattered and stomped on this morning, is now numb.

Dante has to be alright.

He has to be.

The world isn't alright if he's not.

I whisper a prayer as we jump from the cart and then into Mia's little red convertible. I don't know what kind it is and I don't care. I roll up the window and lean my head against it, staring sightlessly at the blurring landscape as we speed past.

Please God.

Please God.

Please.

Please.

Let Dante be alright.

I'll give you anything you want.

Just let him be alright.

I don't know how long it takes us to get to Valese Community Hospital. Time runs together and I don't care about it. All I know is that we've arrived now and I know that because the sign is blue and lit and huge and I am jumping out before Mia's car has even stopped all the way.

"Reece, wait!" Mia calls from behind me.

But I don't.

I run.

I run as hard as I can, until I get to what looks like a reception area with a receptionist sitting behind a computer and people milling about in the halls.

"Dante. Giliberti." I breathe raggedly.

"You can't just visit Mr. Giliberti," she tells me pleasantly, with her pleasant Caberran accent and her pleasant receptionist face. "Your name?"

She picks up the phone and waits for me to give her my name so that she can call whomever she needs to call for permission to let me pass.

"Reece Ellis." I'm still panting.

Her eyes light up with recognition and she sets the phone back into the receiver without calling anyone. She's already been given my name.

"Suite 815," she tells me. Her tone has changed now. "Take the elevator on the right to the fourth floor. It will be on your left."

She's no longer simply polite. Now she's respectful and wondering who the heck I am, but she can't ask. She thinks I'm important.

"Thank you," I tell her and I take off running again. I decide the elevator takes too long and I find the stairs and I take them two at a time for four flights.

Please.

Please.

Please.

I beg God. I don't even have to tell him what I'm begging for. I simply pray that he knows. I don't have enough breath to explain because these stairs are killing me and I can't breathe.

Please.

Please.

Please.

I round the corner of the last landing and burst onto the fourth floor.

The nurses at the nurse's station look at me in alarm but I don't stop, even when they call for me to. I find Suite 815. I burst into Suite 815.

I stop dead inside the door of Suite 815.

Dante is staring at me from a hospital bed.

There are tubes and needles and machines with black screens and green lines.

And he is lying in a sea of white sheets and he's so very pale.

But Dante is staring at me. And his eyes are electric blue against that vast sea of white sheets. And the most important thing is that he is staring at me because that means *his eyes are open.*

Thank you, God.

"Hi," I pant, leaning slightly over with my hands on my knees. I can't breathe. I can't breathe because I am relieved and I just ran up four flights of stairs.

"Hi," he says quietly. "You came."

I stare at him in shock and surprise.

"Did you think I wouldn't?"

I had to. It wouldn't have mattered if the earth was on fire and flooded with flaming lava and brimstone. I would be here if it killed me. I could be nowhere else.

But here.

Right now.

With him.

He shrugs and then winces. And then I notice that his face, his beautiful, amazing face is so scraped. His left eye is black already and swollen. There is a white bandage on his right temple and I can see blood soaking through the bandage.

His hand has an IV in it.

But he is alive.

"You know how I told you that your driving doesn't scare me?" I ask.

He nods, and I think I can see a slight twinkle in his eyes. God, I love it when his eyes twinkle.

"Well, I've changed my mind."

He laughs, then winces and I cross the room and grab his hand as gently as I can.

"You scared me," I tell him softly, and my voice catches in my throat and my eyes fill up with tears. I can't help it. I know I'm strong, but I can't help it. "Are you okay?"

He nods. "I'm fine. Just bumps and bruises. Thank God for airbags and seatbelts."

"Were you going too fast?" I ask, and as I do, I remember speeding along the curves with him the other day and of course he was going too fast.

"Probably," he says. "I wasn't really paying attention. I was thinking about you. And then I was out of control. The brakes weren't working and the tires were skidding. It happened so fast that I couldn't even think."

Except for about me.

He was thinking about me and then he wrecked.

Oh, brilliant.

He wrecked because he was thinking about me.

"I'm sorry," I say and the words start spilling out. "I'm sorry. I should have just talked to you and then you wouldn't have felt guilty and then you wouldn't have gotten into this accident. It's my fault. I'm so sorry."

I'm still holding his hand and he's looking at me with his beautiful blue eyes.

"You're sorry?" he asks in confusion. "*You're* sorry? For what? It's not your fault. None of this is your fault."

"I was being a baby," I tell him. "I didn't know what to say to you and I was trying to be strong but I was so upset that you were kissing Elena."

"Elena kissed *me*," he answers. "I just want to clarify that. And she kissed me because I had just told her that I can't see her anymore. Because I want to be with someone else."

"Someone else?" My voice is small in the large hospital suite and all of a sudden my heart is numb again. This time, it is numb because it is waiting hopefully for words that I am desperately wanting to hear.

"Yes," he nods. "Someone else."

My heart is still waiting.

There is a pause.

Then another pause.

He doesn't say anything so I do.

"Is it anyone I know?"

I look down and he looks up and our eyes lock.

"I should hope so since it is you," he says.

My heart stops.

And then starts again.

And then I bend down and kiss Dante Gili-bear-ti as softly and gently as I can.

"You want to be with me?" I ask this as I pull away and look at him. He smells like iodine and rubbing alcohol and bleached hospital sheets. It's a foreign, unfamiliar smell. And I don't like it. But his hand is strong and he squeezes mine.

He nods. "Ever since you ran into me in the airport."

"You ran into *me*," I answer.

He rolls his eyes and I kiss him again.

Chapter Twenty - One

Ten times.

That's how many times I've visited Dante over the five days that he's been in the hospital. I go in the morning, I sit until lunch. Then I go back to the groves and work until the gift shop closes at 5:00pm. Then I go back to the hospital and sit until 9:00 pm. Then I go home, text Dante when I arrive safely, then do it all again the next day.

Dante tells me that I don't have to.

But I know that he wants me to.

And there's no place I'd rather be.

So many people come to visit. Mia, Gavin, Nate, Nate's dad, Marionette, Darius, Mia's parents, kids I don't know, other members of Dimitri's cabinet, Elena's parents. Even Elena herself comes at one point.

A hundred times.

That's how many times Miss Perfect glared at me while she was here, but she was sugary sweet to Dante and brought him candy. I know she thinks that he and I are just a passing thing, a phase. But I'm the one he wants to be with.

Dante wants to be with me.

We're as different as we can be.

But *Dante wants to be with me. With me. With me. With me.*

And that's all that matters.

Dimitri comes to visit often, obviously. And if he is curious or concerned that I am here so often, he doesn't say anything. He is his usual pleasant, charming self. He's not angry that Dante wrecked his fancy Jaguar. He's just happy that Dante is alright. And that's how a father should be, I decide.

"Why were you driving your father's car, anyway?" I ask Dante as I'm helping him put his things in a bag. He gets to come home today and my heart sings at the thought. And then I smile because I just thought of Giliberti House as home.

"My car was being serviced," he explains as he carefully pulls a soft t-shirt over his head. His chest and ribs and shoulders are still mottled with bruises, marring what is otherwise perfection. His body could truly be a marble sculpture. It's just that perfect. Except now the perfection is bruised. I gulp and look away. His near-miss still terrifies me.

"You've got to be more careful," I announce. "You drive too fast on those curves."

"I thought you weren't afraid?" Dante asks, with his blue eyes sparkling again. "You grew up on farm trucks sliding around dirt corners."

I glare at him. "Don't turn my words around on me. That's true. I did. And I wasn't scared. But that was back when I thought you were a better driver. Now I know the truth, so now I'm scared."

He rolls his eyes.

"Have you heard from Becca?"

He's very good at changing the subject. That's something that I have learned this past week. And we've learned a lot about each other over these last few days. We've had nothing to do but talk in this hospital room. I told him all about Becca and Quinn and Connor and home.

He told me all about Elena, his father, Caberra, and growing up as a Giliberti.

It's been fascinating.

And now I feel like I truly understand him.

He's a really good person who just happens to have been born in a gilded cage.

"Yes," I answer. "I spoke with her again this morning. She wishes you the best and can't wait to meet you."

Dante suggested yesterday that Becca fly here for a week or two at the end of the summer. I thought it was a brilliant idea and so did Becca. She's currently working on hounding her mom until she agrees to let her make the trip. I briefly wonder if Dimitri would call to help our cause, but then I am distracted when

Dante wobbles just slightly as he picks his suitcase up and puts it on the bed.

"Are you alright?" I ask in concern as I rush to steady his elbow.

"I'm not an invalid," he tells me. "I just haven't gotten out of bed for a week. Ooh- now there's a thought." And then he waggles his eyebrows suggestively and with huge exaggeration and I laugh. His pain meds are loosening his normally gentlemanly tongue.

"Normally, that would be an interesting thought, but right now, not so much," I tell him. "Hospital tubes and a drugged up guy don't really do it for me."

"No?" he looks disappointed.

"No," I confirm. "And I'm not thinking about anything of the sort right now. I'm too worried about you for that kind of nonsense."

Lie.

Five hundred times.

That's how many times I've thought about Dante's hands on my body over the past week. He's been lying in a hospital bed and I've been thinking impure thoughts. His ancestors' paintings would surely be glaring at me now. If they could see me. Which they can't.

"Are you ready?" I ask, fighting the blush that is sweeping my cheeks at my ridiculous and impure thoughts.

"Yes. Are you?"

Boy, am I. But that is a loaded question. And now is not the time to think about it.

"I'll have your car pulled around, okay?"

He nods and I leave to ask them to bring his car out of the garage. At his direction, I've been driving it back and forth to the hospital this week. At first I was terrified to drive such an expensive piece of machinery, but now it feels normal. And I can see now how he is so casual about his luxurious things. I'm almost ashamed to say that I've become accustomed to them, too. It's weird. I guess it's human nature. You become accustomed to what is around you.

I help Dante into the passenger's seat and he still seems pale to me. But he's all hopped up on pain medicine so I doubt he's feeling any pain. And because of the pain medicine, he's very talkative on the way to Giliberti House.

"Are you sure that you aren't into Connor?" he asks me for the third time since we left the hospital. I have to smile and shake my head while I concentrate on navigating the curves outside of Valese.

courtney cole

"Yes, I'm very sure," I assure him again. "He's like my brother. He's always been like my brother. He used to pull my pigtails and hide my Barbies."

"I'm jealous of that," Dante announces. "He knew you when I didn't."

And now I'm grateful for the pain medicine that makes Dante talkative. It's revealing a side of him that I've never seen before. A very human, less than perfectly self-assured side. And I like it. It tells me that Dante Giliberti isn't quite perfect.

It makes me love him even more.

The curves and sways of the road combined with the pain meds make Dante sleepy and so he falls asleep, snoring slightly, long before we reach the house. I pull up in front and wake him up and then I help him through the house.

Marionette scampers ahead of us, surprisingly spy for an old woman, and opens the door to Dante's bedroom so that I can help him through it. He's leaning on me and I'm lugging his stuff and helping him walk, all at the same time. The pain medicine makes him groggy and out of it. He'd never let me shoulder all of this weight normally.

But it's okay with me because it makes me feel like I'm finally doing something to help him. I thank Marionette and she leaves me alone with Dante.

In his room.

Alone.

As I help him onto his bed, I realize that this is the first time I've seen his room. I was never in his room at the Old Palace and that's okay. Because I know as I look around, that *this* is his true room, his true space. The place where he is truly himself.

It's navy blue.

And that's so like him. When I think of Dante, I think blue. Like his eyes.

The bed is huge and comfy, filled with dark blue throws and cushions and pillows. There is a handful of photo prints and a camera lying on the foot of the bed, presumably exactly how Dante left them before he left for the Old Palace over a week ago. I glance through them and find that they are pictures of the olive groves and a sunset. Romantic and dreamy. And he is really good at capturing beautiful pictures. I set them down.

The furniture here is heavy and there is a sitting area filled with photos in stacks on the end tables. I can see photos of me from here. And I'm not mad about it anymore. It's clearly something that he loves to do. It's not stalkerish. It's just....him. And he's really good at it.

There is an old picture of his mother smiling from an end-table. She is framed with ornate silver and she is glamorous and beautiful. There is another framed picture of Dante and his father. They are both standing on the edge of a boat, and the name of the boat is beneath them. The *Daniella.* I wonder if that is Dante's mother's name, but I can't ask Dante because he's already snoring from the bed. He's still fully clothed and on top of the covers.

I decide that it is surely his mother's name.

And goshdangit. I said surely again.

"Reece," Dante says softly. He's sleepy and warm and curled up on the bed. He stretches out and reaches for me. He doesn't wince this time when he moves, so he's either doing better or the pain meds are working. Probably a mixture of both.

I cross the room quickly and sit next to him.

"Thank you," he whispers and reaches for my hand. "For staying with me."

His hands are warm and have calluses from working with Darius. I stroke his thumb with mine. And just the mere touch of his skin sets mine on fire. It's pathetic, because he's broken and sore and sleepy. But the emotional toll of the past week has built up and now I'm aching for him to touch me.

His touch is real.

It means that he's fine.

It's a tangible thing.

And I need it.

He needs it too.

I know this because he pulls me down to him and I snuggle next to him, trying to make sure that I don't bump his bruised ribs. He leans into me and kisses me, his lips soft on my own and I sigh into his mouth.

He groans, but not a painful groan.

A groan that tells me that he likes it.

Fire shoots through my stomach and into my heart and my hands start to roam.

They drift lightly over his shoulders, his back, his hips, his butt. He rolls carefully to his side now, facing me and his hands are moving too.

They're everywhere.

And he's kissing me.

And I can't think.

He whispers my name and now I really can't think. I love the sound of my name on his lips. It's surreal. Like a dream.

But Dante's hands are very real and the weight of them tells me that this is definitely not a dream.

And then he moves slightly and winces.

And that reminds me that this is *definitely* not a dream. And he is still injured. We shouldn't be doing this.

I tell him that softly.

"Dante, you need to rest. You're still injured. The doctor said you have to rest."

He looks at me, his eyes all soft and liquid and my heart melts. Because he seems so vulnerable and his fragility in this moment makes him seem even more beautiful than usual. Even more beautiful than the tanned and handsome and confident Dante that he normally is.

"I'm sorry," he whispers to me. And I startle.

"Sorry for that?" I ask in surprise.

"For taking advantage of you. You're trying to help me and I'm taking advantage of that."

He is so serious and I can't help but laugh.

"You're the cripple," I point out. "Aren't I the one taking advantage of *you?*"

He laughs quietly and I laugh, because it's sort of true.

But then again, it's not.

Because he wants me just as much as I want him.

And he tells me so.

And his voice is husky and sexy and I almost melt into a puddle.

"I'll be rested up soon," he tells me. And his voice contains a promise.

A soft and silky promise.

The fire shoots up through my belly again and I nod.

"I know," I answer. I lean down and kiss his forehead and pull the coverlet up over him. "Sleep tight," I tell him.

"Dream about me," he answers as he closes his eyes.

Always, I think.

"Maybe," I say.

He smiles with his eyes still closed and I decide that I could stand and watch him sleep forever. Then I decide that that's creepy and stalkerish. So I quietly walk back to my room.

And I do dream about Dante.

Chapter Twenty - Two

"Holy cow. Would you *look* at him?" Mia breathes.

Our noses are practically pressed against the window of the shop and we're staring into the olive groves. There are tons of sweaty men out there but we're focused on only one.

And sadly, it's not Dante.

It's a guy named Vincent. A summer field hand who Mia has decided that she cannot live without.

As I watch him sweating in the sun with his biceps bulging in the heat as he works, I have to hand it to Mia. If you're going to decide that you can't live without someone, it should definitely be someone as sexy as Vincent.

"What do you know about him?" I ask absently. Because honestly, with looks like his, it doesn't matter.   He's tall, sandy-haired, brown-eyed, muscular and has a smile that girls would kill for. He also fills out his jeans like nobody's business.

"Not much," Mia admits. "His parents live out in the valley, apparently. They're farmers. And so he's an experienced field hand. As you can see," and she motions toward him. "He makes an *excellent and amazing* field hand."

I giggle and so does she.

Coincidentally, he looks in our direction and grins.

And we both sigh.

He's completely sexy.

And Mia has a date with him tonight.

"I wonder how experienced his hands actually are?" Mia wonders aloud.

I know that she's not talking about field-work now and we examine him again. The muscles in his back ripple as he twists on a cherry-picker to prune the trees back. His muscles flex and his hands are deft. We both sigh again.

"Experienced, I'm betting," I finally answer.

"That's alright," Mia replies confidently. "It's just as well. I'm not worried. I can handle anything."

"So says the girl who's never had a boyfriend," I say.

She rolls her eyes and then the next group of tourists come in. We get busy and then I'm even busier watching for Dante, so we stop talking about it. But I know Mia is excited.

And I'm excited too, but for a different reason. Dante was finally released by the doctor to come back to work today, just two short weeks after his accident. His ribs have healed up and his bruises are almost gone. He feels great and I have to say, he looks great too.

Right this moment, he's in the fields too, working with Darius. I find myself hoping that he doesn't over-do it trying to prove himself. I watch as he bends over an olive branch and Darius shows him something on the bark. I have no idea what they're doing or what they're looking at, but Dante looks interested in it.

I hand out a few more cheese samples and look back for Dante.

He's not there.

I sigh and turn back around.

"Looking for someone?"

He's so cocky sometimes. I love that. I smile and fight the urge to drop the tray of samples and launch myself into his arms and wrap my legs around his waist. But I don't want to re-crack his poor ribs. So instead, I smile.

"No one in particular. You here to get a sample?"

"Yep."

I start to hand him a cracker, but he reaches around the tray and wraps his sweaty arm around my shoulders, pulling me to him for a kiss.

He tastes salty but I don't care.

This is very uncharacteristic for him, to show this much of himself in public.

So I enjoy it while I can.

I enjoy it *a lot* while I can.

And I don't care that tourists are watching us and smiling.

He finally pulls away and I'm breathless.

"Oh. *That* kind of sample. I don't give those out to just anyone. So you're lucky today."

He smiles and I decide that I'm the lucky one.

"I came here for a purpose," he announces. "Well, two purposes. One, to get a bottle of water. And two, to ask you out. Would you like to have dinner with me tonight? Alone?"

Alone? What a concept.

We haven't been alone since Dante left the hospital. Marionette has practically been Dante's shadow over the past couple of weeks, fretting about him like a little mother hen. Dimitri has even been here a few times. He felt so horrible about not being able to bring Dante home from the hospital himself. We've had dinner in the main dining room with a group of people every night.

A real-honest-to-god date would be amazing. I nod.

"I'd love that. Where are we going?"

"We'll meet here," Dante says. I try to keep my face from falling. How will we be alone here? But Dante can read my expression and he laughs. "You have to trust me," he tells me. "I'll see you after work, okay? Meet me on the terrace at 6:00?"

I nod. "Okay. I'll be there."

He grins. "Think about me this afternoon."

Always, I think.

"Maybe," I say.

He grins again and disappears through the door after grabbing a bottle of water from the cooler. I can smell his scent lingering in the air even after he's gone and I sniff at it. Mia shakes her head.

"You guys are sickening, just so you know," she tells me.

"And you're not? You and your lovesick moaning and groaning over Vincent?"

"It's not love," she informs me. "It's lust, pure and simple. Get it straight, Kansas."

I shake my head and try to think other thoughts to distract myself. Otherwise, it's going to be a very long afternoon. 6:00 pm seems like a month away. I send a few texts to my mom, Becca and Grandma. Then I smile at a few more tourists. And all of that only took twenty minutes.

Sweet baby monkeys. Scratch that. 6:00 seems like two months away.

But time passes as it always does, even though I'm impatient and jittery and anxious.

At 5:00, Mia and I close up the shop and jump into the cart and she drops me off at the house. "Call me after your date," she says with a ornery grin.

"Call me after *yours*," I answer. She waves and heads to her car and I head into the house to shower.

What should a person wear on a mystery date? I rifle through my closet. I've gone shopping only a couple more times since I've been here. And I didn't use my mom's credit card, either. I used my paycheck from the gift shop. Since my every need is taken care of here, I don't have anything else that I need to buy other than clothes. It's a girl's dream.

I decide on a pair of shorts and a white peasant blouse. I think that if it were going to be a formal date, Dante would have told me. Or sent me a formal gown like he did last time.

"Let me do your hair, ma chérie," a quiet voice says from behind me. I turn to find little Marionette crossing my bedroom. I hadn't even heard her come in.

I once again marvel at her size. She's so tiny, like a little sprite with a gray bun. She makes me feel like an Amazon woman.

"You have a special date with Master Giliberti tonight, yes?"

Marionette smiles at me with her creased grin as she picks up a brush and tugs me onto the bed. She sits next to me and brushes out my hair. And I close my eyes. It's been a really long time since anyone but me has brushed my hair. It's nice.

"I don't know where we're going," I tell her. "It's a secret. Or a surprise, I guess."

Marionette's gnarled little hands run through my hair, feeling for tangles.

"Oh, don't fret, little one," she tells me. "Master Dante is very thoughtful. He's always been. He takes after both of his parents in that way."

"You knew his mother." The realization dawns on me and I turn to face her.

Marionette is nodding. "Ah, yes, I did. A gentler woman than Daniella will never be found on this earth."

Daniella.

So, they *did* name their boat after her.

"What was she like?" I ask. "I only wonder because it makes me sad that Dante didn't get to know her. I can't imagine what that must be like. And I'm very glad that he's had you, Marionette."

She practically preens in front of me at my praise.

"Daniella was a very gentle spirit. She was a free spirit, so beautiful and kind. And she couldn't wait for Dante to be born. She looked forward to it every day of her pregnancy. What happened was a tragedy. It's been a pleasure for me, watching him grow up," she says thoughtfully as she stares past me. "He was such a good little boy. He was sunny and cheerful from the moment he was born, just like his beautiful mama. He's turned into a good man. I'm proud of him. And I don't want to see him get hurt, either. He's had too much pain in his life already."

Marionette's tone has turned stern and I look at her in surprise. Was that directed at me?

"Um, I'm not going to hurt him, if that's what you're thinking," I tell her. "Marionette, he's way out of my league. Way, way out there. If anyone does any hurting, it will be him, I'm sure."

Marionette laughs and I don't see what's funny.

"Ah, little one," she says as she pulls the sides of my hair back and twists them into a clasp. "In that way, you're very like his mother. Very modest. You have a natural glow about you. It's charming. And you don't realize how beautiful you are. And that is charming, as well. A girl like Elena, well, she knows what her strengths are and uses them to her every advantage. I'm very happy that Dante has chosen you. Very happy, indeed. Elena was wrong for him. And I think that you're the right one. But I still don't want you to hurt him. Even inadvertently." She pokes at my shoulder for emphasis.

Inadvertently. She *does* know fluent English. Dante was right.

I tell her so and she laughs again.

"Don't tell anyone," she instructs me. "It comes in handy to pretend I don't understand. Or that I can't hear. I can hear everything, trust me."

Her eyes are eagle sharp and I have no doubt that her ears are, as well. I nod.

"Now then, sweet. You are ready. Don't keep my boy waiting. He's taking you somewhere special."

And she was gone. My word. She moves quickly for an older person.

I have only a few minutes to spare, so I shoot some quick emails to my mom, my dad and my grandma. My grandpa doesn't have an email account, but grandma reads him messages from hers.

And then it's 5:55.

Finally.

I think paint could have dried faster than it took for this day to pass.

I close the lid to my laptop and make my way to the back terrace.

And Dante is already there waiting for me.

The sun is starting to sink over the horizon and Dante stands directly against that backdrop. And I can't decide what is more beautiful. The sunset or him.

He's wearing black slacks and a short sleeved grayish-blue v-neck. And it hugs his chest and makes his eyes look slightly gray and is striking against his blonde hair. Can he get any more beautiful? Seriously. Couldn't God have given Dante just a tiny little imperfection so that he didn't distract me quite so easily?

He sees me and smiles and greets me with a sweet kiss on the forehead, which of course makes my heart automatically melt. I can practically feel it dripping into my ribcage.

"Did you have a good day?" Dante asks politely.

I nod. "Yep. A little slow. You?"

"A tortoise could have crawled faster than today passed," he tells me. "I couldn't wait to see you."

My heart picks up because this mirrors my feelings exactly. And boys back home wouldn't ever say such a thing even if they thought it. Dante is so different.

And could Marionette be right? Is it possible that this beautiful, perfect boy likes me as much as I like him?

"Your carriage awaits," he tells me.

He gestures with his arm and I look and there is an honest-to-god carriage sitting at the steps leading to the terrace. With an honest-to-god beautiful white horse pulling it.

I stare at it in shock. How did I not see that when I first walked outside?

"I thought that Caberra doesn't have horses?" I ask, scrambling down the steps to pet the huge horse's velvet nose. It huffs a pant of hot air against my cheek and I stroke its soft neck. "Yes, you're a pretty baby," I murmur to it.

"We didn't. I had this one brought in for you. You seemed to miss riding," he shrugs casually, like it didn't cost a ton of money to do this incredibly thoughtful thing for me.

I'm speechless. For the first time in… ever. And I tell him that.

"I doubt it will last long," he says wryly and then laughs. And I slap at his arm. And his arm is like a rock. Working out in the fields with Darius has made him even more muscular if that is even possible.

Gulp.

He holds out a hand.

"Would you like to go for a drive?"

Would I ever.

He moves to take my hand and because his eyes are locked with mine, he doesn't see the giant pile of horse poop sitting in front of him. And he steps in it.

We both freeze and he's horrified and I'm horrified and I don't know what to do.

But laugh.

Because it smells so bad.

And he looks so perfect and refined and beautiful and his foot is covered in fresh horse manure and it's even funnier because he's never been around a horse before. It's too hilariously insane.

I start cracking up and then Dante laughs.

He kicks off his black loafers into the grass, and I'm sure they are Italian leather and very expensive, and now one is completely covered in horse poo. The thought of it sends me into a new and fresh fit of giggles.

Dante rolls his eyes at me as he bends down and rolls up his slacks.

"Aren't you going to get another pair of shoes?" I ask when I can finally breathe. He shakes his head.

"Nope. I don't need them. Where we're going, I don't need shoes."

I stare at him, my curiosity freshly piqued.

"Hmm. A riddle," I murmur.

And I take the hand that he offers me once again.

This time, it goes off without a hitch and he helps me into the beautiful little carriage without incident. And I feel sort of like a princess. With a barefoot prince. Dante nods towards someone that I can't see and a groomsman emerges from the edge of the house. He'd been waiting for Dante's signal. He climbs up to the driver's seat and looks back at Dante.

"Where to, sir?"

"To the docks," Dante answers.

I'm busy looking at the carriage. It could honestly have been taken directly out of a fairy tale. It's roundish and plush. And pretty large on the inside, actually. There are a couple of folded up jackets, a picnic basket and a bouquet of flowers sitting on the seat across from me.

Dante picks up the flowers and hands them to me.

"You look beautiful this evening," he tells me. His eyes are sparkling again. "Do you like your surprise? You'll be able to ride him now, whenever you'd like. And you can teach me, too. If you're willing, I mean."

Oh, I'm willing.

Oh. Wait. He meant willing to give horse-back riding lessons.

I'm willing to do that too. Of course I am. He can have anything he'd like.

But I don't say that. Instead, I nod.

"Of course. I'd love to teach you."

Dante settles back into the seat and stretches his arm out on the seat behind me. I lean into it, into his warmth. I've never been more comfortable in my entire life. I tell him that and he laughs.

And life is officially perfect.

The horse's hooves clip-clop on the road and cars pass us. The Caberrans inside of them gawk at us because it's definitely not a common thing to have horses strolling along the highway. I don't see Dante's security detail, but I'm sure they are following us somewhere. But I don't mention it. I don't want to bring up anything annoying tonight.

Because tonight is perfect.

The sun is really setting now and it's beautiful. The oranges and reds and golds are shining over the horizon and onto our skin and everything is romantic and dreamy.

It's like a dream, actually.

I lean up and kiss Dante's cheek and he smells like the ocean and the salt and the sun. And maybe the woodsy scent of the olive groves. I sigh. There's no way that life gets any better than this. I settle back into his side for the drive and he wraps his arm around me.

I know when we are close to the docks because I see sails peeking up into the sky. Sails of every color- white, blue, red, orange, yellow. Boats of all sizes are docked in neat slips along the various piers. The carriage pulls up to a quaint little boardwalk and stops.

Dante climbs barefoot down the little steps with the picnic basket and waits with his hand outstretched to help me down. And then he leads me onto a pier. At the end of this pier, I can see his boat. I know it is his because the name *Daniella* is huge and gold on the stern and I can see it from here.

And it's not really a boat so much as it is a yacht.

A really big yacht.

"Are you ready for that alone time that I promised?" Dante asks me.

I look at him.

And I know that I'm ready for alone time with him.

And that includes anything that *alone time* with him might entail.

I'm readier than I've ever been for anything in my entire life.

I nod and take his hand and he leads me to the *Daniella*.

Chapter Twenty-Three

The *Daniella* is amazing.

It's huge and luxurious and is everything that I ever thought a yacht would be. It's got rooms and furniture and decks. It's filled with chandeliers, crystal, linens, silk curtains. It's pretty much a floating mansion.

It's amazing. That's the only word I can think of to describe it. And in my head, I'm already composing the email that I'll send to Becca about this experience.

I can't wait to see how the email will end.

What will happen here on this boat?

My stomach flutters as the butterflies start flying.

"This is beautiful," I tell Dante needlessly. We step into a sitting area in the front of the stern and I sit on a cushion, looking out over the water. The sea is like blue glass tonight, still and majestic.

Dante sits next to me and picks up my hand.

"I'm glad you're here," he tells me. "I've been thinking about having you to myself all week long."

"Me too," I say. And then I silently kick myself. Seriously? That's all I can think of to say?

Dante doesn't seem to mind. He leans over and kisses me in the most ultra-soft of all kisses.

And the butterflies are back.

But that's okay.

That's a good thing in this situation.

They're just letting me know that something good is about to happen.

Dante runs his hands over my back, so lightly. I lean into his touch, into his arms, feeling the hardness of his chest against mine and I wonder if he can feel my heart beating. If he can, then it is a dead giveaway of how nervous I am, how excited.

The stars shine brightly above us and I've never seen a more romantic setting than this one. I can see the email to Becca now. *Becks, the yacht was amazing, the night was perfect and romantic. We were under the stars and--*

And then I hear voices.

And then I hear voices? That's not how the email is supposed to go.

But I do hear voices. I sit still and listen and Dante does too.

Somewhere, from the inside of the boat, there are voices.

"Is someone here?" I ask. "Is there a crew or…"

Dante shakes his head. "There is a crew, but since we aren't going anywhere, they shouldn't be here tonight. We should be alone."

We are whispering and I wonder what we should do. I know that Dante's security detail will be lingering near the boat and for the first time, it is a comforting feeling and I'm glad that they are here. Somewhere. Wherever they are.

Dante stands up and pulls me behind him. Then he walks softly and quietly and barefoot toward the doors leading into the ship. I am quiet as a mouse as I follow him and I can only hope that no one can hear my heart pounding. Because it is. And it isn't pounding in a good way like it was pounding a moment ago.

We creep into a dining room just as two shadowy figures burst through the doors on the other side of the room.

"Stop!" Dante calls out.

And the two figures stop.

"Dante?"

It's Mia's voice.

What the hell?

"Mia?" Dante sounds as surprised as I feel.

He flips on a light and Mia and Vincent are standing there, looking sheepish and guilty, flushed and disheveled. I instantly wonder what the heck they are doing here and then by the bright red blush staining Mia's cheeks, I *know* what they've been doing.

"Um." I don't know what to say. And apparently Dante doesn't either.

"What are you doing here, guys?" he finally asks. And he doesn't sound angry. Just curious.

"I'm sorry, D," Mia says and her voice is genuine and apologetic. "We wanted to be somewhere quiet. My parents are on *our* boat and Vincent said he would love to see yours, so we came here. I should've asked. I'm really sorry."

Dante is quiet for a moment. But then he smiles.

"It's alright. Just check first next time, alright? I'd hate to accidentally beat you over the head, thinking that you are an intruder."

"I'm too sexy to be an intruder," Mia announces and the tension is broken and everyone laughs with her. "What?" Mia demands. "Green stripes are sexy!" and she flips her green-striped hair with her fingers.

A part of me is incredibly and insanely disappointed that we're no longer alone. I think this as we spread the contents our picnic basket out on the massive dining room table and we all share it.

The four of us.

And then another part is just slightly relieved.

Only slightly.

Because I know what probably would have happened tonight out on the cushions under the stars.

And while I'm so ready for it, I'm a little scared too.

Because I'm a virgin.

But it turns out okay. Seated around one end of the huge table, we laugh and joke and get to know Vincent and it feels like a little party. We eat the expensive cheese and bread and wine that Dante has brought along with the olives, of course, and the little sandwiches cut into triangles.

I notice, too, that the wine is not from the Kontou Winery. Dante gets a point for that. Make that two points. It doesn't make up for the fact that he let Elena kiss him, though. He lost a *million* points for that little maneuver. He'll be making that up for a while. That thought makes me smile.

"Why do you look like that cat who swallowed the canary?" Vincent asks me. He's sitting next to me, and Dante and Mia are involved in an animated conversation about the pro's and con's of 3D movies. I have no idea how they got onto that topic, because I have been lost in a daydream. "Reece?"

Vincent brings me back to earth. I look at him.

"I'm sorry. What?"

"You're in your own little world." Vincent reaches for another little sandwich. I briefly daydream about Dante feeding me that little sandwich. After all, we were supposed to be alone here tonight.

"I know," I tell Vincent. "I'm sorry. I don't mean to be rude. I was just thinking about my summer. Life here is very different from back home in America. Were you born and raised in Caberra?"

I'm proud of myself for making polite conversation and keeping my head out of my daydream. It's quite the feat and I'm doing it gracefully, if I do say so myself.

Vincent nods, then takes a big gulp of the expensive wine. And then another big gulp, draining his glass.

Interesting. Everyone else here, all of the people who know wine and other fine things, sip at their wine. Vincent gulps it. He's clearly not a dignitary's kid.

I pick up my own glass as he tells me about his home in the valley, how his father is a farmer and his mother stays at home. Apparently, they are fairly poor and so he is fascinated by stories about the wealth of Americans. Then I spend a few minutes explaining American economics and social structure and political structure and dispelling a few myths about Americans.

Like, we're not all super rich and morbidly obese and we don't all drive Porsches.

"I drive a used Honda Civic," I finish up. I feel sort of good about that right now. Like the fact that I live on a farm and drive a used car keeps me grounded or something.

"Interesting," Vincent nods. "You're different than I expected. In a good way," he hurries to add. I smile good-naturedly. I've heard that a lot this summer.

After we eat, we talk for a while longer and hang out around the table and then Mia finally, *finally* says, "Vincent, we should probably go. Don't you think?"

Vincent immediately agrees and pushes away from the table.

He turns to me. "Thank you for the lesson on American culture. It was a pleasure to meet you away from the groves."

His smile is sexy and charming and all, but Vincent doesn't hold a candle to Dante. I smile back, though, and Mia and I exchange glances. I can tell that she is sort of happy to leave, too. Alone time is apparently a very valuable commodity. Dante and I walk them to the pier. We watch as they disappear into the shadows and then we turn to each other.

"What just happened?" Dante asks with a laugh. "That was not at all like I pictured this evening going."

"And how did you picture it?" I ask. The waves are lapping gently at the pier and the stars are still twinkling overhead. The air is just turning chilly and I shiver slightly as the breeze hits my bare arms.

"Are you cold? Let's go back on board," Dante says. We walk back onto the yacht and return to the cushioned couches on the stern. He slips a jacket around my shoulders as I tuck my feet under me and then I face him while he settles into the cushions.

"Where were we?" I ask.

I'm nervous. Jittery. And I don't know why. For some silly reason, I feel vulnerable. Like even though I am offering him something that I am ready to offer, it might backfire and crush me. And Dante would never, ever hurt me. I know that. I know it more surely than I know anything else. And I just said surely again.

Drat.

"It doesn't matter where we were," Dante says casually. "This is where we are now. And I like what we have, don't you?"

I nod. Of course I like what we have.

"And I don't want you to ever think that we need to rush things. Not for me, not for anything. Okay?"

Dante's face is so sweet, so serious. So considerate. And I swear to everything holy that I can't possibly love him anymore than I already do. It's physically impossible. My heart can't hold any more love.

And suddenly, it's like an epiphany and it hits me in a white-hot enlightening rush.   Love is all that matters.   Everything else is just details.   Having sex/making love/physical intimacy is going to be great, I'm sure.   Scratch that. It will be freaking awesome. With Dante. But love itself is the important thing.   And I so, so, *so* love him.

"Okay," I nod.   "Did you feel like you were rushing me?"

He considers that as he hugs a pillow to his strong chest.   I find myself wishing that I was that pillow.

"Not purposely. But sometimes, things can be construed differently than they are intended," Dante says carefully.   "I don't want you to ever think that I'm pressuring you.   Because I'm not.   I won't.   I promise.   What we have… it's so unexpected.   And I think it's amazing.   And I'm not going to jeopardize that by trying to rush you."

My heart will soon explode from love for this boy.   I know that much is true.

I shake my head and smile and pick up his hand, grasping it tightly in mine.

"Dante, that is the most beautiful and sweet thing anyone has ever said to me.   Boys back home just don't talk that way.   I love it.   And I love you."

HolySweetBabyMonkeys.

I said the words.

I said the words.

I said the words.

I'm such an idiot. He's going to think that I'm a MariacCrazyPerson. We've only known each other for six weeks. And I said the *L* word. Out loud. To Dante. Giliberti. I'm. So. Stupid.

"I love you, too."

Dante's words are husky and low and sexy in the night and OHMYGOD.

He loves me too.

I can't breathe.

"Reece?"

Dante is looking at me in concern. Because I'm staring at him like an idiot.

"I'm fine," I rush to assure him. "I just felt silly for a second. But now I don't."

"Good," he says. "I don't want you to ever feel silly around me. If I can step in horse manure in front of you, there's probably nothing you can ever do more embarrassing or silly than that."

"Is that a challenge?" I ask with a smile as I snuggle into his arms.

He tightens them up around me and suddenly we've got a full-on, loving embrace going on. Dante kisses my hair and it's so perfect. And the idea of having sex tonight can't be further from my mind anymore. It's been overshadowed by this sweet conversation and the stars and the sea and his smell and the fact that DanteGilibertiLovesMeTOOOOO.

The world doesn't get any better than this.

Chapter Twenty-Four

To: Becca Cline <I.am.a.B@bluejupiter.net
From: Reece Ellis <ReeciPiecie@thecloud.com
Subject: OHMYWORD

Becks,

I told him I loved him. And he said it back. I can't wait for you to meet him. You're going to love him, too.

Xoxo,
Reecie

PS
Don't mention this to my mom. I don't want her texting me twenty times a day for details.

I'm still floating on a cloud.

I barely slept last night, even after being driven back to Giliberti House in the carriage under the stars. Actually, *especially* after being driven back in a carriage under the stars. Dante's arm was wrapped around me the entire way home.

I was awake when the sun came up and started shining in my windows. I carried my coffee out to my balcony and curled up at my bistro table, hoping that Dante would come out to his.

But he didn't.

And I don't have the guts to slip into his room.

Not yet.

I thought about it.

In the night, when I couldn't sleep and I was staring at my ceiling and the moon was passing across my walls and the shadows were moving along the floor, I thought about it. I won't lie.

But then I thought the better of it.

Marionette is a force to be reckoned with. And I have a feeling that she would know the second that I crossed the threshold and there would be hell to pay. She's sweet and adorable, but Dante wasn't lying when he said that she runs Giliberti House with an iron fist. It may be tiny, but it's still iron.

I smile as I cross the room to leave and then I stop still in front of my door.

And smile wider.

There is a white linen envelope lying in front of my door. Someone slipped it underneath. And I can tell from the scrawling bold script exactly who that someone was. The fact that Dante chose to write me an old-fashioned note instead of texting me turns my insides to jelly. It's just one of those little quirks about him that fascinate me.

I open it up.

Good morning, little Sunflower.

I hope you slept well. I had an amazing evening with you last night. I hope to do it again soon, if you will have me.

I have to make a quick trip into Valese to see my father. I promise that I will drive carefully and I will be back after lunch.

I love you.

D.

Several things about this note make me happy.

He calls me his Sunflower. And that makes me happy.

He had fun last night. And that makes me happy.

He actually thought to reassure me that he will drive carefully and that makes me happy. It shows that he is thinking about my feelings. And that makes me super happy.

And he says that he loves me. That makes me so, so, so freaking happy.

Oh- and last, he signs it with a simple D. Not DGG like his previous notes. It seems more intimate and personal.

Reece and Dante.

Dante and Reece.

D and R.

We're a couple.

We're really happening.

I shake my head to clear my thoughts and try to just for a while, think of things other than Dante. It's hard. But I give it the old college try.

I have breakfast with Mia and Marionette in the kitchen. It's so much more casual in there rather than the dining room. And after we stuff ourselves full of fresh croissants, Mia and I pile into the cart and head for the shop.

"So, you didn't end up doing anything last night?" I ask doubtfully.

She shakes her head.

"Nope. After we left the yacht, Vincent was pretty tired so we just went home. It was sort of a let-down. But there will be other nights. Trust me."

She waggles her eyebrows and I am laughing as we round the final curve.

And there, standing on the side of the factory, is Vincent.

And he is talking with Nate Geraris.

What the hell?

Vincent is sweaty and dirty, like he's been in the fields already. Nate, with his white blonde hair and ice blue eyes and his buttoned up shirt and loafers, is pristine and clean and I know he's never been near a field or manual labor in his life.

The little worm.

But what the eff is he doing here? Just because he came for the obligatory visit to Dante's hospital room, does not let him off the hook for being a jerk. He bruised my arm, he lied to Dante. And there's something about him that just isn't right. That's what my gut tells me.

Although, to be fair, my gut could just be angry about the bruise.

"What's he doing here?" I hiss to Mia.

"I've got nothing," she tells me. "I have no idea. I haven't heard from him since he pissed Dante off."

"I haven't seen him since he came to the hospital with his father to see Dante," I say as I unconsciously rub at where my bruise used to be. It's long gone so I have no idea why I'm rubbing at it.

"How was he at the hospital, anyway?" Mia asks as she unlocks the front door of the shop.

"Polite. That's pretty much it. He knew that Dante was still pissed, so he pretty much just said hello and waited while his father visited."

I look over my shoulder and Nate's cold blue eyes are staring at me through the window. And HonestToGod, I feel like shivering. Because his eyes are just that cold.

"I don't like him," I mutter to Mia. "I just don't."

"Not many do," she says cheerfully as she empties out the cash drawer and turns on the various machines.

"What in the world is he talking to Vincent about?" I muse as I cut pieces of cheese into bite-size samples. "It's not like they run in the same circles."

"Probably nothing," Mia answers. "I'm guessing that he came to find Dante and just bumped into Vincent."

I turn back around to look and both Vincent and Nate are gone.

Mia could be right.

But somehow, I just don't think so. A little niggling doubt in me flares up and I honestly just don't think so.

A few hours later, I find that I honestly just don't care. Nate is long gone from my mind.

I've been texting with Becca all morning. Her mom finally agreed to let her come. So in another three weeks, she'll be here. And I can't wait. Cannot. Wait. I chatter excitedly to Mia.

"You're going to love her," I tell her. "Love. Her. Everyone does."

"I'm sure," Mia says as she stares absently out the window. She doesn't seem nearly as excited as I am. I hope she doesn't feel threatened. I know that I'm pretty much her only friend.

"Everything alright?" I ask. She turns to me and her forehead is wrinkled up.

"I think so. It's just that Vincent isn't answering any of my texts. And I haven't seen him all day."

I look at her. "Well, that's weird."

"I know, right?" She drums her fingers on the counter. "Very weird."

"Aren't you supposed to have another date tonight?"

Mia nods. "Yep. So you'd think that he'd answer my texts, wouldn't you?"

"For sure."

Mia is silent now, moping. I find myself getting pissed at Vincent and I don't even know if he's done anything bad yet. It's just that he's Mia's first boyfriend. And he'd better treat her right or I will strangle him myself.

The last tourist group comes through and then we don't have anything else to do and it's lunchtime.

"Go ahead and go to the house without me," I tell Mia. "I think I'm going to ride the new horse over lunch."

She looks at me dubiously.

"Really? By yourself?"

I smile.

"Really. Don't worry. I've done it a few times. Where I come from, people ride horses for pleasure."

"Yeah? Well, you're not in Kansas anymore—"

"Toto," I interrupt and finish her sentence. "Yeah, I've been told. But seriously, go on ahead. I'll meet you back here."

Mia leaves and I lock up the shop and make my way down to where they're keeping Titan. I'm sure he got his name because he is so enormous.

When I get to his makeshift barn, I see that it's not really so makeshift. Leave it to the Giliberti's to do it up right. It's a true little barn, with stalls and troughs and everything a horse would need. It's even got a little tack-room filled with a saddle, bridle, curry combs and such.

I pat Titan and comb him down, then saddle him up. He stamps his foot impatiently, like he's been waiting for me, as I cinch the belly strap.

"I'm sorry, boy," I tell him. "Have you been bored down here? I've been busy with Dante. But I'm here now. And we'll go for an awesome ride. How about that?"

Titan seems agreeable so I swing up onto his back and we set off at a brisk walk down the long driveway of the estate.

He rides like a dream. I'm sure he was very, very expensive. Because that's just how the Gilibertis roll.

Since the last group of tourists have gone and the next group hasn't come through yet, it's quiet and peaceful here on the estate. The birds sing, the trees rustle, the shade feels good on my back. The only thing that could be more perfect would be if Dante were here with me.

And I still need to give him those riding lessons.

I am thinking about that when I hear a car driving behind me. I nudge Titan with my knees, urging him onto the side of the road. He responds in an instant. He has been trained very well.

But the car slows behind us and lingers.

Without looking, I motion for it to pass. I'm riding a horse, for Pete's sake. I know they aren't used to it here, but geez. Just go around.

It doesn't.

I can hear it back there, its engine running and it is not going around me. Then the engine revs a little.

What the eff.

I turn around and Nate is behind the wheel.

His face is serious and his blue eyes are staring a hole in me. He is intent on something. But what?

And then his engine revs once more.

It's loud and Titan is annoyed by it. He skitters a little and I hold fast to him with my knees.

"It's alright, boy," I murmur to him.

But is it?

What could Nate possibly want? If he thinks I'm getting off this horse to talk to him, he's crazy.

He revs his engine again and this time, I turn around and his eyes meet mine. And his are filled with something unsettling and I know that he's not here to talk to me.

And then he revs his engine once again and this time, his car lurches forward. He swerves slightly and bumps Titan's rear flank with his fender as he lunges past us.

Titan bolts. And I'm struggling to restrain him, to control him, but he is terrified and out of control. His hindquarters are digging into the ground as he fights to run.

And then he rears back suddenly and sharply, throwing his head back, and his neck slams into my face. Hard. My nose splatters blood onto his white fur and I can't see because my eyes are watering and then I am flying.

I don't think I hit the ground before everything goes black.

I don't know how long it's black.

But then I'm dreaming.

I see Dante, leaning in front of me. His face is blurry and he's worried and he's saying something, but I can't understand his words. I try to tell him to come closer, but my head is throbbing with a sharp, horrible pain and I can't. He's got his phone and he's talking.

And then he leans toward me again and his hand is in mine.

And I realize that I'm not dreaming.

I can't be dreaming because the pain in my head is too real.

And his hand in mine is real.

"Dante?" I whisper.

"Stay still, Reece," he tells me. He's anxious and scared. I can tell. "Just stay still."

"What happened?" I ask. He's kneeling next to me and he's still holding my hand.

"Titan threw you off."

And then I remember. I remember Nate's gray car and the look on his face and the fact that he purposely spooked my horse.

"Nate," I whisper.

Dante looks at me, confused. "Nate? No, sweetie. I'm Dante."

"Nate was here."

I settle into the grass and I don't feel the need to move because my head hurts too much.

"Nate was here?" Dante repeats, trying to determine what I'm saying. "Reece, I think you're confused. You hit your head, it's bloody."

"No." And the word is painful to say. Physically painful. Because he's right. I hit my head. I can feel the warm blood dripping onto the back of my neck. "Nate was here. He was here talking to Vincent and then he was following me while I was riding. He scared Titan on purpose."

I stop talking because honestly, it just hurts too much to move my mouth.

Dante is staring at me in horror, trying to decide if I am confused or if I know what I'm talking about. He picks up his phone again, but I can't hear what he is saying now because the world is sort of going black again.

No. It's definitely black.

Completely black.

Chapter Twenty-Five

The world is bright.

Very bright.

HolyCowIt'sBright.

My eyes squint as I try to open them.

I can feel the soft bedclothes around me and I know that I'm in my bed. I'm not sure how I got here because the last I knew, I was lying in the grass by the side of the road. And Dante was beside me.

"Reece?"

And he's beside me now.

I open my eyes up and there he is.

Worried. Anxious. Beautiful.

He's holding my hand. One hand. Because the other hand is in a cast.

A cast?

"Dante," I whisper. It feels like I haven't spoken in a while and my mouth tastes funny and all I can muster up is a whisper. "I don't understand. What happened? I don't remember anything. But falling off Titan."

Dante winces, like the memory is painful.

"You're alright," he assures me. "You broke your wrist. And you have a mild concussion."

"Seriously?"

I'm amazed by this. I've never broken a bone in my life. Not when I fell out of the hay loft when I was eight and not when I fell out of the back of my grandpa's farm truck when I was twelve. And we were even driving down a dirt road going 30mph. I rolled into the ditch and didn't break a thing.

So I got my first broken bone from falling off a horse?

I'm so lame.

Dante drops his head onto the bed and mumbles something that I can't understand.

"What?"

He looks up at me and his blue eyes are so very blue, so very contrite. So very guilty.

"I'm so sorry, Reece."

"Why are you saying that? I'm the one who fell off the horse. Not you. I guess you won't want to take riding lessons from me now, will you?" I smile, but Dante doesn't think it's funny.

"It's not your fault. Do you not remember? Before you passed out, you told me that Nate did this to you. My *friend* Nate. He did this to you on purpose."

"What?" I look at him in confusion, but even as I do, the memories start flooding back to me.

Fragments and bits. And then I see Nate's horrible smile as he rams his car into my horse. "Oh my God. He did. Why?"

Dante shakes his head. "I don't know. But I'm going to find out. This wasn't funny. If he thought it was a joke, it is *so* not funny. And coincidentally, he and his new friend Vincent are nowhere to be found. But trust me, I'll find him."

He starts to get up, but I pull on his hand. "Don't leave me."

Dante freezes, looking down at me with concerned eyes and an anxious expression.

"Are you in pain?"

I shake my head. "No. I must be on some serious pain relievers. I just don't want you to leave. Please."

He immediately takes a seat next to me, without question or complaint. "Have you been here the entire time?" I ask. I'm guessing that he has been. And he nods.

"Have you gotten any sleep?" I ask. Because I'm guessing that he hasn't.

He doesn't say anything.

"Dante," I sigh. "You have to get some sleep. Don't worry about confronting Nate right now. Just go take a nap. In your bed. Not in that chair."

He looks at me doubtfully. "But you wanted me to stay."

"That's true. But I'm just going to go back to sleep anyway, I think. So you should get some sleep, too."

Dante studies me for a scant moment longer, then nods.

"Okay. The doctor who came here and set your wrist said that you should stay in bed for at least 24 hours. So, I want you in bed all day today, okay? I have to go to a dinner for the Regatta with my father this evening, but I'll be back. And I expect to still find you in this bed. Understand, young lady?"

He raises a golden eyebrow and I smile. "Understood."

"And you might want to call your parents. I called them and they're really worried."

I groan. And he smiles. "What? They're your parents. I had to let them know."

I groan again.

"I forgot about the Regatta," I tell him. And I had. I remember Elena mentioning something about it weeks ago, but I don't know what it is. I tell him that and he explains.

"It's a huge annual boat race. We've done it here for a couple hundred years. It's a big thing. My dad wants me with him on the *Daniella*. We don't race, but he has to be there to oversee the race. Make an appearance. And tonight, we have a pre-Regatta dinner. It's tradition."

I nod. "I wish I could go."

He's already shaking his head. "You can't. You're going to stay in bed."

"Yes, sir."

"I could get used to that," he tells me with a grin. "Want to keep calling me sir?"

I roll my eyes.

"That's my girl," he says. "I know you're feeling better now."

I smile and he smiles back and then he's gone.

But I'm happy. Because he just called me his girl.

I'm Dante's girl.

It makes me feel so warm and happy that I go to sleep. Of course, the pain relievers might be contributing to that. But either way. I'm warm and happy and Dante's girl. And so I sleep.

* * *

I feel significantly better when I wake up.

My head doesn't hurt.

My arm hurts, but it's broken, so of course it's going to ache.

The sunlight no longer hurts my eyes, so my concussion must be better.

I swing my legs around and sit up, allowing my feet to dangle over the side of the huge bed. The sunlight is striking the wall in a way that tells me that it's late afternoon. I glance at the clock. 4:30. Yep. Late afternoon.

I decide that I've stuck to my promise. I've rested all day. It's a matter of semantics on when exactly *all day* should end. I say it should end now. And there's no one here to argue with me.

I stand up and the room spins for a just a second, but then I'm okay again.

I take a hot bath because the hot shower makes me feel too dizzy. I should take that as a sign to stay in bed a while longer, but I'm stubborn. And I want to get up. Not only do I want to get up, but I want to go to the Regatta dinner. I don't know why, but I just want to see Dante standing with his father and waving to the masses.

I see him every day in work clothes and toiling over the olive trees. It will be awesome to see him in an official capacity because it reminds me of exactly how important he and his father are. It's exciting. Because he's mine. I'm Dante's girl. He said so himself.

I pick up the phone and call Mia.

And beg her to take me with her to the Regatta Dinner.

"No," she says firmly. "I promised Dante that I wouldn't let you leave the grounds. He knew you'd try, you know."

I roll my eyes.

"And don't roll your eyes," she tells me. "You're not supposed to be out of bed."

"I'm not," I tell her.

"You're lying," she tells me. "He said you'd do that, too."

OhMyWord.

This is impossible.

And then I do a really mean thing.

"Mia, you're my very best friend here," I tell her. "Please take me. Please. I feel fine and I'm going crazy here by myself. Everyone is in town at the festivities for the Regatta. The house is quiet. Too quiet. I'm going crazy."

She's silent.

Playing on the best friend thing was mean. Because it means a lot to her. And I do mean it. She's my best friend here. She's the only one I can count on to come pick me up and take me with her. So I tell her that.

"Why is this so important to you?" she asks. "It's just a stupid dinner for the stupid Regatta. It will be here again next year."

"But *I* won't." My voice is pitiful. But it's the truth. And it works. Mia sighs.

"Fine. He's going to kill me. But okay. I'll be there in half an hour."

Yes.

I hang up and get ready as quickly as I can. Even as I do, I know that I really shouldn't be out of bed. But I want to see Dante. I don't know why it's so important.

It just is.

Sometimes love can't be explained.

After my accident, I just feel like I need to be close to someone I love.

I feel... sentimental.

I'm waiting on the front porch when Mia drives up in her convertible with the top down. She looks me up and down.

"Are you sure that you're up for this?" she asks doubtfully. "You look pretty pale, Kansas."

"I'm good," I assure her as she hands me a dress.

"It's black," she tells me needlessly. And Dante's going to kill us both," she adds. But she doesn't sound worried.

"Is everything you own black?" I ask her as we hurry into the house so I can change. She grins.

"I'm trying," she answers. And she's wearing black right now. Her gown is floor length and black. The dress she brought for me is knee length with spaghetti straps. The quintessential little black dress. It pays to own one, I guess, even if it is just to let your friend borrow it in a fashion emergency.

I stick my hair in a chignon again, grab my purse and we are out the door speeding toward Valese.

"Slow down!" I call to her as her little car hugs the curves much too quickly.

"I'm fine," she answers. "I've driven this road a thousand times."

"Yeah? Well, so had Dante."

That shuts her up and she does, in fact, slow down. A little.

But it still doesn't take us long to reach the Old Palace. She tosses her keys to the valet and we find ourselves standing on the front steps. The Old Palace is gleaming tonight, the light streaming from the windows. Richly dressed people are pouring into the doors and all of a sudden, I feel dizzy.

"Are you alright?" Mia asks me, her hand on my elbow.

"I'm fine," I tell her. I will be fine. Just as soon as I see Dante. For some stupid reason, I feel needy tonight. I think it's the stupid pain medicine. It's making me sentimental.

We make our way in and since I'm with Mia, we don't even get questioned at the door. We wind through the crowds and Mia knows the back way into the ballrooms. It's clear that she has been to more than a few of these functions.

We pause outside of the ballroom doors while she adjusts my dress straps and then we slip inside. We are just in time to hear Dimitri speaking about the history of the Regatta, which I listen to half-heartedly while I search the room for Dante.

But I don't see him.

I see Gavin, seated at a table in front. He's with a tiny little blonde date. He sees me and smiles and looks a little confused, like he wasn't expecting to see me. I assume that Dante told everyone that I'm safely in bed right now.

I don't see Nate, the scumbag.

And then my ears perk up. Dante's father is discussing the Queen and King of the Regatta. I watch in interest as Dimitri explains the history of selecting a king and queen every year for the past two hundred years.

And then he announces that this year's king and queen will be Dante Giliberti and Elena Kontou.

Wait. What?

I watch numbly as Dante and Elena walk out to meet Dimitri. Dante is perfect and handsome in his black tux and Elena is beautiful and stunning in a long emerald green gown that matches her eyes just right.

Someone hands them flowers and they wave to the crowd before Elena leans up and kisses Dante's cheek. He smiles down at her and they join hands and bow to the crowd.

And I want to throw up.

Seriously. I feel nauseous.

"Are you alright?" Mia asks quickly. She's watching my face.

"Did you know?" I ask her woodenly.

"No," she answers simply.

And I believe her.

How did this happen?

Why didn't he tell me?

He had to know. He had to know earlier in the day and he chose not to tell me. So essentially, he lied. He lied by omission. Maybe this was the reason that I was drawn here tonight. Maybe I wasn't feeling sentimental. Maybe my heart sensed that something was wrong.

I am staring at them in shock when Dante's gaze accidentally meets mine.

He freezes and dismay clouds his face.

And he takes a step in my direction, but then his father is shaking his hand and I don't wait to see what happens. I can't watch another second of this. I thought he was truly going to stand up for himself and live the life that he wanted... which meant that he wouldn't go through this charade of being with Elena.

I thought he wanted to be with me.

But he lied.

And so I do the only thing I can rationally think of to do.

I run.

Chapter Twenty-Six

The problem is, I didn't learn enough about the Old Palace before I moved out to the Giliberti House. And so I don't have a clue where I am going. I'm all turned around. And even though I have the good sense to take off my heels and carry them as I run, it doesn't do me a lot of good since I don't know where I'm going.

Mia gets caught up in the crowds and so I lose her in the fray.

But that is my intention.

I want to lose her.

I just want to be alone so that I can cry in peace and quiet.

After a few minutes of running aimlessly through empty halls, I find myself outdoors by the pool. It's still and quiet and the water is sparkling under the moon. There is no one here so I collapse into a heap on a lounge.

And I cry.

I cry in heaves and sobs and wrack my ribs and finally my freaking head hurts again from all the sobbing. And I don't even feel pathetic for crying so much because anyone in their right mind would cry in my situation.

I'm in a foreign country, all alone, in love with the Prime Minister's son and he's too afraid to break out of his cage and love me back. Oh, and I practically got stomped to death by a gigantic horse yesterday. I deserve some slack.

Finally, I'm all cried out.

I'm staring numbly at the sky, my mascara dried to my cheeks when I hear rustling and whispering from behind me.

Heaven is pointing in my direction.

And she's standing next to Dante.

She must have seen me running and crying and she found Dante to tell him.

OhMyGodNo. I don't want to see him.

I start to get up to run. But then I realize that I can't run anywhere that he won't be able to find me. He knows this palace a lot better than I do. So, I sit limply back down and wait while Dante walks across the patio to reach me.

There's nothing else I can do.

But he can't make me talk to him.

I'm staring at the ground and I know when he is in front of me because I see the tip of his glossy black dress shoe step into my line of vision.

I blink.

And I stare at the ground harder and with purpose.

"Reece," he says.

I don't answer.

What is there to say?

He lied to me by not telling be about this stupid Queen and King business. And he did that on purpose. I can't trust him now.

So that's what I tell him.

And then I'm silent again.

He sighs raggedly and sits on the end of the lounger. I pull my feet up to my chest so that I am not touching him, so that I'm in no danger whatsoever of touching him, and he sighs again.

"I'm sorry," he tells me. He tries to reach for my hand, but I pull it away. "Reece. Please. I'm so sorry. You don't understand."

He sounds like he is in pain. But I don't care because I'm in pain too.

"Yeah, I know," I tell him bitterly. "Your life is so *complicated*."

"It is," he agrees. "I can't explain it to you. It's just hard. There are so many expectations of me. And I hate to disappoint my father. He's under so much pressure already. It was just a little wave in front of the crowd. And then another wave tomorrow at the Regatta. It wasn't a big deal and I didn't want to make a big deal of it. And that's why I didn't tell you. You were already upset because of my accident and then you had *your* accident and I just couldn't tell you."

I'm silent. Because I don't know what to say. I don't know what to feel or think.

"I love you, not Elena. Elena and I are over. And I did tell my father that I'm not with Elena anymore," he tells me. "And he understands."

"Did you tell him about me?" I ask him. "Does he know that you're with me?"

Silence.

I stare at him in accusation. "You didn't!"

Dante looks at me. "I didn't have to, Reece. He already knew. He could see it from twenty miles away. I love you. Everyone can see it. Everyone knows that."

I'm still silent.

I want to believe him.

"I really want to believe you," I tell him. "But believing you isn't even the problem anymore. Seeing you and Elena up there in front of everyone... you looked like you belong together. You and I...we don't. We aren't a match. Let's just lay it out there. I'm a farm girl from Kansas. You are a VIP with an even more important father. We're not going to work. We're just not."

My shoulders slump and my voice is flat.

And my arm is throbbing.

And my head is spinning.

And my heart is broken.

I just want to go home. Home to Kansas and my mom.

And I tell him so.

Dante stares at me sadly and in disbelief.

"Please don't," he pleads. "Reece. Please. It doesn't matter that we're different. You're everything that I'm not. That's important, right? You're assertive where I'm hesitant, and I'm confident where you are afraid. You're strong when I'm weak and I'm hard when you're soft. People who are exactly the same are boring. We're different and I love that. I love you. And that is all that matters."

"I used to think that love is all that matters," I tell him. "But I just don't know anymore. I don't know if it's enough."

And my heart. My poor heart is breaking and I just want to rip it out and stomp on it because I trusted it to make this decision and now I'm heartbroken because of it.

All of a sudden, I realize that it's raining now and I decide that that that's apropos. My heart is gray and dismal so it might as well get rained on, too. The rain splatters around us and I don't move. I don't care if I'm wet. I don't care about anything.

"We need to go in," Dante tells me. "Please, Reece. You were just in an accident. I don't want you to get pneumonia, too."

But I still don't move. In fact, I lay my head back on the lounge and lift my face to the sky, letting the rain wash over me.

And I'm silent again.

"Fine," Dante finally says. "If you're going to get pneumonia, so will I." He settles on the lounger next to me and lets the rain soak him.

We both must look ridiculous, stretched out next to the pool in formal clothes and letting the rain drench us. We're out of our minds. But Dante stays with me.

And I don't even know how long we are like this.

But finally, after minutes or an hour, I'm cold. It's still raining and my skin is like ice and my teeth are chattering.

Dante looks over at me. "Are you ready now?"

He's not angry or impatient.

He's just wet.

Very, very wet.

I nod.

Dante gets to his feet and then bends to help me to mine. And I let him. I'm too sad and empty to put up a fuss.

He fingers my cast. "You weren't supposed to get this wet," he tells me softly.

"It doesn't matter," I answer. Because nothing matters. Not anymore. I turn and start to walk back inside, but Dante grabs my arm gently and turns me around.

"Reece."

One word. But the tone of his voice. The look in eyes. The pain on his face.

"Please."

Make that two words.

"I love you."

And the three most important words of all.

I crumple onto the lounger and cry again even though I didn't think I had any tears left. And then Dante is next to me, with his wet arms around me and he's whispering in my ear.

And the huskiness of his voice.

The smell of his wet skin.

The beating of his heart against my hand.

All of it.

I don't want to be without him.

Maybe he's right. Maybe love is all that matters. And we can get through our differences. We can get through anything.

And then he's kissing me.

And I'm letting him.

And I'm kissing him back.

Because I love him and he loves me and Elena Kontou doesn't matter.

Dante's hands are all over me, warm and strong and I lean into him, into his warmth, his strength. It's still raining, but we are kissing in the rain and it's sexy as hell. In fact, I think I'll kiss in the rain forever. For the rest of my life. Because it's just that sexy.

"We should go in," Dante says against my lips.

But I don't want to move. I don't want to leave here and re-enter reality. Not yet. Reality isn't my friend right now. I recently lost Dante, got him back, lost him again tonight and then just got him back. I want to linger here in this moment before I risk losing him again, before any more miscommunications separate us.

And no. I'm not making any sense.

I know that.

Dante tugs at my hand and I follow him blindly. Because I'm wet and he's right. We should go in.

But he doesn't lead me back into the main building. He leads me to a pool-house.

It's secluded and dark and perfect.

Once we tumble through the door, wet and dripping, Dante turns to me.

"I don't want to go back to all of those people. I want to be here, alone with you. We can sit here and dry out and we can talk."

His eyes are such a beautiful blue even at night in the dark. And the cleft in his chin is so masculine, so sexy. And I forgive him. I forgive him for not telling me about the stupid Regatta royalty thing because that's exactly what it is: Stupid. And he was just trying not to upset me.

"We could talk," I agree. "Or we can kiss some more."

Dante reaches for me immediately.

"Your wish is my command, remember?"

And I do. I remember the day that he told me that I can have anything that I want. And I know that right here in this moment, I want *him.*

So I tell him so.

And he sucks in a breath and stares at me.

Because he understands exactly what I mean by that.

"Are you sure?" he whispers.

And I nod.

There are cushions everywhere inside this little pool house and I don't take the time to wonder why. I just drop onto the nearest pile of them and pull Dante down with me. I'm on my back and he's hovering over me and his weight is absolutely delicious against me.

Why have I been waiting?

What in the world have I been waiting for?

Because. Being here with Dante. Is Amazing.

He kisses the side of my neck and his lips slide along my wet skin. He clutches me to him and we're desperate, but I don't know why. The emotions from the past couple of weeks have pent up and pent up and now they're exploding.

In a big way.

Dante's tongue is in my mouth and he tastes like wine. And he smells like the sea. And he feels like... Dante. Like home. I moan against his fingers and he whispers into my ear.

"I don't want you think you have to do this."

"I want to do this," I answer. And I do. I really, really do. "More than I've ever wanted anything."

"Me too," he says as he slides against me.

I want to tease him about having nothing more eloquent to say than that, but I find that I suddenly don't care.

This is a pivotal moment in our relationship. In my *life*, actually. And I don't even care about that, about the importance of it.

All I care about right now is him.

It's Dante.

It will always be Dante.

I know that as his mouth covers mine and he rocks against me and the world explodes.

Chapter Twenty-Seven

Okay. So the world didn't actually explode. But it sure felt like it for a minute. I want to e-mail Becca to tell her how my world has changed, but I don't know how to phrase it in an e-mail.

Dear Becks, my world has changed?

Dear Becks, don't tell my mom but I'm not a virgin anymore?

Dear Becks, my fragile flower has been plucked?

OhDearLord. Definitely not that last one.

I'll just wait and tell her when I see her. Even though it's killing me. Because I want to tell her right now.

It's monumental.

It's huge.

The sunshine is flooding my bedroom and I'm still in bed. I'm happier than I've ever been. And I want to get up to find Dante, but I'm too exhausted at the same time. Stupid concussion. Stupid broken arm. Stupid emotional week.

I wiggle my hips just a little, testing.

And I feel a little sore. Down there. But not too bad.

I play the scene over again in my head. The moonlight was slanting in through the windows of the pool house while the rain pelted the glass and thunder rumbled the ground around us. The mountains of cushions were soft against my back and Dante's hands were silky and smooth, his body the perfect weight against my own.

It was perfect.

It was as perfect as I ever thought it would be.

I sigh happily.

There is a light knock on my bedroom door, then it opens.

And there is Dante.

"Good morning." His voice is low and quiet.

My heart skips a beat. He's casual in jeans and a black t-shirt and he's carrying a breakfast tray, complete with coffee and a flower.

I smile.

"My hero. I was just thinking how hungry I am, followed immediately by thoughts of how I'm too tired to go to the kitchen."

Dante shakes his head and sets the tray down on the bed stand, then sits next to me.

"Are you okay?" he asks.

I nod. "My head isn't spinning anymore and my arm doesn't hurt all that much. I'm just a little tired."

He nods seriously and says, "Good. Although I was sort of asking because of last night."

"Oh." My cheeks catch on fire. "Um. I'm fine."

Dante is looking at me seriously.

"I feel like I let the situation get out of control. You were feeling vulnerable because of everything that's happened. And the rainstorm made it seem a little wild and crazy. And I should have slowed it down. And I didn't. I'm a guy and sometimes, I don't think things through. I hope I didn't screw everything up."

He's looking at me worriedly and I can't even believe the words that are coming out of his mouth. And I tell him so.

"Seriously?" I look at him incredulously. "Dante. I've wondered how that moment would feel for years. I wondered if I would feel scared. Or if it would hurt. Or if it would be special. And now I don't have to wonder anymore. Because it was perfect. And I'm glad it was with you."

He's staring at me blankly. Then realization floods his face and it's once again filled with dismay, just like when he saw me watching him and Elena last night.

"Reece," he says and his voice is very, very grave. "Please tell me that last night wasn't your first time. Please."

I look at him. "Did I forget to mention that part?"

And I know that I did. I remember that once upon a time, I wondered how I should tell him. And then I never did.

Oops.

His head drops into his hands. "Oh my God."

And I'm confused. Dumbfounded, actually. "Dante, what is wrong with you?"

He looks up at me between his fingers. "Reece, I'm so sorry. If I had known, I would have made sure it was special. It certainly wouldn't have been in a pool house on lounger cushions."

And now I'm really confused.

"Dante, it was perfect. The timing, the night, *you*, it was perfect. It couldn't have been any more perfect. I wouldn't change one thing about it."

"Are you insane?" Dante asks. "Reece, at the very least, you deserved flowers and a soft bed for your first time. I feel horrible. I cheated you."

"Okay. Well, maybe we can do that another day. And you did not cheat me. Last night was *perfect*. And I don't want to hear you apologize again. Seriously. I will remember it forever. There are girls back home whose first time was in the bed of a pick-up truck. Trust me, last night was special."

Dante looks at me doubtfully.

"I will make it up to you," he promises.

I shake my head and roll my eyes.

"There is no need," I assure him. "Seriously. Now, can we change the subject? This is embarrassing me."

He stares at me for a second, then grabs my hand. "Alright. New subject, but only because I don't want to embarrass you. Do you want to be my date for the Regatta tonight?"

I pause awkwardly.

"Aren't you supposed to attend with Elena?" I ask hesitantly. "As her King?"

"Technically, yes," he told me. "I can walk up there, wave to the crowd and then return to your side. But if you don't feel comfortable, or if it upsets you, I'll tell my dad to appoint someone else. I'm sure Gavin would love to do it."

I smile at that thought. I can just see Gavin hamming it up now for the crowds.

"I'm sure he would too," I agree. "But it needs to be you. It's fine. You can wave with her, just as long as that's *all* you do with her."

"Trust me," Dante tells me. "You have nothing to worry about. I promise."

"Okay then," I shrug. "It's settled. You can wave with Elena and I'll be your date."

"Perfect," he says. "Can I suggest that you rest today? You should take a nap and recuperate. You still haven't rested enough after the accident and the doctor said you should."

"I can rest when I'm dead," I announce as I start to throw the covers back.

Dante rolls his eyes at the stupid old saying and stills my movements with one hand.

"Nice try. Please. Do me this favor. Just stay in bed for this morning. Catch up on emails, do whatever you'd like... as long as it's from this bed."

I pause and give him an evil look.

"Can I do whatever I'd like from this bed?"

"Of course you can," Dante begins and then he realizes my meaning and he grins. "Anything but *that*," he tells me. "You need to rest. Do you promise?"

I slump back against the pillows. "Fine," I pout.

But I'm not really pouting. He wants to take care of me and that makes my heart go pitty-pat.

He leans down and kisses my forehead.

"I've got to go into town and do a few things with my father. But Mia will pick you up and bring you to the Regatta. And once I'm done waving at the crowds, I'll meet up with you. Okay?"

I nod. "Okay. I'll see you then."

Dante turns and strides across the bedroom with his confident long steps, but he turns at the door.

"I love you," he says. And then he smiles and my heart melts.

"I love you, too," I answer.

And he slips out of the room. I pick at my breakfast for a while and sniff at the flowers that he brought. And I drink the coffee.

Then I curl into my pillow and take a little nap. After the bumps and bruises from this past week, I'm going to need some beauty sleep for tonight.

* * *

I'm super glad that I slept most of the afternoon.

I decide that as I'm jostled about by the crowds overlooking the Bay of Valese. I'm still tired, even though I slept for hours. Even though I'm standing here with the sun on my shoulders surrounded by a festival-like atmosphere and anxious to see Dante. In spite of all of that, I'm still tired.

I'm so lame.

But I'm excited, too. I can't help it. Everyone around me is excited and their excitement is contagious.

Apparently, the Regatta is a big deal thing here. There are streamers and signs and balloons and street vendors. It's a huge party and everyone is happy.

Hundreds of boats have signed up for the big race. I can see all of their sails billowing in the breeze as the boats line up for the start. Apparently, the winner gets $10,000 and the annual trophy, which is a huge sailboat made from crystal.

It's sitting on a giant pedestal now on the edge of the beach.

I can see it from here, glittering in the sun.

"There's Dante," Mia tells me, nudging my arm.

I look and sure enough, there he is.

The Daniella is floating out in the middle of the bay, although it is moving just a little closer to shore. I can hear the metallic sounds of a microphone being tested. And Dante just stepped out onto the deck of the yacht. He's turned around now, talking to his father.

I look around, at the happy faces, and I'm glad that I'm here. There is a band playing happy music. I can't understand the words of the songs because they're singing in Caberran, but the music sounds happy. People are dancing in the streets and a little boy next to me tugs at his mother's arm until she buys him pink cotton candy from a street vendor. I smile at him and then for some reason, I look past his mom, into the crowd.

And on the edge of everyone, through the sea of strange faces, I see Vincent.

He's standing alone, observing the festivities.

I shake my head.

"Hey look," I tell Mia. "It's Vincent." She hasn't heard from him since the night on the boat. He hadn't even answered any of her texts. And she deserves to know why.

"Jerk!" she snaps, glaring at him. "I'm not wasting my time, Reece."

I start to say something else, to encourage her to confront him, when another face appears next to Vincent.

A face with white-blond hair and ice-blue eyes.

Nate.

I suck in my breath.

Vincent drops his head to say something in Nate's ear and it is clear that they are together.

Again.

There is something strange going on here.

My mind immediately starts spinning, trying to fit pieces together. Nate and Vincent. Vincent and Nate. They shouldn't be together. They have nothing in common. Yet, they must. But what?

My mind spins.

What do they have in common?

What?

The Regatta?

Mia?

Me?

And then my gaze brushes across the *Daniella* and I know.

Dante.

Of course it's Dante. They were whispering on the grounds of his estate. They are together now at the Regatta that he is hosting. Vincent is probably who Nate was talking to that day on the beach when I overheard him talking about Dante.

What are they planning?

What the eff are they planning?

I look at Mia and she is staring at them too. And I can see on her face that she is also trying to figure it out.

"What's going on?" I ask her.

She shakes her head. "I don't know."

I look back at them and they are gone now, disappeared into the crowd. And then I catch one glimpse of Vincent's back. He's headed down to toward the beach. And before I can think, I start shoving through the crowd to follow him. Mia is close on my heels.

"Excuse me," I tell people as I shove them. "I'm sorry. Excuse me."

Vincent doesn't notice me because he's still far enough ahead of me.

I wind my way down to the beach and I see Vincent ducking down in a secluded area about fifty yards away.

As I run toward him, I look at the *Daniella*. Dimitri, Elena and Dante are all on the stern of the ship and I hear Dimitri begin talking into the microphone. Dante and Elena are waving at the crowd.

And I no longer care if Vincent sees me, because I can feel in my heart that something is very, very wrong here.

Vincent bends down, kneeling on his knees in the sand and I see wires in his hands.

Wires.

He looks up and sees me at the same time as I see something small and black in his hands. And it is attached to the wires. He's alarmed and starts to get up and I whirl around.

"Dante!" I scream. Mia starts screaming too and we're screaming at the top of our lungs. But so is the rest of the crowd. Everyone is clapping and screaming and whistling and Dante can't hear us over the rest of them.

I look over my shoulder and Vincent isn't chasing us.

Weird.

And the look on his face is weird, too. It's almost happy. And he is messing with the little black thing in his hands.

Everything is in slow motion now.

I turn, screaming for Dante again and this time, his eyes meet mine. He's standing on the stern of the *Daniella* and his beautiful blue eyes meet mine.

And then his boat explodes.

Chapter Twenty-Eight

Fire is everywhere in the bay.

The *Daniella* is in pieces.

Mia and I are screaming and everyone around us is running.

Vincent is gone.

And I have to find Dante.

I run toward the water and plow into it, pushing away a piece of fiberglass that is floating next to me. It's charred and jagged and I know it's a piece of Dante's boat.

I start crying as I plunge into the water and I try to swim but someone is holding onto my foot.

And then they're pulling my foot.

I turn and find a security guard. He's pulling me out of the water and telling me that we have to go. We have to go right now.

Apparently, Dante had a security detail assigned to me after all.

I argue and struggle because I have to find Dante.

But the security guard won't let me go.

"Mia!" I scream. "Find Dante."

She looks dazed and confused and I know she's in shock. And so am I. And Dante hasn't emerged from the water. Neither has his father or Elena.

In my panic to find him, I start fighting against the security guard again. I'm hitting him with my cast and I'm so afraid and hysterical that I don't feel the pain.

He scoops me up and throws me over his shoulder.

And he carries me away from the water. Away from where Dante must be. He steps over the shattered remains of the crystal Regatta trophy. The tiny pieces glimmer in the sun like jewels.

"You don't understand," I cry. "I have to find him. Please. Please put me down."

But he doesn't.

I twist around to look behind us and now I don't see Mia. And I still don't see Dante. And I can hardly see anything because tears are blurring my vision.

The bay is in shambles. All of the boats that were lined up for the race have caught fire from the explosion and there is mass panic and chaos as some people evacuate and others try to extinguish the flames.

I squeeze my eyes shut and bang my hands uselessly against the security guard's back. It doesn't help. He acts like I'm not even there. He just continues to carry me through the crowds and up to the street where a black car is waiting. He speaks into his earpiece and then deposits me into the backseat of the waiting car.

He looks down at me as he's fastening me into the seatbelt. His eyes are kind and through my panic and confusion, I almost feel badly about hitting him so many times. But he doesn't seem to mind. Maybe, in all of the chaos and hysteria, he didn't even notice.

"It will be alright," he tells me. He slaps the top of the car twice and it speeds away.

And they're taking me away from Dante.

"Please stop," I beg the driver. I know from his black suit that he is a member of the security team, too. "I have to hunt for Dante. Please."

"I can't, miss," he tells me, without taking his eyes from the road. "I have orders. This is your evacuation plan."

Evacuation plan?

I have an evacuation plan?

Through my confusion and tears, I stop and try to think.

"Where are you taking me?" I ask. "Back to Giliberti House?"

The driver shakes his head.

"No. This is a Code Red Evacuation. You are to be taken to a plane immediately. You'll use the Prime Minister's private jet and it will fly you to London. We'll be at Heathrow in less than four hours."

"We?" I meet his eyes in the rearview mirror.

"Yes, we. You and I. I have orders to not leave your side until you are with your father."

I feel numb. This can't be happening.

"How do I have an evacuation plan?" I ask simply. I can't think of anything else to ask. This is happening so quickly.

"Everyone close to the Prime Minister has one," he tells me.

"Where is Dimitri?" I ask. "And Dante? Did you see them? Are they okay?"

"I don't know, miss." The security guard averts his eyes and I don't want to think about what that might mean.

I'm getting frantic again. I stare out the tinted windows of the car and we're speeding away from the coast, away from the bay, and away from the last place that I'd seen Dante.

"I can't leave here. Don't you understand?" I am practically shouting. "I can't leave Dante."

"You have to," the security guard tells me. "You don't have a choice. It's not safe here. This is what Dante wants. He approved this plan of action for you."

"He wanted you to take me away?"

I am shocked. And I sit limply as the security guard nods.

"In the case of an assassination attempt, yes. He approved this plan to remove you from Caberra."

Assassination.

Attempt.

I am stunned.

Because it happened so quickly, I hadn't had time to think about it. Vincent tried to assassinate Dimitri. And Dante was with his father. And Nate had to have been in on it. That's why Nate and Vincent have been together lately. That's the connection.

That's who Nate had been talking about on the phone that day.

And this was all about Dimitri.

It wasn't Dante at all. Dante was collateral damage.

Dante was.

I'm already speaking of him in the past tense.

I gulp.

"Is Dante dead?" I whisper.

The security guard looks at me through the rearview mirror and then looks back at the road.

"I don't know."

And then I can't speak anymore because I am crying. I try to cry quietly so that I don't get hysterical again. I curl into a ball on the seat and I cry until we pull into the airport hangar.

The security guard opens my door and unfastens my seat belt, then helps me from the car.

"I'm Daniel, miss. And I'll be by your side until I hand you off to your father. We'll call him en route. I won't let anything happen to you."

I nod and my eyes are red and burning and the tears are still running down my cheeks. You would think that I would run out of tears but I haven't. My feet move numbly on their own accord as Daniel escorts me onto the plane. I walk past the lone flight attendant without saying a word.

Ordinarily, I would be astounded at the lavish airplane. I would be in awe of the luxury that surrounds me here. But right now, in this moment, I don't care. I curl up on a leather sofa and cry some more.

Daniel covers me with a soft blanket and he sits across from me. He stares out the window and he lets me cry.

I can't think of anything other than Dante.

I see his face, his smile, his hands. I hear his voice. I hear his laugh. I see the look on his face as he balanced above me in the pool house. And then I see the look on his face right before the *Daniella* exploded. His eyes were soft, because he'd just found me in the crowd. I'll never forget that look.

It was probably the last time that I'll see it.

I know it.

And the last thing he'd said to me this morning was *I love you*.

That makes me cry all the harder.

This can't be happening.

Yet it is.

All of those times that Dante tried telling me how complicated his life is... I didn't listen. I got frustrated and annoyed. But he was so right. His life was complicated.

And now it's over.

OhMyGod.

I'm not going to think like that. I'm not going to think that Dante is dead until someone tells me the actual words.

But the fire. There was so much fire.

And my heart knows that no one could survive that.

I picture the piece of fiberglass that floated past me in the bay and I remember how jagged and charred it was. And Dante had been standing on top of that. And if it is in pieces then so is...

OHMYGOD.

I can't think like this.

I can't.

I squeeze my eyes shut and try to think of nothing at all. But it's hard.

Impossible.

And so I torture myself with images from the explosion, Dante's face, his smile and pretty much everything about him for the entire four and a half hour flight.

The plane lands at Heathrow International Airport and I watch sightlessly as we taxi into the hangar. Because it's a private plane, I get to bypass customs and security and I walk down the tunnel into the terminal.

And my dad is standing there.

And I start running.

He grabs me and holds me and I cry onto his shirt.

"Daddy," I whimper.

From behind me, I hear Daniel.

"You'll be fine now, miss," he tells me. And he turns to get back onto the plane.

I let go of my father and grab Daniel's arm.

"Thank you," I tell him simply. And then I hug him. He seems surprised, but then his arms close around me and he hugs me back.

"I'm sure they will contact you as soon as they can," Daniel tells me solemnly. "They'll let you know what is going on."

I nod and I don't even ask who "they" are. I don't care. As long as someone contacts me, that's all that matters.

Daniel turns and leaves and I turn back to my father.

"Are you alright?" he asks worriedly. And he's so anxious that he's forgetting to use his fake British accent.

I shake my head and start to cry again and my father doesn't know what to do. Because I was supposed to have been a boy and he doesn't know what to do with a crying girl. He pats my back awkwardly.

"I want to go home," I whimper. "Can I go home?"

"To Kansas?" dad asks quietly.

I nod. "To Kansas. Right now."

He sits me in a chair and goes to the find out when the next flight is. And it turns out that there is a flight leaving in an hour with a layover in Amsterdam.

He buys me a ticket.

And then he sits with me until it takes off.

I don't have anything. Everything I took with me to Caberra and everything that I bought while I was there is still at Giliberti House.

"I'll contact them and have it shipped," Dad promises me.

I realize too that my cell phone is still in Caberra. I dropped my purse on the beach when the bay exploded.

"I'll let your mother know," my father tells me after I inform him of that. "I'll let her know that you're on your way. It will be okay, Reece. Everything will be okay."

"No, it won't," I whisper. "I'm sick of everyone telling me that it will be okay all of the time. It won't be okay. Not this time."

He pats my back for a while longer because he doesn't know what to say and then it's time to board and so he walks me to the gate.

"Fly safely," he tells me. And his accent is back now. I hug him tight.

"I love you, daddy," I tell him before I turn to walk onto the plane.

"I know," he answers. "I love you, too."

I hand my boarding pass to the flight attendant and I can't help but think about doing this very same thing when I flew out of Amsterdam. Dante was on my flight. And everything changed. He changed everything.

And now he's gone.

I gulp back a fresh bout of tears and I drop into the seat.

I curl up and put my head against the window. I watch the flight crew loading luggage beneath us and I realize that I haven't once panicked about flying this time. I'm not afraid anymore. And now it doesn't matter. Because I'm empty inside.

Nothing matters.

I close my eyes and embrace the empty feeling in my heart.

It's numb and cold and alone.

And I know I will feel that way for a long time to come.

I listen to the pilot telling us how we have a one and a half hour flight until we reach Amsterdam, which is where I lay over for a few hours. I close my eyes.

And somehow, I sleep.

And I am so tired and emotionally drained that my sleep is dreamless.

I wake up when the person next to me nudges me and tells me that we're here and ready to deplane. I nod and say thank you.

And I wait my turn patiently to get off the plane.

And I trudge down to the terminal.

And I step out into the terminal into the masses of swarming people.

And I look up.

And there is Dante.

He is standing in front of me.

And my heart stops.

Chapter Twenty - Nine

I'm running.

I'm in Dante's arms.

And he's kissing me.

He smells like smoke and fire and carnage. And he's dirty and his clothes are torn.

But he's here.

And he's alive.

Dante is alive.

"You're alive," I whisper over and over. He's still got his arms wrapped around me and he's not letting go.

He pulls away slightly and looks down at me.

"I'm alive," he confirms. "And you're a hard person to catch."

I stare at him.

"It's your fault," I tell him. "You designed my evacuation plan. What the hell is an evacuation plan, anyway? And you were supposed to have the security detail taken off of me. And what the hell happened? How are you alive? Everything was on fire. And is your dad alright?"

We realize that we are once again impeding the flowing traffic, just like we did when we met here the first time. Dante leads me to a nearby seat and we sit and he explains.

"My father is fine. He's in the hospital with bruises and minor burns. The explosion threw us far away from the boat, so when it burned, it didn't hurt us. Elena is in the hospital with burns, also."

"Are you burned?" I immediately begin checking his perfect body for signs of injury. But there is barely anything there for a few little scrapes and a lot of soot.

"I'm fine," he tells me.

"What happened?" I ask in confusion. "I don't understand."

"Nate paid Vincent to rig the yacht to explode. Nate's father is the Deputy Prime Minister. Do you know what that means? It means his father would be the interim PM if anything should happen to mine. And then more than likely, if he did a good job, he would be appointed the permanent PM. And Nate knew that. At this point, it doesn't look like his father knew anything about this. But the investigation is ongoing, of course."

I am appalled. I knew that there was something about Nate, something off, but I had no idea that he could be so cold and calculating. And poor Mia. She had really been into Vincent and he was just using her to get to Dimitri.

I mention that to Dante and he nods.

"Yes. Remember that night on the *Daniella*? Vincent was the one who suggested to Mia that they sneak onto my boat. He was just casing it out to see where to implant the explosives. And my car accident? I was driving my father's car. They think that Vincent probably rigged the brakes. That's why I couldn't slow down on the curves."

And I feel sick.

What a cold and calculating thing to do.

And then after that, Vincent sat there and had dinner with Dante even though he knew that Dante would die with Dimitri if all went according to their plan to blow up the boat.

OhMyGod.

"That's horrible," I murmur. I am curled into Dante's side, clinging to his arm and I doubt that I am ever letting go of it.

"You're alive," I say again in wonder. I look at his hand and it is long and real and strong. "You're alive."

"I'm alive," he nods.

And my heart is singing. It's singing Caberran songs that I don't know the words to. It's singing my favorite songs from when I was a kid. It's singing bubblegum pop nonsense from the radio. It's singing anything it can think of to sing because it is just that happy.

Dante is alive.

And that is truly all that matters.

"What do we do now?" I ask him. "Are we going back to Caberra?"

He stares at me.

"No." And he hesitates. "*We* aren't. Reece, you're going to Kansas, just like you were planning. I'm going to return to Caberra because there are going to be investigations and trials and whatnot because of this whole mess. So I have to be there. But I don't want you there right now. We aren't completely sure that Nate and Vincent were the only two people involved. I can't risk your life. You're going somewhere safe."

I freeze.

My heart stops again.

"Without you?" I whisper. "No."

I just got him back. There's no way in hell that I am going to fly to Kansas when Dante is alive and well and sitting next to me holding my hand.

No.

Way.

In.

Hell.

"Reece," and Dante's voice is firm. "I'm not risking your safety. I was frantic earlier when I couldn't find you. I've never been as scared as I was today. And not for myself—I was scared for you. And I disobeyed my own evacuation plan to get to you. Russell is furious."

I finally notice that Dante's security team is situated at strategic locations around us. And Russell is only a stone's throw away. And Dante is right. Russell doesn't look happy.

But then, Russell never looks happy.

"But Dante," I begin but Dante is already shaking his head.

"No buts," he tells me. "We'll figure something out later, but you can't be in Caberra right now. It's not safe."

And I know that's it. His decision is final and he's not going to change his mind.

"This is not goodbye," Dante adds. "It's just goodbye *for now*. I love you and you love me. We'll figure something out."

"We'll figure something out?" I ask dubiously. "Like what? I'll be thousands of miles and an ocean away. You're going to forget about me."

And now I sound pathetic.

But hey, my boyfriend almost just got blown to pieces and I thought he was dead. I deserve a little latitude.

"Reece."

Dante is looking into my eyes and there is dirt smudged on his cheek. I reach up with shaking fingers to wipe it away and he grabs my hand and kisses it.

"I love you. I love everything about you. I love the way you laugh and your American accent and the way you never doubt that you can do something. You just always assume that you can. I love that. I love *you*. And we will make this work. There is no one for me in the entire world but you."

How can I argue with that?

"Okay," I whisper. And I lay my head on his broad shoulder and soak him in because I've only got him for a couple more hours.

After a few minutes, we get up and walk to a little restaurant in the airport.

And for the next two hours, two hamburgers and four sodas, we talk and laugh and I stare at him because I still need to reassure myself that he is safe and sound.

And beautiful and strong.

But then it's time to go.

And nothing is fine.

"It will be okay," Dante tells me as he reaches over and tucks my hair behind my ear.

"That's exactly what Daniel told me," I say.

"And Daniel was correct," Dante points out. "And so am I."

"Okay," I nod.

But my heart is breaking. Because it's been through a lot lately and honestly, I just don't know how much more it can take.

Dante walks me to the terminal. And he kisses me gently as they announce that the passengers are loading.

"I don't want to go," I tell him painfully. And it *is* painful because my heart isn't finished breaking yet. "This is horrible. This does not feel *okay.*"

Dante smiles and it looks like he is forcing it.

"It's not fun," he admits. "But think of it this way. Two hours ago, you thought I was dead. And I'm not. So everything is fine, remember?"

Well, if he wants to put it that way.

I nod. And he kisses me again and I walk into the tunnel leading to the plane.

I turn and look and Dante waves, blowing me a kiss.

He makes blowing a kiss look sexy.

But I roll my eyes anyway and pretend to catch it.

And then he rolls *his* eyes.

I laugh and turn around so that he doesn't see me crying as I walk away.

* * *

Kansas is hot.

Kansas is freaking hot.

Kansas is hell's kitchen hot.... As in the devil standing over a hot stove stirring boiling tar hot.

And that Is. Freaking. Hot.

The heat plows into me like a brick wall as I walk out the backdoor of the farmhouse letting the screen door slam before heading out to the barn.

As I walk into the barn, where it isn't a bit cooler, only somewhat shadier, the barn cats scatter at my presence. Mischief nickers from his stall, but I'm not here to ride him right now. I'm here for privacy. I see my grandpa through the back barn door. He's out in the pasture working on an irrigation head, so he'll be tied up for awhile.

I'm carrying my laptop and I climb up into my dark little cubbyhole in the hay loft. It's breathtakingly hot up here, but it's the only place that I can be alone lately. And it's just close enough that I still get the wireless reception from the house.

I pull up my email.

And my heart quickens because there is a note from Dante.

To: Reece Ellis <ReeciePiecie@thecloud.com
From: Dante Giliberti <DGGiliberti@caberraPM.gov
Subject: I miss you

Kansas,
Just a note to tell you that I miss you. Giliberti House isn't the same since you are gone. And so I'm staying at

the Old Palace for now. It makes it easier with all the legal stuff going on for Nate.

We found out for sure this morning that Nathaniel didn't know anything. But he's so mortified by the scandal that he tendered his resignation. I feel badly because I like Nathaniel. He's a decent guy.

I hope that all is well in Kansas and that you haven't forgotten about me. How's Quinn, by the way? (No, I'm not jealous. Well, maybe just a little).

Anyway, I'll call you tonight. I miss the sound of your voice. I can't believe you've been gone for three weeks already. It feels like forever. But I'll talk to you tonight.

All my love,
Dante

I sigh and close the laptop. I should answer, but it makes me too sad to email him. It makes me feel so alone when I remember that he is thousands of miles away. I want to look at him and talk to him and smell him. I just want to *be* with him. Is that so much to ask?

I stare down at my arm and twist the sunflower bracelet on my wrist. Thank God I was wearing it the day of the Regatta. Because it's here with me now and every time I look at it, I'm reminded of Dante.

As if everything else doesn't remind me of him, too.

"Reece?"

I hear Becca calling for me just a scant second before her brown hair pokes up over the top of the hayloft ladder.

"Why do you come up here?" she demands as she climbs up. "It's hotter than hell up here."

"It's hotter than hell down there, too," I tell her.

She's only wearing cut-offs and a bikini top, so she ought to be cool enough. I tell her that and she rolls her eyes.

"Today was the car wash for Student Council. You were supposed to be there. Did you forget?"

Crap. I nod. "I totally forgot. I'm sorry. But I wasn't even supposed to be here right now, so surely it isn't that big a deal."

"No, it's fine," she agrees. "But I would have liked to have you there. All Drew and Jason did was stare at me and Alyssa while we did all the work."

"Well, if you didn't want people to stare, you shouldn't have worn a bikini," I tell her absently.

In my head, I'm already composing an email to Dante. I have changed my mind about answering him. Even though it makes me sad, it's better than dealing with this trivial kind of B.S. And it's funny. Now that I've come back from Caberra after Dante was almost killed, everything sort of feels like it's B.S. It's sort of good. It makes me realize the important things in life.

Like, oh, *life*.

"Helloooooo? Reecie-Peecie? Helllllo?"

I come back to earth and stare at Becca.

"I'm sorry," I tell her. "I was thinking about something else."

"Don't you mean some*one* else?" she rolls her eyes. "I love you, Reecie, but all you do lately is think about him."

I have to give her that.

"I'm sorry," I apologize. "Really. I just miss him. It's really hard."

And Beck's eyes soften up then, because she knows. She misses Quinn like crazy too. They're still broken up because it's for the best but Becca is miserable.

"It's alright," she tells me. "Do you want to go into town tonight and get some ice cream? I think we both need it. Chocolate chocolate chip. With chunks. And cookie dough. And maybe hot fudge, too."

I nod. "Sure."

I really don't. But what else am I going to do? Sit in my room and mope? Listen to my grandpa's radio program about the price of hogs? I think not. I have some dignity left.

"Okay," she answers as she crawls to her feet and back down the ladder. "I'll see you tonight."

"K," I answer.

And I'm alone again.

I make my way back inside and sit down at the kitchen table. My grandma is making fresh lemonade, which of course reminds me of Caberra.

Only my grandma doesn't put mint leaves in hers. I almost tell her that she should, but then I don't. I don't need another thing to remind me.

As if everything doesn't remind me of Dante and Caberra anyway.

"Honey," my grandma says as she turns around and hands me a fresh glass.

"I know you're miserable. But it will be okay. Your grandpa and I were separated by thousands of miles when he was in the Army and we turned out okay."

I stare at her. "Grandma, that was during a war. Everyone was separated. I think that's a little different."

"Perhaps," she says as she sits next to me and looks at me with her wise old eyes. "But probably not. Separation is separation, no matter how you look at it. And absence does make the heart grow stronger, you know. It's cliché, but true."

"It can't make you stronger if it kills you," I mutter.

She pats my hand.

"You'll be okay," she tells me again before she gets to her feet and goes to the sink to wash dishes.

I'm really tired of hearing that.

My phone buzzes in my pocket and I pull it out. Becca probably wants to change our plans for tonight already. She's so freaking fickle.

But it's not her.

It's Dante.

Whatcha doing?

I smile.

Burning alive in the heat. How about you?

Two seconds go by.

Oh, same. I just wanted you to know that I love you.

I smile again because I know how this game goes. We've been playing it for three weeks. One of us will say I love you.

Then the other person says, *How much?*

And then the other makes up some insane and crazy amount of love.

More than the ocean is large.

More than a shark loves human limbs.

More than Gavin loves his reflection.

More than baseball players love steroids.

More than chocolate, more than wine and way, way more than anchovies.

More than yesterday, but less than tomorrow.

It's a crazy and corny game, but we do what we have to do to keep from going insane.

Because this distance thing? It really sucks.

So I play along today, even though I'm feeling pissy.

How much? I type.

Dante doesn't answer immediately which annoys me. I'm really in the mood to hear how much he

352

loves me. Because I miss him SoFreakingMuchIMightDie. Seriously.

"This much."

It's his voice.

I whirl around and he is actually here.

In my kitchen.

This can't be real.

But there he is.

Dante is standing in the doorway, filling it up like only Dante can. His blue shirt sets off his blue sparkling eyes. And OHMYGOSH. I'm going to have a heart attack.

My grandma is standing next to him and she looks surprised, too. But she is nowhere near as surprised as I am. My mouth is hanging open and then I remember that I can move.

I leap from my seat and into his arms.

"Dante! What are you...how are you... I mean. OHMYGOSH."

And I'm kissing him.

And I know my grandma is behind him but I don't care because I've missed him more than a PMS'ing woman misses M&M's. So I tell him that.

"Touching," he says wryly as I cinch my arms tighter around his neck.

And kiss him again.

And inhale his Dante smell. The earth, the sea, the sun.

It's him. It's truly, truly him.

"I can't believe you're here," I tell him. "*How* are you here?"

He shrugs. "My dad said that things have wound down enough that I could leave. So here I am. He knows a few people, you know. People in the International Foreign Exchange Student Program."

He's silent as he watches me.

And I am watching his blue eyes sparkle. OhMyGosh I have missed that.

Wait. What?

I comprehend what he just said.

"Foreign Exchange Student Program?" I repeat. "You're here to stay?"

I can't believe my ears. This can't be happening.

But I think it is.

He nods.

"That's how much I love you," he tells me. "I'm coming to hotter-than-hell's-kitchen-Kansas for my senior year so that I can be with you. That's how much."

I'm stunned.

"That's a lot," I admit. "I think you win."

He laughs and picks me up and I wrap my legs around his waist. Then I bury my face in his neck like I wanted to the first time I met him. And at this point in time, I don't seem insane like I would have back then. I just seem like a girl who's in total love with her boyfriend.

The joy is bursting out of me. I can't contain it and I just want to laugh.

I feel that giddy.

"I'm glad you're here," I tell him. "Where are you staying? Who are you exchanging with?"

Because everyone knows that's how the program works. A kid from a foreign country comes in, and a local kid goes out.

"The McKeyan house," he told me. And then he grins.

And I have to laugh and shake my head.

"Well played," I tell him. "You got rid of Quinn McKeyan. I *told* you that he wasn't going to be an issue. I don't have a crush on him anymore."

"Well, a smart man doesn't take any chances," Dante tells me seriously. And I laugh again.

"So, Quinn is going to school in Caberra?" I ask. "I don't know how you put that together so quickly or without me knowing, but I don't care. I'm just glad you're here."

"Oh, I know some people," he shrugs. Then he grins impishly again. And I could seriously watch him smile all day.

All. Day. Long.

No lie.

"So," Dante stares down at me casually like he's not holding 124 pounds in his arms. "What's a person do here for fun?"

"Have you ever heard of cow-tipping?" I ask him innocently. He shakes his head and I explain and he looks at me dubiously. And I can't blame him. It does sound like a contrived thing.

"Well, instead of cow-tipping, we could go security guard dodging," I suggest, as I stare through the back window at Russell casing out my farmhouse.

Dante laughs.

"Security-Guard-Dodging? That's my girl."

And he grabs my hand and we dart out the front door, leaving Russell standing in my back yard as we run outside and jump into my car.

And happiness bubbles up in me again and I grin.

Because Dante is right. I'm his girl.

I know it's true because Dante Giliberti left paradise and came all the way to Hell's Kitchen to prove it.

And because of that, I finally know that what Dante has been saying all along is true. Love is all that matters. It's all we need.

I smile and turn the key and we tear off down my driveway as dust billows behind us.

And I know that Dante was right about something else, too.

Everything really will be okay.

About the author

Courtney Cole is a novelist who lives near Lake Michigan with her domestic zoo (aka family), pet iPad and favorite cashmere socks.

Dante's Girl is her first light-hearted contemporary romance. Her previous works are paranormal romance and suspense.

She plans to continue The Paradise Diaries with book two next year.

To learn more about Courtney, please visit www.courtneycolewrites.com

Acknowledgements

I have to thank my husband and kids first. Because they put up with me when I lose myself in the worlds that I create. They are very, very patient with me. And thankfully, they don't mind having take-out for dinner.

I also have to thank Tiffany King and M. Leighton. They are my Ink Sisters, my Writerly-BFF's and I don't know what I would do without them. They keep my sane and offer me so much advice. I love you both. Because you're awesome.

Ash, the Bookish Brunette. Thank you for reminding me that Kansas chicks are awesome and feisty. I should know, since I am one too. Haha. Thank you for being my muse for Reece.

Dani Snell. Thank you SO FREAKING MUCH for the amazing and awesome and incredible cover. It's everything that I didn't even know I wanted — and more. It's amazing. You're incredible.

And thank you to my readers. THANK YOU. You are so kind and wonderful and I love you all. Thank you for reading my books. Thank you for loving my books. You're the best readers ever.

CPSIA information can be obtained at www.ICGtesting.com
Printed in the USA
LVOW102117230912

299995LV00008B/47/P